Also by Thomas M. Disch available from Carroll & Graf:

*334*
*Camp Concentration*
*On Wings of Song*

Also by John Sladek available from Carroll & Graf:

*Roderick*
*Roderick at Random*

# BLACK ALICE

**Thomas M. Disch
and John Sladek**

Carroll & Graf Publishers, Inc.
New York

Copyright © 1968 by Thomas M. Disch and John T. Sladek

First Carroll & Graf edition 1989

Published by arrangement with The Karpfinger Agency, Inc

Carroll & Graf Publishers, Inc.
260 Fifth Avenue
New York, NY 10001

ISBN: 0-88184-506-X

Manufactured in the United States of America

'Who are *you*?' said the Caterpillar.

This was not an encouraging opening for a conversation. Alice replied, rather shyly, 'I—I hardly know, Sir, just at present—at least I know who I *was* when I got up this morning, but I think I must have been changed several times since then.'

'What do you mean by that?' said the Caterpillar, sternly. 'Explain yourself!'

'I can't explain *myself*, I'm afraid, Sir,' said Alice, 'because I'm not myself, you see.'

'I don't see,' said the Caterpillar.

*Alice's Adventures in Wonderland*
LEWIS CARROLL

Alice was beginning to get very tired of sitting by herself on the trunk, and of having nothing to do. This was the first day of vacation—she should be having *fun*, for heaven's sake! She looked up the asphalt road for the familiar grey dot that would become Miss Godwin's Saab, and sighed. She turned around and watched a fat, furry caterpillar crawl about furtively beneath a canopy of ivy leaves. The caterpillar was banded yellow and black; the ivy was a vivid, early-summer green; the bricks of the wall that circled St. Arnobia's were a dull red, brick-red. Alice didn't approve of so much colour. It was in poor taste. So, very carefully, she pried the caterpillar from the brick wall and let him crawl about on the pleats of her new dress.

But that was soon boring too, since the caterpillar showed no interest in conversation. Miss Godwin was forty-five minutes late! If only Alice had thought to leave out one book when she'd packed her trunk so that she would have had something to read now. If only the sky would clear, so she could start getting tanned. If only, if only, if only Miss Godwin would come.

She began to fidget.

*You're fidgeting*, she told herself. *How many times must I tell you not to fidget?*

Miss Godwin was so late that most of the other St. Arnobians were already gone. Alice had had to sit and watch their departures and pretend not to be dying of impatience. The younger girls had screamed and jumped about like absolute wild Indians, and prattled on about every little thing that had happened since the Easter holiday, not even stopping their mad chatter to wave good-bye to Alice. By contrast the seventh and eighth graders were as composed as stone statues. They kissed their parents demurely or offered a white-gloved hand to be shaken. They sat up straight in the seats of their cars, conversing with the indolent grace of goddesses. Next year, Alice realised, with a sensation almost of swooning, those goddesses would be her classmates. They didn't know it yet, but Alice was going to skip seventh grade. After Miss Godwin's summer tutoring, she would go straight from sixth grade to eighth grade. From the academic point of view, of course, she had nothing to worry about. She was better in arithmetic and reading and even in art than most of *this year's* eighth graders. But the idea that she would be an eighth grader herself—a creature of such flawless elegance, of such *maturity—that* was a really overwhelming idea. It was like finding yourself suddenly twelve years old instead of eleven.

While she waited, Alice had studied the older girls carefully, noting especially the way they climbed into a car. Instead of scrambling in headlong, they would first sit on the edge of the seat, then swivel around ninety degrees, drawing their legs into the car in one smooth motion. Elegant wasn't the word for it! No doubt they'd learned to do it in Miss Boyd's etiquette class, since they all did it so perfectly. Eighth graders had etiquette every day, but sixth graders only had one hour a week (unless you counted dancing classes) and that had been barely time to learn introductions. Still, practised or not, there was no reason why Alice couldn't get into Miss Godwin's Saab in a ladylike way. Miss Godwin had a sharp eye for such things.

A red, needle-thin dragonfly darted about in the grass by Alice's feet, and she lifted them up to the top of the trunk nervously. A fine mist of perspiration prickled her cheekbones and brow. The asphalt road was empty as far as one could see.

She sighed and checked her watch. Her father had given it to her on her eleventh birthday in March, a brand-new Lady Bulova with two small diamonds. Miss Godwin was *one hour and five minutes late*. The ominous thunder-heads that had been building up all afternoon covered the sky now from horizon to horizon. She did hope Miss Godwin would come soon, before the rain ruined her dress, which was linen in a retiring shade of beige. Bix box pleats came down from the yoke, and a matching belt fastened below the waist with a button. Alice adored the dress, but she worried, after seeing the other girls in their holiday dresses, whether it might not be too old for her, and wanted Miss Godwin's opinion. Miss Godwin, unlike some other governesses Alice could mention, had exquisite taste.

Governesses as a breed were awful creatures. Either they wore space shoes like fat old Mrs. Buckler or ugly straw hats with silly ribbons like Miss Stuck-Up from England (who had only lasted two weeks, because it turned out that she drank). But Miss Godwin was really wonderful. Really really. Good-looking, young, easy-tempered—and talk about cultured!

Why, she'd taken her Bachelor's degree at the Sorbonne in Paris! She spoke much better French than even Mr. Limberley at St. Arnobia's, and she'd read *all* of Victor Hugo! Alice sometimes could wish that her parents were as cultured as her governess. Maybe if they had lived for a while in Europe, they'd have been more like Miss Godwin—more full of life, more happy, more *real*. Miss Godwin certainly was real.

'What *can* be keeping her?' Alice said aloud. Then, remembering that that was her worst habit, almost bit her tongue off as a punishment. Some years ago (two), in the dark days of Mrs. Buckler, Alice used to talk to herself all the time, but now she was supposed to be over it. Actually she'd never talked to *herself*; she'd talked to Dinah, who was sometimes her imaginary sister and sometimes a cat.

A moving speck appeared on the farthest hill crest, then vanished as the road dipped. In the hot, hazy air the distant stretch of asphalt seemed to ripple like a pool of water. A mirage. Alice knew all about mirages. Someday she would go to the Sahara and see one of the big desert mirages—a whole city created out of the warm air. Someday, when she was grown, she would go *everywhere*. The prospect of being grown-up hung tantalisingly before her, just out of reach, beckoning. A mirage.

The approaching car was not a Saab. It was just another old Cadillac. It pulled sedately in through the wrought-iron arch of the gate, and a stiff-looking couple emerged from the back seat. Becky Horner's parents, Alice guessed. Becky was in the Infirmary with poison ivy from the seventh grade's General Science field trip two weeks ago. Alice was sure that Becky was just putting on about how sick she was so that the other girls wouldn't be able to see her with calomine and bandages all over her legs. (Becky had sat in the poison ivy.)

The Horners passed within a dozen feet of Alice without even nodding to her. When they couldn't see her, Alice stuck her tongue out at them. Miss Godwin said it was childish to be a snob, but that didn't seem to stop an awful lot of adults from being snobby. Alice probably had more money in her trust fund that Mr. Horner would earn in his whole life, but from the way Becky turned up her nose at Alice you would have thought she was the janitor's daughter. Just because Alice's parents didn't belong to the same clubs that the Horners belonged to! When grown-ups could be so stupid, sometimes it seemed the course of wisdom to remain a child.

It was quite dark now for mid-afternoon. Thunder rumbled distantly. *If it rains*, Alice told herself, *I shall cry*.

It started to rain, but Alice had no chance to cry just then, for another car appeared, a clunky, copper-coloured Buick. It slowed and stopped right in front of Alice, who was sitting on her trunk, chin in hand and elbows propped on her knees, looking into raindrop-speckled dirt at the shoulder of the road. Miserably she felt each rain drop that soaked into the crisp linen of her dress.

'Alice Raleigh?'

She looked up at the man leaning across the seat of the Buick. He was an older man, who wore a cheap black bow tie and an unconvincing smile. Not exactly what one would call a gentleman.

'Yes,' she said, 'I'm Alice Raleigh.'

'I'm Reverend Roland Scott. You just call me Father, Alice.'

He got out of the car by the right-hand door. He was tall and his black suit was too loose in the shoulders, too snug at the waist, and inches too short. Even so the cuffs were frayed. She couldn't help staring at him: he was such an *improbable* priest. Priests never had as much hair as that—and such greasy hair —and his sideburns were so long that reminded her of one of those men that drove around in town on Saturdays on motorcycles making so much noise. But the worst thing, the thing that was really uncomfortable, was his eyes. They were the same summery green as the ivy, and despite the fixed smile on his pale lips, *they* did not smile at all.

He extended his hand, and after a moment's hesitation (for hadn't Miss Boyd made it very clear in Etiquette that a gentleman *does not* offer his hand to a lady?) she took it. Immediately after she'd shaken hands she wondered if perhaps she had not been supposed to *kiss* his hand instead. Miss Boyd had said nothing about meeting Catholic priests.

'I'm a friend of your Uncle Jason,' the priest said, 'and I've come to take you home as a favour for him. Miss Godwin had trouble with her car, and your uncle, knowing that I live near here, phoned to ask me to escort you home.' He said all this in a stiff, deliberate manner that reminded Alice of one of the younger St. Arnobians reciting a Bible passage. It would be letter-perfect, but somehow one suspected that he didn't know the meaning of half the words.

Once more he extended his hand, as though to help her in the door of the car. He wore a ring on his middle finger—a black stone with a design traced on it in gold: a pair of compasses spread open above clasped hands.

'Are you ...' she began, before she realised what an indiscreet question it was, for she knew from her father, who was a Mason himself, that Catholics weren't allowed to join the order. And a priest... ?

'Yes, my child? What is it?'

'Are you ... going to take my trunk?'

'Certainly, child. But you don't have to wait out here in the rain, do you?'

His grip on her hand tightened, and he began tugging her forward to the door of the Buick. At just that moment a terrible flash of lightning split the sky and almost immediately afterwards the thunder sounded, seemingly on all sides. Alice, startled, pulled away from the priest, but the wet dirt on the shoulder of the road was slippery, and the soles of her brand-new patent leather pumps were smooth as glass. Before she knew she was falling, she was on her back in the mud. The priest said something terribly unpriest-like.

Somebody else said: 'Dear Lord, *will* you look at that!'

The three Horners, each of them with a big black umbrella, stood at the door of their Cadillac regarding Alice gravely, as one might look at a stray—and slightly dangerous—animal broken from its leash. But as soon as Alice had turned to look at them, they turned their eyes away, pretending not to have seen her. Mr. Horner helped Mrs. Horner into the back seat with such a deal of pomp and circumstance that he might have been helping her on to a throne. Alice was furious: with the rain, with the mud on her dress, and now, overridingly, with the smug Horners. For once she knew what to do about it. She scrambled up from the mud and ran towards the Horners.

'Becky!' she shouted. '*Dear* Becky! You can't go away without saying good-bye.'

'Hey!' Reverend Scott shouted after her above the downpour. 'Hey kid! Where you going?'

Alice, spattered as she was, embraced her dear Becky and planted a wet kiss on Becky's fat cheek. Becky squealed with outrage, dropping her oversize umbrella, which began to blow away.

'Dear Becky,' said Alice with satisfaction. 'I just wanted to say good-bye and to say how sorry, how really upset I was to hear about your poison ivy and about the arithmetic test you failed. But I hope you have a good holiday now that it's all

13

over. Maybe we'll see each other this summer?'

'I doubt it,' said Becky, as her father pulled her into the back seat, while the chauffeur went off after the umbrella. 'We're going to be in Majorca, you know, and I don't suppose you'll be *there*. But I'll see you next term, I'm sure.'

'Say good-bye to your little friend, dear. We must be leaving.'

'Good-bye,' said Becky, swinging the door shut. Just before the latch caught, she added, *sotto voce*, 'Brain!'

Between the tears in Alice's eyes and the rain everywhere else, the Horners' Cadillac seemed positive to swim away. Alice was heartsick—not just at hearing the detested nickname tossed in her face once more, but also because she knew she had merited Becky's rudeness by her own. What had she hoped to gain by being rude to Becky, who would, after all, be a fellow eighth grader next year?

Wouldn't old Mrs. Horner be just *green* if she knew that? But even that reflection didn't seem greatly to cheer Alice up.

Hearing the sound of a car's engine turning over, Alice ran back to the road in time to see Reverend Scott drive away in his clunky Buick. It was strange enough, for the moment, to make her forget her misery. For a moment she suspected that he had stolen her trunk, but no, it was still there beside the brick wall where it had been all the time.

She sat down on the trunk and made herself stop crying so that she could talk things over with Dinah like two sensible people.

'Now, for one thing,' Alice began, 'I'm quite sure he's not a priest. He doesn't look like a priest, you know. And he's wearing a Masonic ring.'

'If he's not a priest, then what do you suppose he is?' Dinah asked. It was Dinah's way always to be asking questions.

'A child molester,' Alice declared gravely.

Neither Alice nor Dinah had any very clear idea of child molesting, but it would be a very terrible thing, to judge only from Alice's mother's guarded remarks on the subject, to fall into the hands of such a person.

'And yet,' Dinah observed, 'he *says* that Uncle Jason asked him to come. Uncle Jason would not be likely to send a child molester. And another thing—how would he know that Miss Godwin would be late?'

'Do you think Miss Godwin sent him, then?' Alice asked in turn, a little shocked with such a bold proposal.

14

'No. I don't know *what* to believe, Alice. I honestly don't.'

'I suppose we shall have to tell Mummy and Daddy.'

'Oh dear,' said Dinah, 'they'll probably forbid us to go out to the beach on our own if we do that. We'll have to spend all our time indoors, and we'll *never* get a tan.'

Dinah and Alice considered this for a while in silence. They imagined coming back to St. Arnobia's next term as pale as two ghosts, and there would be Miss Stuck-Up Pig-Face Horner as brown as a walnut after a summer in Majorca.

'It would be the grown-up thing . . .' Dinah began tentatively.

'. . . not to tell anyone about it,' Alice concluded firmly.

'Not even Miss Godwin?'

'Not even her. After all, Dinah, we're *almost* twelve years old.'

Just as they had come to this agreement between them, the tardy Saab came into sight down the asphalt road. When it stopped before the gate, Alice scrambled in to hug Miss Godwin without the least thought of being ladylike. 'I thought you'd *never* come,' she wailed, pressing her wet face into the soft fabric of Miss Godwin's suit. 'I waited and waited. Oh, it was awful!' Now that she knew the worst was over, she began crying in earnest.

'Poor darling! I'm so sorry, Alice honey, but the car just wouldn't start. I took it in to the garage, and they kept poking around in the motor and telling me to wait a minute more when they meant an hour. I am so sorry, darling. I *tried* to call the school, but the operator said the line was out of order. I suppose the storm did it. But, honey, why didn't you go inside to wait when the rain started? You didn't have to stay out here and spoil that pretty new dress. In fact, we'd better get you changed out of that, or you'll catch a cold.'

The rich timbre of Miss Godwin's voice was filled with an undoubtably sincere concern. Alice's sobbing grew subdued, rhythmic, and comfortable. It was warm in the car (Miss Godwin had turned on the heater) and dry and so nice to be called honey and darling. Usually Miss Godwin was too proper to address Alice as anything but *Mademoiselle*.

One of Miss Godwin's hands stroked Alice's long blonde curls, while the other dug into her purse for a lace-edged handkerchief and dabbed at Alice's eyes with it. The handkerchief was a pale daffodil yellow; the hand was the colour of a Hershey chocolate bar, and the almond-shaped nails were silvery-white.

After the trunk had been loaded into the Saab and Alice had been rubbed dry all over and put into another dress, they set off north for Baltimore. Alice had left off crying and sat squeezed into the right-hand corner of the seat, staring at the steamed-over window. Abstractedly she drew a face on the glass, adding the eyes last. The fresh green of the summer fields shone through where she had made dots for the eyes, and for a moment she saw him again: the bow tie, the greasy hair, the vivid green of the eyes.

*Where would I be now,* she wondered, *if I'd got in his car?*

Kidnapped—that was where! When she'd read Robert Louis Stevenson's book on that subject, she had thought it would not be an altogether undesirable thing to be kidnapped. Now she was less sure.

'Miss Godwin, if I told you a secret, would you promise not to tell Mommy and Daddy?'

'Tell me your secret, and I'll tell you if it's the kind I can keep.'

Alice laughed. 'Then, you'll have to guess. Whose face do you think this is that I drew on the window?'

Miss Godwin glanced at the scrawled face. 'Whoever it is has two eyes, a mouth, a nose—*perhaps*, and hair on top of his head. Doesn't sound like anybody *I'd* like to know.'

Alice arched one eyebrow enigmatically and erased the face with the palm of her hand. 'Now you'll never know. It will be a mystery!'

She settled back into the seat to listen to the whine of the tyres on wet concrete (they were on the main highway now) and the quiet ticking of the windshield wipers. The rain was heavy now, the sky so overcast, that many of the cars on the highway had turned on their headlights. Suddenly Alice realised that she was very hungry. She hadn't had a bite since the cookies at the going-home party that morning.

'I don't know about you,' said Miss Godwin, reading her mind, 'but I'm famished. Perhaps Mademoiselle would favour a light repast?'

'Peut-être,' Alice replied majestically, and then giggled.

Miss Godwin pulled up the gravel drive to Buddy's Bayshore Drive-In. 'The *hambourg avec moutarde* is recommended,' she noted, examining the menu that was fixed to a metal pole outside, after putting on her reading glasses. 'And to drink—the wine of the country, of course. Two malted milks *chocolade*.' Miss Godwin handed Alice the intercom speaker,

16

but though Alice was pleased to be given the responsibility, she was giggling too hard to order.

When Miss Godwin placed the order, Alice studied her admiringly, as she might have gone through the pages of a fashion magazine. It seemed incredible that anyone so *chic* would bother to spend her summers tutoring one seventh-grade girl. One *eighth*-grade girl, that is. Why, Miss Godwin had even been a model in Paris for one of the most famous designers!

That was a secret between Miss Godwin and Alice and Uncle Jason. Miss Godwin didn't want Alice's parents to know about that, since Mrs. Raleigh had definite ideas about Negro servants and their 'place'. She found it hard to bear that Miss Godwin should have a Master's degree (and, almost, a Ph.D.), but she could never have countenanced the thought that her child's governess had once been a Paris model.

A skinny, pasty-faced boy with a front tooth missing brought the hamburgers and malts out to the car. Alice's stomach growled, and Miss Godwin discreetly overlooked the fact. It was altogether minutes before Miss Godwin had tucked in the napkin about Alice's dress and opened the door of the glove compartment, in which there were two tidy niches to hold the malted milk cups.

Observing how daintily Miss Godwin ate her hamburger, even leaving part of it on the side of her paper plate, Alice decided she would do the same. Maybe that was why Miss Godwin had such a good figure. It was time for Alice to start watching her figure, or she'd end up like Mrs. Buckler. (Not to mention her own mother.) But before she knew it, she'd eaten the last of her hamburger and the tail end of her pickle and drained the chocolate malt until it was nothing but noise.

Chapter 2

*Oh, what a rogue and peasant slave am I!* thought Roderick Raleigh, apropos of nothing in particular. Most times Roderick had a much better opinion of himself than that, but in moments of melancholy (and nothing was so liable to bring on melancholic moments as finding oneself, as now, at the corner of 11th Avenue and Boston Street, before the three-story brick residence and office of Jason Duquesne) one tended to recall the sublime words of the Swan of Avon. *Is it not monstrous . . .*

At this point one tended *not* to recall the exact sublime words, but their tendency was very clear to Roderick. Was it not monstrous that his brother-in-law, Jason Duquesne, should live in such a home as this—the oldest brick residence in the city of Baltimore—amid what could only be called baronial splendour, with surfeiting riches heaped all about, while *he*, Roderick Raleigh, who was so much better equipped, by nature and upbringing, to appreciate such graces, should have to come begging for crusts of bread at Jason's carved oak door? Was that not monstrous? If that wasn't about the limit of monstrosity, then Roderick Raleigh didn't know what was.

'Are you getting out, mister?' the cab driver asked.

'Yes, yes, of course.' Roderick glanced at the meter. $3.55. The last time he'd taken a cab from Exmoor to Jason's it had cost only $3.25. The driver had probably *deliberately* chosen a longer route. Accordingly, when the driver had given him his change from a five, Roderick only tipped him twenty cents, and when the driver ventured to protest, he gave him a brief, though not unpassionate, sermon on the importance of honesty in small things. Roderick took such a pleasure in sermonising that he often wondered if he had missed his true vocation. Perhaps he should have been a man of the cloth, instead of . . .

Instead of what he was.

At thirty-nine Roderick Raleigh was still looking trim as the day he had (almost) graduated from college. If one were generously disposed, one might have called him handsome, though his handsomeness was in a rather outmoded style. The pencil-thin moustache, for instance, was strongly reminiscent of the later Errol Flynn. He had allowed his temples to grey exactly as much as Cary Grant's. His suit was well cut, costly without ostentation, and, by contemporary standards, rather drab. No one could challenge his tango, but when he heard fast music his impulse was to lindy rather than to twist. And often enough his true impulse was to go to a table and sit down and catch his breath. But for all of that, Roderick Raleigh still considered himself, if not a young man exactly, not an old man by any means. And not middle-aged either. At thirty-nine Roderick Raleigh was *mature*, neither more nor less.

Roderick climbed the four brick steps of the stoop, swinging his walking stick jauntily and whistling a Victor Herbert march tune. He stopped to adjust his tie and smooth the hair at his temples. (The thicker, jet-black pompadour above always looked after itself; for $400 it had damn well better.) He raised the walking stick to press the doorbell, but at the last moment another impulse controlled him and he mashed the steel tip of the walking stick, as though by accident, into the brass plate above the doorbell. The resulting scratch cut across the *D* of *Jason Duquesne* and the *y* of *Attorney-at-Law*.

*I must apologise for that*, Roderick told himself, for he was, as nearly as he could be, a true Southern gentleman with a sense of the proprieties second to no one's. Gently, he passed a leather-gloved finger to the bell and listened to the harsh notes of the antique chime.

He stood to the side, leaning on the iron railing, and examined the view across Boston Street. A horrendous procession of high-rise, government-financed apartment buildings—featureless, red-brick slabs, one just like another—spread up and down the length of Boston Street as far as Roderick could see. At first, when the ugly buildings had started going up five years before, Roderick had been secretly pleased. He was certain they offended Jason as much or more as they offended himself, and Jason would have to live with them every day. He would have only to glance out of his office window to see them, the great, gaunt *memento morts*, monuments to human ignorance and the triumph of bureaucracy over architecture. On more mature consideration, Roderick had found less cause to rejoice. Jason, who was pushing sixty and had already had two small strokes, would not last more than a few years more (by Roderick's calculations) and then the house on Boston Street would revert to Roderick and Delphinia. Or, more exactly, to Alice, since it was she, unfortunately, and not her parents, who was after Jason sole heir to the Duquesne millions.

*Ugliness,* Roderick reflected, *is everywhere now.* Then, as he was in the habit of editing his own thoughts, amended that to: *Uglification is rife.* Except that instead of ugliness they called it Urban Renewal. It was worst in New York, but it had spread up and down the coast quick as the pestilence. It had conquered Baltimore. It had even, he could remember, got down as far as Norfolk.

Strange, how Norfolk kept getting into his thoughts so much lately. And that last evening there ... he could remember the dilapidated house on that nameless street by the tidewater ... and the ugly modern furniture ...

Everyone had been in such a rush to be modern then. And where had it got them? Where were they all gone to now—the fraternity brothers, the floozies, the high-old times? *Golden lads and lasses must, Like chimney sweepers, come to dust.* That was the moral of the story, if it had any moral at all.

Impatiently, Roderick pressed the doorbell again, then turned back to confront the drear land of Urban Renewal ... He smiled, remembering.

'*They* call it urban renewal,' Bessy said, chuckling and jiggling the immensity of her bosom, 'but I know what *I* call it. I call it a doublecross. After all the graft I laid out to get hold of that place on East Main ... why, it makes a person positively sick at her stomach.'

'Then why do you keep laughing about it?' Roderick asked.

'Because it ain't never going to work, sweet child. Men—and sailors especial—are going to go round tomcatting no matter how much you renew the urban. They can push us off East Main, but they're only going to come looking for us later somewhere else, and I don't see the point, moving it from one street to another. Men is men, and a pretty girl ...'

'... is like a melody,' Roderick concluded gallantly.

Bessy smiled and patted Roderick on the knee. 'You'll get yours in a minute, honey. Just you be patient and drink up that black coffee. Now, you'll forgive me, won't you—I have to look in on the parlour. Sounds like those brothers of yours are chopping the place into firewood.'

Bessy left the kitchen through the swinging wooden doors, and for one crazy moment looking at her wide hips and huge, drooping buttocks Roderick had thought yes, he might enjoy taking her upstairs after all. What would Bogan have had to say about that? But then Bessy turned around, showing her full bulk in profile, and Roderick's unseemly desire quickly ebbed away, to be replaced by the more vivid and abiding emotion of hatred. Christ Almighty, how he hated Donald Bogan!

He took a penknife off his key chain and wiped the blade on the gabardine of his trousers. He cut a good three-inch gouge into the still-unmarred wood of the door between the kitchen and the parlour. Then, very carefully, he traced a long curve intersecting the vertical gouge at each end: *D*. The *B* was harder to make since the curves were smaller, but he worked slowly and, so to speak, lovingly. When he'd graven Bogan's initials for posterity to witness, he started on the initials of their fraternity.

It was the second night of the Kappa Kappa Kappa Annual Howl. The first night (the *only* night so far as the University authorities knew) was given over to more innocent pleasures: water-skiing and coeducational baseball in the afternoon, followed by an evening of dancing, light drinking, and, typically, light necking. Roderick's date had been Delphinia Duquesne, only daughter and sole heir of Morgan Duquesne of Baltimore. Despite their living now in Maryland (where Duquesne held an important seat in the state assembly), the Duquesnes were essentially a Southern family. The scuttlebutt at Tri-Kappa was that Duquesne practically *owned* two whole counties in the west part of Virginia, not to mention real estate in Richmond and Baltimore. Delphinia herself was as Southern as fried grits, and a mite prettier. She'd been 'finished' at St. Arnobia's, outside Charlottesville, and gone from there to a girl's college that was *so* exclusive that a daughter of Jefferson Davis had actually been refused admittance once upon a time. Such, at least, was the proud tradition. With a background like that one could overlook her looks (which weren't *bad*, really) and her age (she claimed twenty-eight; thirty-one was likelier), and excuse a certain amount of flightiness. In fact (and Roderick had been trying to convince himself of this proposition for weeks now), it wouldn't be at all hard to fall in love with a girl like Delphinia Duquesne.

It is one thing to fall in love with a southern belle; it is quite another to make out with her. So, when the brothers of Kappa Kappa Kappa woke up late next morning to take their sweethearts to depot, they were feeling chilled, hungover, and *mean*.

They picked up a keg of beer on the way back from the depot and worked on that till four in the afternoon. Then Roderick drove over to the other side of town and bought five quart-size Mason jars of bootleg gin. It would have been quite possible, and almost as cheap, to buy perfectly legal gin just twenty miles away, but what was the fun of that? As the fraternity charter stated, the brothers of Tri-Kappa believed in preserving Sacred Tradition. The bootleg gin was a ritual.

'Man, that sure's rotten stuff,' said Donald Bogan, ritually smacking his lips over the gin. Bogan, a short, fair senior who always spoke as though he were addressing a public meeting, was Tri-Kappa's unchallenged authority on the art and science of boozing. At twenty-four his face had already taken on the bloat and tinge of an alcoholic.

'You said it, man,' echoed Warder, the frat president. 'And you want to know something else rotten? last night was rotten. Man, I was as horny as a bullmoose. I feel like I been three years on a desert island with my hands tied behind my back. I mean, Roddy boy, what say we start off down to Hampton Roads and pay our little call on ol' Bessy?'

'Yeah,' said another pledge. 'I wouldn't mind changing *my* luck. How about it, Hot Rod? What you got lined up for us?'

Roderick, as the poorest and least 'connected' of his many brothers (mainly the sons of lawyers, bankers, and state politicos), was under the obligation to work his way through college, and his work consisted mainly in procuring, on the average of once a month, gin and women for his brothers. It was Roderick's belief (and it was well-founded) that his continued membership of Tri-Kappa depended solely on his talents as a provider of these necessaries at reasonable prices.

'How many?' Bogan asked loudly.

'Enough,' Roderick promised. 'Seven or eight.'

'Including ol' Bessy herself? How'd you like that, boys? I bet she ain't more than sixty years and not *much* more than three hundred pounds. The opportunity is still open. Now who will grasp it? How about you, Hot rod?' Like everything he said, Bogan's laughter seemed to come out of a public address system: it was loud, depthless, and rough-edged.

'No thanks, Bogan buddy. I haven't had as much gin as you have. I don't think I'd be up to it. I'll leave Bessy to you.'

Bogan glowered mirthlessly, as the drunken laughter continued around him. Bogan did not like Roderick. Roderick did not like Bogan. Twice Bogan had tried to have Roderick ostracised, and each time Roderick had made him look like a fool. And last night he'd made him look the biggest fool of all, because his date for the dance, Delphinia Duquesne, was the same girl Bogan had brought to last year's Howl—and afterwards bragged that he was engaged to.

The thirty-one brothers from Kappa Kappa Kappa had piled into six cars and driven the fifty miles into Norfolk in about as many minutes. There were cathouses, of course, within walking distance of the campus, but if they'd gone there they'd have missed the fun of racing down U.S. 64 stoned out of their minds, another sacred tradition. Besides, Bessy's whores cost half of what they got at the U, due to Roderick's canny use of the fraternity's bargaining power.

Bessy came to answer the door, flashing her professional good cheer and bogus jewellery, and chattered to the boys while she took a quick head count. 'Well, well, if it ain't the boys from *that* fraternity!' (She'd been warned never to speak the name of their house aloud in the brothers' presence, since most of them worried about blackmail, police raids, and newspaper publicity and liked to think, therefore, that Bessy thought they were merchant sailors on leave.) '*Isn't* that sweet? Girls!' she called out, 'come see what the colleges is turning out.'

When all the boys had gone into the parlour, Bessy took Roderick aside and scolded him for bringing more than he'd promised. 'With only eight girls, we're going to be at work all night.'

'You know as well as I do you'll be working all night in any case. So what's the fuss?' Roderick smiled appeasingly, and Bessy sighed resignedly as he paid out the fee they had contracted for. They entered the parlour together.

'Okay, children, have fun,' she said, giving her girls the go-ahead sign.

Ordinarily that would have been it, but Bogan was still feeling mean, and Bogan never got mean without wanting to give a public demonstration of it. 'I want *two* of your best tonight, mammy.'

'Two? Lord, ain't that being a mite greedy? We're a little short on supply tonight, honey, as you can plainly see.' She waved a massive hand in a sweeping gesture that made the shiny lavender material of her dress crackle electrically. It was plain to see: there were four frat brothers for every girl. The older boys were already making their choices and heading for the stairs, while the younger ones had settled on to chairs and couches to wait their turn.

'Hell with that noise,' said Bogan. 'I want what I want when I want it, and by damn I'll have it!' He strode across the room and pulled a tall, light-skinned girl away from a freckled senior.

The senior said something rude, and Bogan (who had commandeered, as his second choice, a black, rather homely girl that nobody had got to yet) said something ruder.

'Well now,' said Bessy brightly, when all the girls had been taken upstairs, 'why don't I make the rest of us a nice fresh pot of coffee?'

'Coffee!' sneered a freshman. 'I want a drink! He fumbled in the pocket of his blazer for the thirty-cent cigar he had bought days before in anticipation of this moment. After he'd bitten off the wrong end, he found himself unable to light it.

Someone started singing the University anthem. Roderick felt sick. It was the room that did it. Everything in it was new and in the worst possible taste. The green leatherette sofa on which four freshmen were sitting seemed to have come here from some dentist's waiting room. It was flanked with blonde, tiered tables with wrought-iron legs and glass-protected tops. On each table stood a vivid orange plaster pagoda of a lamp. The carpet was as white as an advertisement for laundry soap, but right near the tip of Roderick's oxford was a small dark stain. Blood or coffee, Roderick touched a finger to it. The synthetic material of the rug felt crinkly, like wadded-up cellophane.

He got to his feet and concentrated on not giving in to a sudden, dizzying sensation of nausea. He was disgusted with the whores, with the whorehouse, with ...

Himself. Last night he'd whispered protestations of eternal love into Delphinia's ear; tonight he'd come to hire some poor, broken-spirited girl for an hour of joyless love. Never again, he told himself. This would be the last time, absolutely. After all, one was bound to get a disease in the long run.

Feeling a little better with this matter decided, he leaned back and rested his hot cheek against the wallpaper, where clumps of red and yellow roses wound around a trellis up to the warped mouldings. Across from him above the green sofa was a portrait of Robert E. Lee. Three seniors came downstairs and went out to the cars to drink more gin and exchange lies.

Three juniors went up the stairs. Robert E. Lee winked at Roderick.

Roderick went into the kitchen. Immediately he felt better. 'What about that coffee?' he asked Bessy.

'Why, love you, child, I already brought that around and you said no. Sit you down and tell me how you like it. Cream and sugar?'

'Black.' He sank into a ricketty wooden chair and Bessy poured him a cupful.

'Whyn't you go upstairs and look see what your friend Bogan's up to, Roderick? You know where that little peephole is. He's taking way too long by my estimation.'

'That's his problem. There's nothing I can do to hurry him up. Say, Bessy, how come you moved here from East Main? I liked your old place a lot better. It was more ...'

'Homey?' Bessy suggested, pointing at the framed embroidery sampler above the icebox: GOD BLES OUR HAPPY H.

Roderick nodded.

'Well now, that's a long story.' Bessy lowered herself into a protesting kitchen chair. 'You see, Roderick, I been urbanly renewed!' And she had begun telling Roderick the long story.

... Roderick had just put the finishing touches to his own initials on the kitchen door when the screams began coming from upstairs ...

Jason's English-trained Negro butler answered the door. 'Mr. Raleigh! Mr. Duquesne will be delighted to see you, sir. If you'll wait a moment in the library ...'

The library was a dark, musty, pleasant room. The curtains were always drawn now to blot out the sight of the housing development. Roderick loved this room—the smell and touch of it, the warmth and the mass of books about him: the eighty heavy volumes of the code of Virginia in uniform leather bindings, the *Corpus Iuris Secundum*, the crumbling spines of an eighteenth-century *Codex*. Here was the world that Roderick had been intended for. This was the world that he would have occupied (in the capacity probably of a full partner) if only it hadn't been for someone with the initials D.B. Roderick took down one of the nearest volumes and began reading the almost-meaningless, magical words.

'If you're checking the inheritance laws, you're wasting your time.'

25

Roderick spun around, snapping the lawbook shut. 'My dear Uncle Jason! How are you feeling, sir? You *look* quite fit. Are you over that little . . . indisposition?'

'Thank you, I am quite well.' Uncle Jason's thin dry lips were twisted in a customary half-smile. 'How nice of my brother-in-law to pay me a call just to inquire after my health. Or was there something else?'

'As you know, sir, we have not always understood the terms of the trust fund in the same light. We have varied.'

'We have,' Jason agreed, waving Roderick to a chair. He seated himself behind his expansive desk and folded his blue-veined hands over his waistcoat. 'And to come down to it, you want more money, isn't that it? Isn't that always it? Now, please be so good as to skip the preamble—we both know it quite by heart—and proceed directly to the absurd pretexts. For I presume you've invented new ones or you wouldn't be here.'

'You're being unfair, Uncle Jason. If you only knew how hard Delphinia and I have tried to live within our meagre allotment. We've martyred ourselves. We've gone without. We've pinched pennies.'

'One million pennies a year is a lot of pinching, Roderick—when you have, as it were, free board and room.'

'Ten thousand dollars it not enough, Jason. It wouldn't be enough for just one of us.'

Jason began chuckling, not at all sympathetically. 'Then why don't you, strange as the idea must at first seem, go out and take a *job*, Roderick? The trust has nothing to say against it. You know, my dear young man—and forgive me if I seem to patronise, but I am fully a generation older than you—there is something I have never been able to get across to you these many years, and that is—this is *not* your money. You have no claim on it. Nor do I. I am merely the executor of my father's will. The money belongs not to you, nor to Delphinia, nor me, but to Alice, your daughter. The will is very clear and, as we all know by now, it is unbreakable. It says: "The remainder of my money and property is to be held in trust until the child or children of my daughter, Delphinia, reach the age of consent. The executor shall see to the proper upbringing and education of such child, or children, and . . ."'

'I know, I know,' muttered Roderick, who was pulling nervously at his gloves. 'The trust also states clearly that Delphinia and I are to be given the means to raise Alice as befits her station. Which is impossible on ten thousand a year. Double that amount would be scarcely enough. That's what I've come to see you about. Delphinia would have come with me but, as it happens, she's laid up in bed.'

Jason sighed. 'What else have you ever come to see me about, my boy? I declare, you and Delphinia have been provided for to the outermost limits of the will already. I can't let you get into Alice's money one penny further, not for *any* reason.'

'Jason, be reasonable. As Alice's father—which seems to be my only legal reason for existing—am I not expected to belong to certain clubs? To participate in civic functions? If not for my sake, then for Alice's?'

The old man waved his hand impatiently. 'Participate all you like, Roderick. Run for mayor, if that suits you. But don't expect Alice's trust fund to finance your campaign.'

'That's not what I mean, damn it! I mean ... joining clubs ... establishing valuable social contacts for her future ...'

Jason slapped his open hand on the desk with surprising force for a man of his age. His pale grey eyes sparkled with feeling, but his face was composed as he said, a moment later: 'No! I will *not* dole out money for you to join another country club, if that's what you mean. And I doubt that your daughter would find much profit in the "valuable contacts" you're liable to establish with that money. That money is not your entertainment fund, Roderick. It is Alice's living, her dowry, if you'll excuse such an old-fashioned notion, her *future*. Have you no sense of proportion, man? The most valuable contacts she can have right now are with her father and mother. She needs above all to grow up loving people and being loved, to think of someone besides herself, to rid herself of those unwholesome fantasies. That girl has been through a terrible ordeal. How you can come here *now*, after all that has happened? No, I will not talk about that with you, Roderick—it would only make me angry and fretful. We understand each other, all too well, I fear.'

'It's because I worry about Alice ...' Roderick began.

'Poppycock. You worry about yourself, and my sister worries about herself and her imaginary ailments. If it were otherwise, Alice wouldn't be in the state she is today. You are a selfish, frivolous man, and Delphinia is a selfish, frivolous woman.

'No, don't run away, Roderick. Hear me out. You'll continue to get your ten thousand a year for as long as Delphinia or you are alive. You may fritter your half of it away on night-clubs and "valuable contacts" if you wish, and Delphinia may feed hers to her hypochondria, but you'll not get one penny more! Not one penny!'

Instead of having risen at the end of this speech, the old man's raspy voice was lowered to a hush. Jason wasn't one to idly bluster, Roderick knew. This had been a serious statement of policy, and it boded ill. He stared with pursed lips at the only outward sign of Jason's upset—a purplish vein that pulsed in his high, soulful forehead. Then, bowing his head in a curt farewell, Roderick turned away and headed for the door.

Outside, Roderick's fists unclenched about his walking stick. His jaw relaxed then, and the flush of anger faded to a dull glow of resentment. Whistling the same Victor Herbert march tune, he walked to the Hotel Chesapeake Cocktail Lounge, ten blocks away. He would not let himself be cast down. Actually, he hadn't expected anything to come of his visit to Jason, but he had owed it to Delphinia to try. As soon as the bartender saw him come in the door, he began mixing a martini, dry, on the rocks.

Chapter 3

Were the dear little canaries trying to say something to Delphinia? Were they trying to say:

> Just a minute, Delphinia dear,
> And your own dear Rodipoo will soon be here?

It would be a comfort for her to believe it. She'd been waiting for him to return from Jason whole *hours* now. The Lord knew, she had few enough comforts to support her. Wasted by illness, conspired against by doctors, scanted by her husband, and scorned by her only child—it was a harder life than a woman of delicate constitution should have had to bear. She lifted her eyes to heaven—as much in accusation as in prayer . . .

. . . And saw the cracks in the ceiling. By now Delphinia knew every one of them by heart. Directly over the bed was a great patch of chipped paint that resembled a horse and rider, posting. Over to the left, above the escritoire, was a lady in hoop-skirts, as clearly defined as if she'd been painted there by an Old Master. Beyond that, in the northeast corner, was a face that could be a man's or a woman's, depending on Delphinia's mood and the events of the day. Once, unwisely, she had complained to Jason about the cracks in the ceiling (hoping he would relent and let them have the house on Boston Street for themselves), and he had sent plasterers in to repair the cracks. Delphinia had had some difficulty explaining why she'd sent the plasterers away.

Such a day: Delphinia's back hurt! The canaries were starving! Rodipoo was taking *forever*! She wanted to stamp her foot from sheer pique, but there was nothing to stamp it against but the contour mattress. Her bed was so monstrously big that when she sat halfway up in it her foot was a yard away from the foot-board. It made her feel like a little girl sometimes.

The bed was such a *nice* bed—an heirloom that had been in Delphinia's family for ages. Her mother's grandmother was supposed to have rescued it from the burning of Atlanta, single-handedly fighting off Sherman's henchmen. It—and maybe the cameo clasp on the neck of her nightgown—was the only remnant of what had been a proud old Southern family.

There was still money, of course, but it was new money,

money without a tradition to ennoble it. Her father, Morgan Duquesne, had made his fortune speculating in tobacco futures and real estate back in the 'twenties. Still, tradition or no, if Delphinia could have had that money, she would have been much happier. She would have *given* it a tradition. Her pale thin fingers twiddled on the counterpane as the thought of how she might have ennobled that money: elegance, chandeliers, a tremendous staircase, gardens; parties every Friday night—not parties—*balls!*—invitations to all the best homes—which she might ignore if she so chose! *Dozens* of coloured servants, including a butler just like that sonofabitch at Jason's, and a chauffeur in livery. Relaxing on the veranda in the evening, friends dropping in to gossip and admire the elegance, the chandeliers, the ...

Dreams! She would never have that money. The injustice had been done, and now it could not be undone. She would spend the rest of her life a *prisoner* in her own bedroom. It was like a romantic old story, the sadness of it ...

Delphinia had never been a strong woman, and the shock of her father's will, coming as it had hard on the heels of Alice's delivery, had turned her into a permanent invalid. She could still remember the fateful afternoon when the will had been read, the musty office, and that terrible, sly smile of Jason's when he came to the part that had disinherited her. Her father had warned he would do it, but she had never taken him seriously. Jason must have put her father up to it. Jealous Jason. Otherwise it was too incredible. She must remember and tell that to her lawyer. They should *sue* Jason for alienation of affections.

Actually, they should have sued him long ago, because when the will had been read, Delphinia had swooned right on top of one of the heavy oak chairs in Jason's office and injured her spine. He *had* been thoughtful enough to pay the hospital bill for X-rays and such. (Or had that been just some mode of his foxiness? Just a clever way to sidestep his legal *responsibilities*?) After the hospital, the arthritis had set in, and Delphinia had to be confined to her bed. No matter what nonsense the doctors talked, Delphinia had faith that she would be delivered from her cross some day. It was all a matter of finding the right doctor. If only Jason would let her make a trip to Europe to consult specialists ...

It wasn't *fair*! And it always came back to Jason! Jason, smiling that sly, lawyer's smile of his, telling her she wasn't *really* sick! If only he knew the pain she suffered every day from the arthritis—not to mention a stomach as delicate as a butterfly's. Jason, sending around his quack doctors for 'checkups'. Doctors? Spies, rather, whose only interest was in seeing how close to death's door she was and then reporting back to *him*!

Delphinia poured herself a glass of icewater from the pitcher on the bedside table, shook one of the useless pink tablets into her palm, and swallowed it with a sip of water. Gasping from the exertion, she set the glass back on the porcelain tray. A few drops of water spattered on to the surface of a tortoise-shell hand-mirror. After wiping it with a tissue (it was exactly for chores like this that she *ought* to have had a maid of her own), she began to examine her features as carefully as an augerer would search for omens.

*I'm pale as a white rose,* she thought. A single, delicate vein showed upon her ivory brow like an ornament. A hairdresser came in once a week to rinse lavender into Delphinia's long, greying hair and do it up exactly as it had to be done. It was worth the effort—everyone said her hair was like a work of art. She had the pale grey eyes of a Duquesne, but hers seemed to have taken on the delicate lavender tint of her hair, or of the vein in her forehead. Or of the vivid purple shadows beneath her eyes? The shadows came from lack of sleep and would vanish if ever her illness were cured and the insomnia went away.

The coral rosebud of her lips which she had put on fresh an hour before, puckered and drew near to the friendly, flattering mirror, but before they could touch it, she heard Rodipoo's familiar tread in the hallway—why did he always seem to *march* everywhere?—why couldn't he just stumble around like everybody else?—and Delphinia had barely time to set aside the mirror and fluff the artificial nosegay pinned to her nightgown before he came in the door.

'Rodipoo! *Quel surprise!*'

Rodipoo looked sullen and out-of-sorts, and he *slumped* in the genuine imitation antique Louis Quatorze chair beside the bed, which was most unlike Rodipoo to do. The canaries had suddenly gone wild with anxiety, and Delphinia knew that something terrible had happened.

He told her everything he'd said to Jason or Jason to him. She could scarcely bear to listen. Rodipoo got angrier and angrier. His shoulders hunched, and his chin came jutting forward aggressively. He looked like a bulldog. How could a man do so little exercise and remain so strong-looking? Why, he looked more like some Norfolk sailor than a Southern gentleman who'd never had to do a day's work in his life.

It had been just this—the lower-class burliness coupled with a gentlemanly manner—that had first endeared Rodipoo to her. It had been a mistake to fall in love. She should never have given in to his demands for an elopement. But how was she to have known he'd been expelled from college two weeks short of graduation? He had deceived her. He knew she would have never eloped with him if she had thought he wasn't the sort of young man a Duquesne could be proud to marry.

When Roderick was done telling his same old story, Delphinia lowered her eyelashes contemptuously. 'You're drunk,' she said. 'Were you drunk when you went in to see him? Is *that* why you were so ready to surrender to his base conditions?'

'Delphinia, there's no need for *us* to fight. We have enough real problems without tearing each other apart again.'

'Oh, it's all very well for *you*! But do you ever think what it must be like for *me*? To lie here, day after day, with nothing to look at but a cracked ceiling! Oh, I wish I were able to leave this bed. I wish *I* could go to Jason's office and lay it on the line to him. I can promise you that *I* wouldn't go creeping away with my tail between my legs, like a beaten dog! God, I wish *I* were the man in this family. If I had my strength and health about me, there is nothing *I* wouldn't stop at to get what justly is *mine*. *Murder* would not be too much . . .'

'Delphinia, you're being silly, and you're going to end up in a state.'

'That money is *my* money. It belongs to *me*. And it's your fault that I don't have it. If I'd married a *decent* man—if you hadn't *lied* to me—Daddy would not have cut me out of the will. It's your fault that we're practically starving!'

'It's nobody's fault but your father's. You might as well try to blame it on Alice, who wasn't a year old at the time.'

'I do! It *is* her fault! What does *she* need all my money for? Why does she need a full-time personal servant, who costs I don't know how many thousands for the three months of the summer, when I lay here at death's door with no one to look after me? Who's the sick one—me or Alice? She's not sick. She puts on an act to get attention. *I* should know what sickness is. My life has been nothing but one long sickness. So don't talk to me about *Alice*! Schizophrenia—my ass! What's schizophrenia compared to arthritis?'

Delphinia developed this train of reasoning at some length, but when she looked up from behind her lace hankie, damp with tears and sweat, she discovered that Roderick had tiptoed out of the room. It was just as well. She needed to rest after the emotional ordeal she had been put through. Eventually the canaries quieted down, and the house became so still that Delphinia could hear, somewhere outside in the garden, Alice singing a French song about a fox and a crow.

*Mes sincer's compliments, cher monsieur du Corbeau*
*'Dans ce chic habit noir, Ah! que vous êtes beau!*
*Et si votre ramage egale vos atours,*
*Vous êtes la phénix des fôrets d'alentour.'*
    *Sur l'air du tra la la, la,*
    *Sur l'air du tra de ri de ra*
    *Tra la la!*

Alice glanced up quizzically at Miss Godwin, for the little flourish of grace notes that she had added as her own contribution had got lamentably out of hand.

'Your French is improving, Mademoiselle,' Miss Godwin observed tactfully. 'And now that you've shown me you still remember La Fontaine—which I never for a moment doubted —why don't we get down to the business of state capitals? What is the capital of Alabama?'

'Montgomery.'

'Of Alaska?'

'Juneau. Miss Godwin, there something else I had to talk to you about this morning.' Miss Godwin half-closed the book on her lap and pushed up her reading glasses with an impatient forefinger. 'It's a personal problem. Remember, you said I was always supposed to tell you about anything like that right away —instead of talking to Dinah.'

'You haven't *been* talking to her lately, have you?'

'No,' Alice said. Quite honestly, for it had been fully a week since she'd had her conversation with Dinah sitting in front of St. Arnobia's in the rain. 'No, I waited till I could talk to you this morning. It's about Mommy. You see ... I don't think ... I mean, I wonder sometimes ...'

'Yes?'

'If she loves me.'

'Of course she does, Alice. She loves you very much. What makes you wonder about it, though?'

'Well, I've been home a week now and every time I go to her room she's got something else wrong with her and doesn't want to see me. The only question she had to ask about school was if I'd had the same desk she'd written her name on thirty-five years ago. When I told her all the furniture was new, she started to cry.'

Miss Godwin bit her lower lip, then, with conscious effort, smiled. 'Do you remember last year, Alice, when we went to the zoo and I explained about all the different kinds of love in the world? How the mother-bear will cuff her children about to show the way she loves them, how the eagle's children never see their mother at all, because she's always hunting for their food and is only home at mealtimes . . .'

'Like Daddy,' Alice interjected, smiling.

'Some love is very loud and noisy like a cage of monkeys, and other love hides away like a crab in the sand, afraid to show itself. We can never just walk up to somebody and say— love me the way I want to be loved. We have to wait for them to do it in their own way at their own time.'

Alice sighed. 'I *suppose* so . . .'

'Now, your father—*he* certainly pays attention to you, doesn't he?'

'Yes, sometimes. Although it's funny about Daddy. He's very nice to me and all, but sometimes I get the impression that he doesn't know who I am. He's like one of those people at the Museum, the ones who see a statue and walk around it and finally turn and ask someone else: "What do you think it *means*?" '

'And no wonder, Alice! It's been nine long months since he's had a good look at you. You're inches taller and kilowatts brighter, and you must seem like an entirely new girl to him. You do to me.'

'Really? I mean, do you really think I've *improved*?'

'Now, *that's* fishing. You know the rule about fishing for compliments. Tell me the capital of Arizona.'

Alice closed her eyes and tried to remember the pictures she'd made up to make it easier to remember that one by. *Ariz* were the first four letters of Arizona, which was almost the same as *aris*ing. And who was the bird La Fontaine had mentioned? The bird that arose out of his own ashes every thousand years?

'*Phénix!*' Alice proclaimed triumphantly. 'The capital of Arizona is *Phénix*.'

'And Arkansas?'

'Little Rock.'

And Geography was the capital of Dullness. If only there were some way to make it really interesting, the way math and science were interesting. Bored but not unhappily (because it was nice after all, to be home, with intelligent people to talk to), she recited state capitals and stared at her arms, first one way and then another, to see if she'd started to tan. No, it was hopeless. She was still as pale as . . .

A white rose.

Across from Alice, putting her pallor to shame, Miss Godwin was a veritable festival of colours in her orchid-and-green floral-print, Speckles of sunshine filtering through the willow branches brought out bright tints of copper in the dark skin of her face and arms, and behind her a border of young marigolds echoed the same ruddy tone.

A few yards up the garden path stood the house itself— Alice's house. A simple white wood box of two and a half stories, it had a quiet middle-of-the middle-class air about it. The Raleigh house and the others spaced out along Gwynn River Falls Drive had known a brief moment of glory half a century before when the patrician element of Baltimore had made their country homes there, but now the suburbs were encroaching, the patricians had decayed or moved out, the fabulous gardens were being divided into lots, and the carriage houses were being rented as homes.

Just a few feet on the other side of the Drive was Gwynn River Falls, now little more than a marsh, due to the unrelenting dryness of recent years. It was June, but the screen of willows along the shore had a Septemberish look, and the sweet corn in the fields on the other side of the river was scant and unpromising. At the further end of this field a car had stopped on the dusty county road. The man in the driver's seat was looking across the river at the houses along Gwynn Falls River Drive through high-powered Japanese binoculars.

'It's too open,' he said to his companion, a tall Negro youth masked in sunglasses. 'And there's too much traffic on the highway.'

'Ain't that what I said all along?' the Negro commented.

'Well, it wasn't *my* idea either, you know.' The man in the driver's seat lowered his binoculars to reveal eyes as vividly green as the leaves of the cornplants.

'Don't sweat it,' said the Negro. 'Let's split.'

Jason Duquesne was behind the library curtains watching the cars go by on Boston Street and trying to ignore the monumental awfulness of the development just across the street. A copper-coloured Buick stopped for the signal, and only a few cars behind it was Miss Godwin's Saab. Jason waved out of the open window, and Alice threw him a kiss.

When the butler entered the library to announce their visit, Jason was decorously installed at his desk, pretending to read Miss Godwin's twenty-four-page report.

'Show Miss Godwin into the library, and tell my niece that we'll join her in the parlour in just a while. Oh—and James...?'

'Sir?'

'Tell my niece that a certain book with a peppermint drop on it may be of interest to her in the meantime.'

Miss Godwin was wearing a fluffy pink dress, a wide-brimmed pink hat, and an unconvincing, but still sweet, pink smile. Jason had never been able to put her at her ease when they were alone together, although when Alice was with them all her constraint disappeared. As though the woman were only comfortable with children.

It had been just the opposite with Mrs. Buckler, Alice's governess of two years before. Jason had got on splendid with *her*. They had discussed Alice's progress in her studies, her health, her character, and Mrs. Buckler had seemed to be the most sensible, refined, and conscientious of women. The old hypocrite had taken Jason in for almost a year, and the consequences had been disastrous. When Mrs. Buckler had not been entirely indifferent to her eight-year-old charge, she had been nasty, devising subtle cruelties that would make Alice appear to be in the wrong. The girl had retreated more and more into a private world of pretence and fantasy to escape the treacheries of her governess—a retreat that would inevitably have led to out-and-out psychosis, if it had not been for Jason's tardy awakening to his niece's condition and Mrs. Buckler's true character. He could still remember that Christmas morning two years ago when he had paid a surprise visit to the Raleigh home and found Alice sitting alone beneath the gigantic, tinsel-decked evergreen and 'giving away' all her gifts to Dinah, who would, ungratefully, break them up or tear them to pieces. The psychiatrist in New York who'd examined her had said it was a very close thing, a matter of only months perhaps. How, Jason had always wondered, could her parents have seen her playing and talking with 'Dinah' every day and never suspected?

Yes, all things considered, Miss Godwin was an improvement. If only she had been a little less ... Negro-like ... Jason would have been more comfortable with her, but he hadn't been able to bring up the subject with Dr. Wirth at the clinic in New York, and it had not seemed to make any difference to Alice, who was used to dealing with Negroes on terms of equality, since Dinah, when she had not been simply a cat, had been a coloured girl. So, despite a certain residual uneasiness, Jason could not help but be grateful to the Negress for what she'd done.

'Are you feeling well, Mr. Duquesne?'

'Oh dear, have I been sitting here woolgathering? Excuse me. Yes, thank you, I'm quite fine, though I may add that from a meteorological point-of-view, there may be general cause for anxietal behaviour, eh? Due to the inspissation of the liquid element. Wouldn't you say so?'

'I beg your pardon?' The fashion-show smile was definitely slipping away.

'I was just trying to demonstrate, Miss Godwin, the way in which language sometimes interferes with the normal processes of communication. I refer especially to this latest, and least comprehensible, report on my niece's condition. Twenty-four pages written in the obscurest dialect of *Sociology*.' Jason flicked through the report. 'What am I to make of 'approach to group-response orientation"? Or—and this is my favourite—"redirection of sublimed and non-sublimed anxietal behaviour"? I am told you understand your work, Miss Godwin, but I assure you no one else ever will at this rate. You make the cure sound worse than the disease. A machine would not describe another machine so coldly as you describe Alice in these pages.'

'*Mister* Duquesne!'

'Oh, now I've done it. Forgive me. I don't mean to be curmudgeonly, but I've been sitting here all afternoon inventing *bon mots*. But if you *would* just take back this report and translate it into English for me, I'd be grateful. You see, I understand that "verbal behaviour" means speech, and I *think* "affective projection" is daydreaming, but for most of the rest of it I'm really at a loss. A single page of conclusions is enough, just something to let me know if she's better, and what danger there is of her falling back into the unfortunate condition from which you've rescued her. I give you credit for that, Miss

Godwin, but when you write your reports, just tell in an old-fashioned way whether Alice is a good girl and whether she will grow up to be worthy of her fortune and her name.'

'You will have such a report tomorrow, sir. In the meantime, let me assure you that Alice is much better. St. Arnobia's has done her a world of good. Only the most exceptional and unlikely circumstances could precipitate a return to ... her former condition. I think Alice is strong enough at this point to stand up to even another Mrs. Buckler, though God forbid she should have to. And I had thought, sir, that I'd said as much in Section Eight, the summary.'

Jason cradled his forehead in his fingers, avoiding the governess' eyes. 'Excuse me, Miss Godwin, I've not only been unfair to you, but dishonest as well. No doubt you've seen through me all this while. It wasn't your report that upset me; it was something else entirely. Perhaps you're a good enough psychologist—or fortune-teller—to be able to tell me what that was, eh?' Jason smiled a crooked, self-mocking smile.

'Perhaps I can. Would it be that you've had another fight with Alice's father?'

'Bravo! Yes, he's been around trying to weasel more money out of the trust. The way those two vultures circle around that child's inheritance! I used not to worry about it so much, but since this whole Buckler affair, I'm afraid that their attitude will poison her character, drive her back into the old fantasies.'

'Then let me assure you, Mr. Duquesne, that it simply isn't the case. Alice has—what shall I say that isn't jargon?—adjusted beautifully. I've been particularly attentive of her relationship with her parents, and though it is not ideal, Alice's character will probably be strengthened by it in the long run. She's stopped living in daydreams and started living in the world of ideas. She is learning things at an incredible pace and has a logical sense that astounds me more each day, even knowing her I.Q. I don't know if I should say this—but she may already be brighter than her parents.'

'Ha! That's no very great distinction, is it? I've never yet lost an argument to Roderick—and as for my sister Delphinia ... well, we always used to be charitable and say she inherited the family *looks*. As for Alice ...'

'As for Alice,' Miss Godwin broke in, 'I suspect she's growing terribly impatient with us. Why discuss my report, when the subject of it—or' (with an arch smile) 'should I say *Exhibit A*?—is waiting for us in the next room?'

38

'All right,' Jason agreed, chuckling, 'let's examine the evidence.' He walked behind her to the parlour, where James was about to lay the tea.

'Dear, dear Uncle Jason,' Alice trilled, coming forward exactly as Miss Boyd had coached her to, with her right hand slightly lifted for her uncle to press to his lips. 'How delightful to see you again!' But at the last moment all her etiquette deserted her, and she found herself disgracefully clinging to the old man's neck and kissing his face all over. Then, a moment later, she was as calm as one of the Fates, sitting beside Jason on the settee.

'You've grown, my dear, I'm delighted to say. I have to stoop far less this year to kiss you. But you still look exactly like Alice in Wonderland.'

And indeed, she might have stepped right out of a Tenniel illustration with her navy-blue dress and contrasting apron, her knee-length stockings and patent-leather pumps. A clear case of Nature imitating Art.

'I must thank you, Uncle, for letting me look at your book.' She nodded at a battered-up edition of *Just-So Stories* on the table before them. 'As you know, Kipling is one of my favourite authors. And it seems to be *very* old.'

'It's a first edition, Alice, and it's yours. That is, if you'll pour the tea and do a good job of it.'

'A first edition! Of Kipling! Really? Oh, Uncle!'

After she had gathered her etiquette about her again and tea was over, Uncle Jason paid Alice the supreme compliment of challenging her to a game of chess. He offered her a two-rook handicap, which she loftily refused.

'Excuse us, Miss Godwin,' Jason explained, 'but it's been nine months since I've had a go at this young lady, and I suspect she's been polishing up her endgame in the meanwhile.' Miss Godwin appeared to be quite content with her copy of *Realités*.

For the sake of probability, Jason usually trounced Alice, but today Alice played particularly well. She took his queen, without his quite intending she should, and later, when she made her most masterly move (and he could tell from the glint in her eye that she *knew* it was brilliant) he threw up his hands in mock despair. 'The Defence concedes.'

She was still not tanned! Three weeks of holiday were gone, and she was not a bit darker than the day she'd left St. Arnobia's. The problem was that she didn't have the patience to lie around on a beach doing nothing. Maybe only very dull people could get suntans.

'Miss Godwin, *why* can't I get brown?'

'Hm? Oh, yes.' The governess was writing in her black leather notebook, the cup of coffee on the breakfast-nook table before her forgotten and cold. Alice noticed that her governess had put just enough cream in her coffee to make it the same shade as her skin.

'Do you think *I* could get brown, if I drank coffee instead of milk?'

'What? No, the food we eat has little to do with the colour we are.'

Alice giggled. 'Oh, Miss Godwin, you haven't been listening to me at all, or you'd know I was teasing. Are you writing another report on me? You'll have to give me a very high score for stupidity for asking that last question.'

Miss Godwin continued to make out the report, imperturbed. Alice's father came into the breakfast nook wearing a blue seersucker suit from a few years ago that had become a little tight about the waist. His face was puffy from lack of sleep, and he'd forgotten to put on a tie.

Miss Godwin and Alice greeted him, and he replied with a growl from deep in his chest. Emmie brought him a carafe of hot coffee and poured the first cup. After moistening his lips, he could speak. 'God—that sun. Turn it off!'

Miss Godwin reached over to the cord and twitched the venetian blinds shut. Roderick essayed a smile and felt tentatively to see if his toupee was in place. It was. His smile became more assured.

'My, you're up early today, Daddy,' Alice observed over the edge of her milk glass. This was the first time all summer that they'd had breakfast together.

He nodded, sipping at the hot coffee, then asked, still gruffly: 'Why are you so dressed up? Is this a holiday, or someone's birthday?'

Alice was delighted that he'd noticed her dress. It was cut

exactly like Miss Godwin's, with a full skirt flaring out from the hips, except that Alice's was turquoise while Miss Godwin's was canary yellow. Miss Godwin also lacked a puffy bow on her derrière. Alice's loose blonde curls were caught up in a ponytail by a smaller bow of the same material. 'Do you like it? It's for art class, though I do have to wear a smock over it when I paint. I always have art class on Saturday at the Museum.'

'Oh, really?'

When it appeared that her father had nothing further to say, she re-opened the book beside her breakfast plate and began reading to herself. It was bad manners to read at the table, but both Miss Godwin and her father seemed too preoccupied with their own bad manners to care. After a few moments she giggled.

'A funny story?' Roderick asked, in a manful effort to appear human, despite the hour.

'Sort of, Daddy. It's a math problem.'

'Math? Oh—arithmetic, you mean. Yes, I remember the stories in my old arithmetic book. *A* giving part of his apples to *B*, and *B* never having as many as *C*, and so on. Very distressing situations. They never amused *me*.'

'We have a new way of teaching math now, Mr. Raleigh,' Miss Godwin said. 'The children are taught logical constructs instead of the old, tedious number-juggling. The new math teaches them to think and, just incidentally, it's much livelier. For teachers as well, I might add.'

'Is that so?' Though Roderick was clearly more interested in his coffee than in the new mathematics, Alice began talking in a rush to explain it all to him, ignoring her governess's warning glances.

'Oh yes, Daddy, it's fascinating. Look at this problem I was just reading—it's about parents and their children,' She read aloud from the book: '*There are more adults than boys, more boys than girls, more girls than families. If no family has less than three children, how few families are there be?*'

His weary lids lifted to show more of the reddened whites of his eyes. 'Is *that* what you're studying?'

'Mm-hmm. How many, Daddy? Do you know the answer? Think!'

He rubbed his hand over his face and scratched his moustache, mumbling about parents and their children.

'Shall I read the problem again, or do you give up?'

'Now now, babydoll. Your Daddy's a very tired man this morning, and he's a little slow on his mental feet.'

'Drink your milk, mademoiselle,' Miss Godwin said brusquely. 'You have to be at art class by nine.'

Alice gulped down her milk in one long swallow, then began explaining the problem while there was still time. 'Daddy, listen—there are more adults than boys, and more boys . . .'

'All *right*! But I still fail to see what there is that makes you laugh.'

'Because I could see the answer right away. It looks hard, but it's really simple. If there were *two* families, there would have to be three girls and four boys—but there would only be four adults. So there have to be more than two. If there were *four* families, there would be at least five girls and six boys, eleven altogether. So one of the families would only have two children. And it would be worse for more than four families. So the answer has to be three?'

Alice giggled happily at this piece of induction. Miss Godwin rose from the table, closing Alice's book. 'Come, Miss Logician, we're going to be late.'

Roderick lighted a cigarette and waved bye-bye. Or so Alice thought. To Miss Godwin it had looked more as if he were waving out the match.

Roderick blew a smoke ring and watched it expand till it hit Alice's empty milk glass and broke up. Yawning, he pulled her math book towards him and turned the pages at random. Eight-thirty was a beastly time to get up in the morning.

Because Miss Godwin's Saab was back at the garage for repairs, they had to take a bus to the Baltimore Museum, which suited Alice perfectly. Buses were more fun than cars. On Saturdays the Gwynn River Falls bus was always full of screaming teenagers in bright clothes on their way to the municipal beach. Alice would be at the beach herself—in the afternoon—where she would meet her friend Dorothy, after she'd had lunch at Howard Johnson's. She knew it was considered gauche, but despite herself she still liked Howard Johnson's best of all the restaurants in Baltimore.

She sat very quietly on the green plastic seat so that she could hear the Number One Song in the Nation which was blaring out of three transistor radios that boys on the bus were holding outside the windows. At home she wasn't allowed to listen to the Big Beat stations, so she was always hungry for the sound of it. Some of the older girls wore shorts, some stretch pants—all in the wildest electric blues and oranges and fuchsias. One girl had a blouse that was candy-apple red. Very vulgar, Alice thought. She wondered what Miss Godwin would say if she used candy-apple red on her nails. The boys on the bus were excruciatingly handsome—though Alice wasn't really interested in boys. They wore blue jeans that were practically in rags and the longest, longest blond hair—and they were *so* brown. She decided she would try to recapture the vivid chaos of the scene in art class. But however was she to get the feeling of the Number One Song into the painting? From the bus stop it was three blocks to the Museum. Miss Godwin would take her to the door, then go further downtown to take care of her shopping.

This summer the children's art teacher was an older New York woman who said her name was Lonnie Braggs. Miss Braggs was, to Alice's way of thinking a complete ninny. She strolled around in riding breeches from student to student, praising everyone's work indiscriminately, no matter how bad it really was. Last week she'd told Alice that her collage was as good as the Braque on the third floor of the Museum, when Alice knew perfectly well it was a wretched mess. Even the *pasting* had been botched. When she'd pointed that out to Braggs (who didn't like to be addressed as '*Miss* Braggs'), Braggs had said: 'The crucial thing, darling, isn't what it *looks* like or how *neat* it is, but how honestly it expresses your emotions. Self-expression—that's the ticket! When I said it was as good as Braque, I meant it was as *honest*.' How could you ever talk to someone like that? Maybe Braggs really did believe what she said and wasn't able to tell any difference between a good painting and a bad painting.

When they reached the side entrance to the Museum, Miss Godwin took Alice's hand. 'I'll see you at this door at twelve o'clock exactly. Our table is reserved at Howard Johnson's for half-past. Remember, when you paint, to look sloppy and wildeyed. From what I've heard of your Miss Braggs that'll put you right at the head of the class. *Au revoir*.'

'Miss Raleigh? Miss Godwin?' A tall Negro in livery strode up to talk to them and touched his cap. 'I am Mr. Duquesne's chauffeur. Mr. Duquesne has had a stroke, and you are to come with me to his house.'

'Uncle Jason!' Alice shrieked. 'Oh, *not* Uncle Jason.'

Miss Godwin held her hand very tight as they walked to the

waiting limousine. The chauffeur helped them into the spacious back seat. His lips showed no more expression than a cat's, and his eyes were hidden behind heavy sunglasses.

'Is he going to die?' Alice implored. Without answering, the chauffeur closed the back door and got in behind the wheel. The back seat was closed off from the front by a glass window.

Miss Godwin found the microphone that communicated to the driver and switched it on. 'Will you describe Mr. Duquesne's condition, please?'

The chauffeur spoke into another microphone, and the sound of his voice seemed to come out of the floor of the car. 'I can't say, ma'am. I didn't see his Honour, myself. The doctor's with him now. It was the doctor gave me my orders.'

'I see. Thank you.'

Alice almost made the mistake of giggling when it occurred to her that Miss Godwin should have ended the discussion by saying 'Over and out.' It was really a magnificent car. Much bigger than the Horners' old Caddy. Funny, that Uncle Jason had never mentioned having such a car. Maybe he'd been saving it as a surprise. But why did he want a car like this when he hardly ever left the house? And a chauffeur!

It was terrible, his having another stroke, and it seemed very strange and ominous that he should want to see her immediately afterwards. Unless—but Alice didn't want to consider that *unless*.

The limousine came to Boston Street and drove right on past. 'Say,' Alice shouted, 'that was Boston Street! He should have turned left there! I think the driver must be lost. Don't you think you should tell him he's lost, Miss Godwin?'

But Miss Godwin made no reply. She stared straight in front of her with a queer, tense expression that Alice had never seen before. At last Alice herself picked up the microphone, pressed the button, and said: 'You're going *the wrong way*. You've gone *past* Uncle Jason's street. It was blocks ago!' But the microphone must have been broken, for the chauffeur didn't answer or even look around.

It wasn't until they entered the waterfront district that Alice knew the man had been lying all along. They hadn't been going to Uncle Jason's at all. Alice was being kidnapped! At last! How thrilling!

Chapter 5

The only seat in the bus left unoccupied was the one beside Mrs. Elizabeth McKay, and in a sense that was occupied too, at least in part, by her spillover. In the space still left free in that seat she had deposited her bag, a bountiful cloth carryall as ample as herself. Now, as the bus pulled into its Baltimore terminal, she replaced the sheaf of pamphlets with which she had whiled away the hours from Norfolk into the top of the bulging satchel.

She waited till the last white-uniformed sailor was off before she attempted the narrow aisle herself. The cleaning man helped her down the steps. Such courtesies were paid her more and more often of late, and it could not be out of respect simply for her bulk, for she had been carrying *that* around for a good fifteen years already. No, they could see, somehow, that she was dying, that she was as good as dead. Their courtesy was a funereal gesture, like tipping your hat to a hearse.

'Well, you're no spring chicken yourself, honey,' she thought sourly, as she smiled good-bye and thank-you to the cleaning man.

Having wrested the carryall away from a porter, she found herself a taxi outside the terminal, and without really giving it a thought (for her corns and bunions were crying aloud for mercy), she threw open the back door. Too late she saw that the driver was white.

Before she could mumble an apology, the white man had lifted the canvas bag out of her hands and settled it on the front seat. 'Where to, ma'am?' he asked.

Startled, she could not remember, for a moment, where it was she had to be. She entered the cab reluctantly. When she did find her voice, it was scarcely audible, and she had to repeat her destination: 'The Royalton Hotel.'

Well, this certainly wasn't the Baltimore *she* remembered! As soon as the shock of it had worn off, she found herself resenting the driver. If he'd been coloured, she could have taken off her shoes.

Reaching the Royalton, she overtipped ridiculously, and the driver, out of appreciation or from that same sense of her decrepitude, carried the bag to the desk of the hotel. Settling it down, the topmost pamphlet tumbled out. It's blurred, four-colour cover represented what seemed to be a rather thickly wooded golf course; above this a jumble of various lettering tried to disguise the advertising throwaway as a magazine: SUNRISE, a Magazine for Those Who Care. *Special Hot Weather Problems Issue!* Then, beneath in a flowery script, the epitaph: 'There shall be no more death.'

'Thank you,' she said tartly, snatching it back, fearful that he would notice the mailing address glued in the lower right-hand corner: *Green Pastures Funeral Home, North Tidewater Road, Norfolk. Va.*

'Hell of an hour,' the sleepy desk clerk commented, as she signed the register. (*Elizabeth Brown*, with a special curlicue at the end and a circle instead of a dot over the *i*.) He was a white man too, though the old bellhop who took her bags up the creaking, carpeted stairs was just the colour you'd expect.

'Many white men stay at this hotel?' she asked nervously.

' 'Bout half of 'em's white. You got no cause to worry.'

Seemed as if Baltimore was getting as integrated as that heaven she remembered some preachers used to talk about, with black and white singing the Lord's praises and glory hand in hand. Hah! Wasn't but one place, here or hereafter, ever really got integrated, and that was a cathouse. White and black, they paid their dues and they took their fun.

The two flights of stairs were longer than she was prepared for, and by the time she was in Room 323, she didn't have breath left to thank the man. Within the thick envelope of her bosom, her heart was pounding like an air-hammer. Without troubling to unpin her hat, she sank down on to the thin mattress of the iron bedstead and sat perfectly quiet until the battleship-grey walls of the room had stopped their sideways spinning.

It wasn't, Room 323, anything to write home about, but she wouldn't be needing it beyond eight, nine o'clock that night. Twelve hours, at the most.

It would have been nice now to take a hot shower, but she'd taken a room without bath. Just a sink in the one corner and the can across the hall. She was paying for the room out of her own pocket, and she wasn't about to spend a nickel more than she had to. Let Harry and the others ... (she had her own reasons for not naming, too precisely, those others to herself) ... let *them* throw away their money on booze and high living. You can't expect the young people to do anything else with it, after all. For her own part, she knew where *her* money was

46

going. A perpetual plot with a Remembrance Beacon burning day and night. Because it didn't matter a jot nor a tittle if you had yourself the biggest splashiest funeral in town, with a handcarved Italian marble headstone to boot—if you didn't own the plot outright, it was all a vanity. Come ten, twenty years, they'd maybe dig you up again to make room for the next in line, and your last state would be no better than your first. There was a plot, she had seen it many times, at the edge of the coloured Baptist Cemetery in Nansemond County, such a plot . . .

Sighing—but only from the weariness of her bones; not, today at least, from resignation—she began unpinning her hat and taking out hairpins. The tight bun of her frizzled iron-grey hair loosened, and her whole aching body seemed to ease. Sweet Jesus, yes, that was better. Enough better that she was able to get over to the sink and wash her face and brush her teeth, which were full of the Planter's Peanuts she'd eaten all night on the bus. She lingered a moment before the fly-specked mirror admiringly. It was not her face, of course, for there wasn't much of that left to sing about, but her tooth, a single gold upper incisor, that she regarded. She remembered how, when she'd come home with that tooth, she'd bragged to Maybelle that someday she'd have a whole head full of gold teeth. It certainly had seemed like it, in those days.

There are a lot of girls who, when they've got the money, can't think of ways to get rid of it fast enough. Though their boyfriends can, sure enough.

Not Bessy McKay, not her. She'd kept her money in a safe deposit box in the biggest old bank in Norfolk, right on through the war. Then, when the next boom came, in '48, she'd been ready for it. Her own house, McKay's, with a dozen of the prettiest black girls and high-yallers in the Confederate States of America. Clean, too. It was in the classic style, was McKay's, harkening back to the days before Prohibition, when Norfolk had been at its finest. Bessy's girls didn't have to go out hooking in hotel lobbies or honkytonks, no indeedy. And when there were conventions, they'd practically *hold* them in Bessy's house. Navy officers, college boys, policeman—you name it, they'd all paid their visits. Of course, she had had to move out of the centre of town in '50, everybody'd had to, but her second house, on the tidewater, was every bit as grand if not more so. And modern? Oh, very.

And then . . . well, it did say that the Lord would destroy the houses of the evil, though when it came to that she could have advised the Lord, if He'd have listened, of many houses eviller than hers ...

And where had it all gone to, the money? All the time she'd had to *work* for it, she'd grudged every nickel, but when it started coming in from every side, she'd just stopped bothering. A little here and a little there: clothes, a treat for the girls, loans to friends who drifted out of sight or vanished into prison (Harry Dorman, that sonofabitch, still owed her five hundred, and be damn she'd get it back this time!). And liquor.

And liquor. She fumbled around in the carryall for the bottle, which was wrapped in the little calico dress, screwed off the cap and let a good, burning swig ride down, smoothing the flutters in her stomach. Then another, for luck. She was going to need it. How had she ever got caught up in this crazy scheme anyhow?

But the whiskey had the answer to that question ready to hand, and it came floating up before her, the image of it, like a bundle of helium balloons sailing past the delighted eyes of a child: the flower-decked cars; the richly crusted bronze casket; her own folded hands and sweetly smiling lips; the marble stone and the angel faces; the inscription, *O Lord, I am not worthy!*

Miss Godwin was sitting there as stiff as one of those Egyptian statues at the museum, arms and legs composed in neat right-angles, hands clenched about the little yellow handkerchief in her lap. Alice wondered if she knew yet that they were being kidnapped, for her anxious expression could have been just as much for Uncle Jason's sake as for their own. If she didn't know, would it be safe for Alice to tell her?

The best course, she decided, was to say nothing and watch the way they were driving very carefully so she would be able to retrace it, if need be. It was rather careless of her kidnappers, she thought, not to have blindfolded herself and Miss Godwin.

The limousine pulled into a huge municipal parking lot, half empty because of the weekend, and pulled up beside a copper-coloured Buick. The Negro chauffeur (except he probably wasn't *really* a chauffeur) got out and opened Alice's door.

'Can my governess come with me, please?' she asked of him, for she did feel a teensy bit uneasy.

'C'mon, kid.'

Miss Godwin leaned down and kissed Alice on the forehead.

48

'You had better do what he says, mademoiselle. Promise me you'll be brave.' Alice promised. While Miss Godwin pretended to wipe away an imaginary tear from the corner of Alice's eye, she handed her, without comment, the book of *Just-So Stories* that had been in her big canvas carryall. Alice had been intending to impress Miss Braggs with her first edition that morning.

'*C'mon*, kid.'

Miss Godwin pushed Alice out the door. Then, for the first time really, Alice was frightened. For the man in the driver's seat of the Buick had eyes as green as the pulp of a lime. It was Reverend Roland Scott. He smiled, acknowledging her recognition.

She wanted to scream, as she would have wanted to scream in a scary movie, but because there was nobody else screaming she found she could manage nothing more than a puppyish yelp. The Negro chauffeur lifted her up by her arms and placed her beside the driver of the Buick. She managed to keep hold of the book. He slammed the Buick's door shut, then the back door of the limousine, and, getting in behind the wheel, he drove off into the flat, asphalt distance. Miss Godwin pressed her nose against the back window to wave good-bye.

The Buick followed after a few minutes. When it was turning from the parking lot into the street, not moving fast yet, Alice tried the handle of the door. It had been locked without her noticing, and there seemed to be no way to unlock it. She tried to wind the window down, but that wouldn't work.

The Reverend Roland Scott (except, of course, he probably wasn't any more Reverend than the Negro had been a chauffeur) laughed. Alice began to scream, more from anger than fear, and the Reverend Roland Scott cuffed her.

'*That* wasn't very nice,' she said.

'Don't scream.'

'You didn't have to *hit* me.'

'That wan't anything, kid. That was a lovepat. You behave now, or you *will* get hit.'

She began silently to cry. Tears dripped down on the frayed cover of *Just-So Stories*. Her kidnapper, as she might have expected, paid no attention. He was a heartless brute. They were leaving the waterfront district and entering an area of slums and cheap hotels, though not the worst slums certainly that Baltimore could offer.

'Am I kidnapped?' she asked, just to make sure.

'Uh-huh. Relax, kid. It ain't going to be as bad as all that.'

Taking his own advice, her kidnapper drew out a package of filter cigarettes from his shirt pocket (Alice noted the brand carefully), punched the car lighter, and, in a moment, lit up. 'Now,' he said, exhaling two thin jets of smoke from his nostrils. 'A little kidnapping doesn't have to be bad at all. If you behave. In no time at all you'll be back home again.'

'Oh, I'll behave,' Alice promised, crossing her fingers. 'Will I get back home today? You see, I have to meet a friend at the beach this afternoon.'

He chuckled. 'Not today exactly. But soon.'

Catching herself chewing on a hangnail, she slapped her own hand so that it stung. It was a ritual she'd almost forgotten, from years and years ago, when her father had cured her of thumb-sucking the same way.

She regarded the pale flesh of her arms regretfully. Good heavens, at this rate she'd be all summer getting a tan, for her kidnappers probably would keep her indoors all the time. She wondered how long it would take and how much money they were asking for her. It didn't seem the right moment yet to ask.

She worked loose a page of *Just-So Stories* and stuffed it behind the seat cushions. It would be, she hoped, a valuable clue. And good enough for stinky old Reverend Scott if he were caught with it!

The Buick pulled down a narrow, garbage-strewn alley and stopped by the doorway of a wornout-looking brick building. A crudely-lettered sign above the door said: Royalton Hotel Service Entrance.

The kidnapper glared down at Alice with his green eyes and whispered (though there was nobody nearby to have overheard): 'Now are you going to come along without a peep—or will I have to use this?' He showed her the pistol.

She shrank back into the corner of the seat and promised, this time, *really* to behave. All four nail-bitten fingers were in her mouth up to the second knuckle.

He nodded and touched a button on his door. 'Get out,' he commanded.

Reaching for the handle without seeing it, Alice opened the door and slid out of the car. She stood statue-still until he'd come around and taken her hand. 'If anyone inside sees us, you call me Daddy, understand?'

'Yes, sir.'

'Yes, what?'

'Yes, Daddy.'

But the lobby of the Royalton, once they were inside, was as empty as a St. Adnobian classroom at five o'clock. He smiled, and flicked the butt of his filtertip into a metal ashtray, where it disappeared through a hole in the top. Alice bit her lip fretfully. She had hoped to get the cigarette butt for herself, as a clue.

'Just like I hoped,' he said. 'Saturday morning. Ain't it beautiful?'

'Yes, Daddy.'

Hand in hand, kidnapper and kidnapped climbed the narrow service stairs. Patches of paint of some indecipherable colour clung to the grey wood along the untrodden edges. Then, down the third-floor corridor, tiptoe on the faded carpet, beneath which the floorboards rose and fell, creaking, so that Alice got the disquieting impression that the Royalton was put together as haphazardly as the tree house she had climbed up into last summer, right over Gwynn River Falls. How had she ever dared to do that!

They stopped outside Room 323. He knocked and said, 'It's me—Harry.'

Therefore, she reasoned, Roland Scott was an *alias*. Or, at least, Roland was.

Heavy footsteps padded to the door, making the wooden floor groan. A key grated in the lock. The door opened.

'Here. Good-bye. Nobody saw us.' Harry pushed Alice into the room. The door slammed behind her and was locked. Turning around, she found herself before simply the biggest woman she had ever seen (with the possible exception of Mrs. Buckler) who, with a rather flirtatious gesture, dropped the room key into the hollow between her monumental breasts.

'Hello there, honey,' she said. 'I'm Bessy.'

'Really?' Alice asked. 'Or is that your *alias*?'

'Now ain't that a silly question? Because if I say it's my name, you'll just have to believe it is. But as a matter of fact, honey, it is my name, and no foolin'.'

Bessy smiled, almost bashfully, and went to rummage in the canvas carryall on the chair beside the dismal double bed. Alice had a chance to look around the room. The dim overhead bulb revealed nothing but greyness overlaid with dirt: grey walls, grey floors, grey curtains over grey windows that looked across an airshaft at grey bricks. Aside from the bed, the only furniture was rickety sticks and slabs of pine, which formed, in

51

different combinations, chairs, a table, and a dresser, all painted grey. Above a sagging sink in one corner a mirror reflected greyness. Everything looked too dirty to touch, so Alice stayed where she was, in the middle of the room.

Bessy returned and thrust her hand, pink palm up, under Alice's nose. 'Here honey, you swallow these.' Two pills, the smaller white and innocent-seeming, the larger, an ominous red lump of what looked to be solid plastic. Poison?

'If you please, I'm forbidden to eat things that strangers give me,' Alice said in a flat voice.

The woman laughed, and her golden incisor flashed. 'If I please! O sweet Jesus—if I *please*!' She sat back on the bed, holding her left hand over her jiggly breast.

'All right now, you listen to me, honey, and listen close— you're going to be staying with me three days, maybe longer. If your ever-lovin' daddy don't come up with the ransom money right away, we may be stuck with each other I don't know how long. Now you're a bright little girl. You tell me how you're going to eat and drink if I don't give it to you. Huh?'

Alice saw the logic of it. She was utterly, helplessly, hopelessly in the black woman's power. If they meant to kill her—if it *were* poison, Alice could do very little to prevent it. And if it weren't, why then there was no need to make a fuss.

She swallowed the two ghastly pills. She would have liked a glass of water, but she mistrusted the murky glass on the ledge by the sink.

And Harry had told her that kidnapping didn't have to be bad! Bad? It was worse than being vaccinated, almost.

'Were they poison?' she asked. She could feel the larger pill still stuck halfway down her throat.

'Just medicine, honey. To calm the nerves. Now, you just lay down there on that bed, while I get about my work.' She began emptying out her carryall. Alice's head hurt. She wished the hotel didn't exist. She wished that nothing was real but her and Dinah. Not the dirty grey room. Not the big black woman. Not anything. But that wasn't healthy, wishing things not to be real. She had to remember to live with her environment, the way Miss Godwin said.

The black woman was still taking things out of her satchel. A steel thing. Shoes. A red thing. Clues . . .

Then the greyness swallowed her whole.

Waking, her stomach hurt awfully, as though it were a kettle full of boiling water, and she had an *incredible* headache. Was this what migraine was like? No wonder her mother hated it!

'Feel bad, Dinah honey?' a voice asked, not unfeelingly.

She remembered the greyness, the room, the woman. But was she Dinah now? Dinah, who didn't exist?

A great black hand, surprisingly firm, took hold of her arm and pulled her into a sitting position. The bed was all covered with newspapers. How queer! 'Come on, honey, sit up. That's it. We gonna do your hair.'

The woman was holding scissors. Alice watched her groggily. The scissors snipped, and curls fell to the newspapers on the bed, and snipped . . .

'No!' Alice shrieked, pulling away. Her hands felt at the back of her head for the ponytail, now irreparably lost. Bessy clapped one hand over Alice's mouth and pulled her back to the bed with the other.

Snip, and another lovely long lock fell to the newspapers. It would take months, *years*, to grow it back.

The hand eased away from her mouth. 'You gonna keep quiet?'

'Yes. I hate you though.' A tear trickled down her cheek. Snick. A wad of hair fell and stuck to the wetness.

'Now we're gonna curl your hair a little bit, won't that be nice?'

'I'm not going to talk to you,' Alice announced. She watched Bessy plug the cord of a peculiar appliance into the wall socket beside the bed. It was little more than a steel rod with a plastic handle. It smoked! Was Bessy going to torture her? 'What *is* it?' she asked in a whisper.

'This?' Bessy spit on her forefinger and touched the smoking rod gingerly. The wet sizzled. 'This is just a li'l ol' curling iron, Dinah honey. It won't hurt. All I'm gonna do is give you curly hair, so you'll be pretty. All right?'

Knowing that Bessy was doing this to prevent the police detectives from being able to identify her, Alice nodded. It was all part of being kidnapped, apparently.

'My name is Alice, you know,' she said.

Bessy paid her no heed. The curling iron touched her hair, and there was a sound like Rice Krispies, only louder. Alice flinched. 'It smells *awful*,' she protested.

'It *do*, don't it, but it's gonna look real sweet.' Bessy chuckled. 'You wait and see if it don't.'

When her hair was nothing but stiff, wiry curls, Bessy pulled Alice to the sink and told her to close her eyes real tight. A cold, thick liquid was brushed into the resisting curls, and a new and worse stench was added to the old. It seemed to go on for hours, first the cold squish, then hot water, then more cold squish.

At last there was the welcome hum of a hand hair dryer and the balmy rush of hot air across her itching, burning scalp. Bessy gave her a towel for her face. When she was all dry, she peeped open her eyes fearfully to see what her hair would look like in the speckled mirror. She stared, dull-eyed, frozen with shock.

The face in the mirror was not the face of Alice Raleigh. The tight black curls of Bessy's handiwork framed a face of deep, gingerbread brown, from which two pale blue eyes, the sole remnant of the real Alice Raleigh, stared out desolately. The mouth in the mirror opened wide to scream, but Bessy was ready for that. Alice bit at the hand covering her mouth, she clawed and kicked and writhed, all to no purpose. She was so little, and Bessy was so big.

The huge hand that covered her mouth covered her nose as well, so that she couldn't breathe, the other hand held two more pills, a white and a red, in readiness. When the hand came away Alice had to gasp for air. The pills popped into her opened mouth, and the hand came down again so that she could not spit them out. In defeat, Alice swallowed.

In a few minutes all her resistance was gone. She wanted nothing but sleep, but Bessy would not let her lie down.

'Come on, Dinah, we got to get you changed out of that dress.'

'I'm not Dinah.'

Bessy, heedless, handed her a short red dress with piping on it, a dress that was not only fearfully shoddy and faded, but years too young for Alice. Or for Dinah?

If only she could *think*, but her head was reeling so that she had all she could do to keep balanced while Bessy changed her out of the turquoise dress and into the red check.

To *think*: why, for instance, was she black? Had Bessy *painted* her while she was asleep? Was that possible? She dawdled, pondered, dozed.

'Upsy-daisy, Dinah darlin'. We going to leave this fair city now.'

The sunlight coming in through the window was the last muddy dregs of the summer afternoon. Alice could barely make out the individual bricks on the other side of the airshaft.

Bessy plopped her on to the bed and pulled off her shoes and long white stockings and gave her, instead, a pair of scuffed-up saddle shoes, with no socks at all.

While Bessy busied herself carrying the newspapers and shorn hair into the toilet across the hall, Alice regarded herself sleepily in the mirror. *Was* it herself, that figure in red, its kinky hair awry, chewing a brown thumb, blinking improbable, drowsy blue eyes?

'What's this?' Bessy asked, holding up *Just-So Stories*.

'It's my book! Don't throw that away!'

Bessy carefully pushed the nondescript book into the bottom of the carryall.

As in a dream, Alice was led out of the door, down a different staircase, out into the dusky streets. They walked forever till they came to the Greyhound Bus Station, where, at the candy and souvenirs counter Bessy bought a twenty-nine-cent pair of sunglasses. Alice was glad to have them, for the terminal was painfully bright. You could sleep while you waited on the orange plastic benches, and in the bus you could sleep even better in the soft snuggly seat next to the window, with Bessy's overlapping middle serving almost as a sort of blanket.

With something like surprise, Alice realised that the whining noise she'd been hearing ever since they'd left the hotel was her own voice. She hadn't meant to whine, but rather to scream, to tell the people about her who she was.

The light in the bus went on. A man came down the aisle, crying, for some reason, the single word 'Pillows!'

It was enough. She wakened and struggled to her feet, pushing away the imprisoning fat of her abductress. 'I'm white!' she screamed. 'Look at me! I'm white! I'm white!'

Bessy pushed her back into the soft seat. The lights went off. Alice tried to say more, but her voice was only a pathetic squeak.

'Look at my eyes,' she whispered. 'My eyes are blue.'

'I'm sorry,' Bessy announced to the bus at large. 'I'm awful sorry, folks. My little Dinah here ain't never been away from her home before, has you, Dinah honey? And this trip up north has got her all upset. You've got to excuse her, folks.'

But no one appeared to be listening to the apology. No one appeared to have heard Alice's outburst. None of the whole embarrassing incident had, as far as *they* were concerned, even happened.

Chapter 6

Frank Yerby was Delphinia's favourite author, and of all his novels the one that Delphinia liked best was *The Foxes of Harrow*, a tale that was, according to its cover, 'charged with all the passion and violence of the Old South', Delphinia could never get enough of the Old South, but this novel had something that none of the others did. Delphinia discerned in the unhappy life of Odalie, the mistress of Harrow, a remarkable parallel to her own, and she could never read about Odalie without wanting to cry. Like that unfortunate woman, Delphinia was descended of a fine old French family proud of its heritage; she was of a passionate yet sensitive nature, and beautiful and frail as a spring flower. Like Delphinia, Odalie was of so refined a nature and so delicate a constitution that it was, if not impossible, then very, very difficult, for her to fulfil her conjugal duties.

Of course there were differences too, but they were superficial. Delphinia, for instance, was not, due to a cruel jest of Fate, the mistress of Harrow or of anything like Harrow. As for Rodipoo, it was hard to say exactly how much he resembled the master of Harrow, Stephen Fox. He *was* still handsome (though, it is true, his hair did not glow like fox-fires); he *was*, most times, a gentleman and considerate of his wife's finer feelings. She decided that, despite everything, she loved Rodipoo every bit as much as Odalie had loved Stephen Fox.

As though to put this decision to the test, Rodipoo came into the bedroom and, after a perfunctory greeting, took a seat by the window. They sat in silent communion as the room grew dusky, Delphinia loving Rodipoo, and Rodipoo, presumably, loving Delphinia.

At last, growing bored, she handed him the book. 'Would you read a bit of this aloud for me, darling? The light is going, and I feel one of my migraines coming on. I left off where Odalie said, "I've come to be your wife ... if you still want me."'

Indulgently, Roderick read aloud to his wife. Even blurred by whiskey his voice could send shivers through her. So refined, so gentlemanly! A pity that he would never be able to go before the bar! What jury could resist such a voice? She had never understood what had happened exactly, why that career had been denied him. There was, for those who would believe it, that ugly story that her father had tried to make her listen to, after she'd come back from the elopement and he was trying to persuade her to seek an annulment. Roderick had assured her it was a tissue of lies. Donald Bogan had been the guilty party, Donald Bogan, whose father was a judge on the State Supreme Court; Jealous of Roderick and Delphinia's love, he had shifted the blame for his terrible act to his unsuspecting fraternity brother. Roderick's family, though genteel, could do nothing to save him; Delphinia's father, who might have helped, simply *refused*! Yes, it was a terrible injustice; it reminded her strongly of what happened to Mack Lefevre, the hero of *Trammermill* (another novel of the Old South). Mack Lefevre had been sole heir to Trammermill, a fine old Southern plantation, but then one day he had a duel with . . .

A slight worry-frown creased Delphinia's pale brow, as the sound of running footsteps distracted her from the train of her thoughts. The footsteps were too heavy to have been her daughter's, and surely all the servants would know better than to stampede up the stairs. All of them *except* . . .

As Delphinia suspected, it was the governess, Miss Uppity Godwin, who came stumbling into the room—without knocking!—looking quite as though she'd been through a tornado. Roderick leaped to his feet, and Delphinia had to bite her lip to keep from reprimanding him then and there. Standing up for a coloured servant, indeed! But it wouldn't do to mention it now, in front of Nell Godwin. Not, it seemed, that she would have noticed, for she was running off at the mouth a mile a minute, in a manner quite impossible for Delphinia to understand. Alice was learning to talk the same way, like some damn Yankee Northerner. It was really a disgraceful exhibition, and all of this on top of the agony that her migraine was causing her!

'Oh my God!' said Roderick, running his hands through his toupee. 'Oh, Jesus!' Such language!

'Yes,' continued Miss Godwin, 'and then I was locked in the car with him all the rest of the day. It was to give them time to take her wherever they had to. Didn't you *wonder* where we were?'

'I asked Emmie this afternoon, and she said you were taking her to the beach.'

Miss Godwin wrung her hands. 'I tried to find out something. I tried to talk with him, but he wouldn't say anything, not a word. It's my fault for having believed him and gone into the car, but when he said that Mr. Duquesne was ill, I didn't think . . . Oh, it was so awful, I'm so sorry!'

'Kidnapped,' said Roderick. 'Kidnapped!'

Delphinia was beginning to understand what had happened.

Miss Godwin began crying into a soiled yellow handkerchief and sank into the imitation Louis Quatorze chair. Really, that was going too far! Without so much as a by-your-leave!

'Kidnapped?' asked Delphinia, in a sceptical tone. '*Who* is kidnapped?' She leaned forward in her sickbed, unmindful of the arthritis that would ordinarily have made this movement impossible. She clawed the silk comforter off her legs and demanded imperiously: 'What the hell are you talking about, Nell?'

The canaries, always responsive to the moods of their mistress, began to screech and flutter, while the governess, scorning to answer, sat there in the Louis Quatorze chair and snuffled into her handkerchief.

Delphinia swung her legs out of the bed. 'What are you talking about, Nell? Where's my baby? Answer me, damn you! Where's my little Alice?' A little unsteadily, for she was not used to walking, Delphinia tottered across the room and caught hold of the governess's shoulders and began shaking her. 'What have you done with my baby?' she screamed into Miss Godwin's face. 'Kidnapper! Child molester! I knew it would end this way, the minute I laid eyes on your black face.' She lifted a hand to slap the Negress, but the effort of rising from her bed had so over-taxed Delphinia's weakened frame, that she collapsed to the floor before she could carry out her intention.

Roderick helped his wife back to her sickbed, after which all three of them seemed somewhat calmer.

'What shall we *do*?' Roderick wanted to know.

'They warned me that you weren't to go to the police, Mr. Raleigh. They said they'd find out if you did. But I don't know what else can be done.'

'They? Who are *they*? You only mentioned a Negro chauffeur.'

'There was another man that drove the car that Alice went off in. I couldn't get much of a look at him.'

'Oh, my poor darling *baby*!' Delphinia crooned mindlessly. 'Oh my little Alice! They've taken her away; she'll be raped, she'll be murdered! The niggers have stolen my baby and they're going to enslave her innocent white body and lock her up in a bordello . . .'

'Delphinia, please shut up,' Roderick said sternly. 'These fantasies of yours are embarrassing.' His wife's mounting hysteria seemed to act as a dampener to his own emotions. 'If Alice is kidnapped, we shall have to ransom her. It is as simple as that. I'll see Jason tonight. I presume they gave you instructions on how we are to get the money to them?'

Miss Godwin lit a cigarette to steady her hand. 'Yes, Mr. Raleigh, they did. And that was why I said it would probably be necessary to bring in the police. You see, the ransom they're asking is one million dollars.'

'A million dollars?' Jason's mouth fell open, and a flush overspread his hollow cheeks. 'Why, it's absurd!'

'My sentiments entirely, Uncle Jason. Of course, it's evident that they have the trust fund in mind. It was never entirely a secret that Alice had been liberally provided for. When we contested the will, the story must have been in every newspaper from Baltimore to Atlanta.' Roderick was quite calm now. He sat with his hands resting loosely on his knees, staring fixedly at the four golden balls whose spinning powered the glass-encased clock on Jason's desk. It was ten-thirty. Only the way Roderick's jaws were clamped tight-shut betrayed the tension he was under.

'It can't be done, Roderick. It would be literally impossible to have that much money in cash by Monday evening. Alice's money is in bonds and real estate. It would take *months* to liquidate such a sum.'

'We have to do *something*.'

'Yes, yes, of course. A hundred thousand? Mightn't they content themselves with a hundred thousand?'

Roderick's hands tightened about his knees. His voice grew shrill. 'Don't ask *me*, for heaven's sake, Jason! How should *I* know what will content them? Maybe they'll be satisfied with *ten* thousand a year, like Delphinia and I have been. Or maybe they won't stop once they've got the million they ask for. Maybe they'll murder Alice no matter what we do. Maybe they already have. But, God *damn* it, Jason, I wish you wouldn't talk about this as though it were a new investment for her portfolio. Her *life*—and maybe her sanity—are in your hands.'

The old man lowered his gaze, as though Roderick had

touched a sore point. 'Yes, I know, but we must try to keep our wits about us. I'm Alice's lawyer, as well as her uncle, and I must regard things in both lights. As her lawyer, I may say that I have been dealing with criminals of all sizes ever since I was called to the bar, and it has been my experience that the bigger a criminal one has to deal with the less of a fool he will be. To judge only by the asking price, these are the biggest kind of criminals. Now, wouldn't it be foolish of them to kill the goose that lays their golden eggs? I'm sure the only reason for their haste is that if the whole business is concluded in less than three days, it will not necessarily be considered a Federal crime, whereas *after* three days it automatically becomes a matter for the F.B.I. That would account for the Monday night deadline. No, believe me, the best policy is to string them along at least one more day. After that...' Jason trailed off weakly.

Roderick's gaze was directed squarely at his brother-in-law now, and when he spoke, he seemed to be choking on his own sarcasm. 'After that? Yes, Jason, after *that*? What would you say the odds are she'll still be alive then? Better than fifty-fifty? How much of a gamble should we take on it? Two-to-one, in our favour? How much, Jason?'

'I'm sorry, Roderick.'

'And *I'm* sorry—to have troubled you. I thought you'd know better than me what to do, but I see I was mistaken.' He reached for the telephone on Jason's desk.

Jason put his hand over Roderick's preventing him lifting the receiver. 'What are you doing? Who are you calling?'

'The police, as I should have done an hour ago.'

'Shouldn't we talk about that first? I mean—is it wise, Roderick—considering? If they find out...'

'How are they to find out if only the two of us know I've called?'

'Perhaps they're watching your house. I don't know, Roderick. But we must be careful. We must consider the risk to Alice.'

'A moment ago you were cavalier enough about *that*.'

He pulled the receiver away from Jason and dialled O. 'I want the police,' he told the operator. 'This is an emergency.'

'You're right, of course,' Jason mumbled. 'Of course you're right.'

Roderick described the situation succinctly, twice, first to the desk sergeant, then to his superior. After hanging up, he retrieved his hat and walking stick from the chair by the door. 'Good-bye, Uncle Jason. I must return home. The police will be there shortly.'

'If I can be of any help . . .'

'In that case, I'm sure, the police will let you know.' He was half out the front door when Jason called out his name. 'Yes?' he asked briskly. 'Yes, what is it, Jason?'

'Nothing,' the old man replied in muffled tones. He had wanted to tell Roderick to be brave, to keep his chin up, but after all, it was advice he could more suitably have offered himself.

*I'm too old,* he thought, *for this kind of thing.*

A million dollars! Most people had no idea what an immense sum of money a million dollars was. Only if one had worked with large sums for as long as Jason Duquesne had did one have even an inkling of its magnitude. A million dollars . . .

He paced the carpet in front of his desk, following a well-worn triangular path. At eleven-thirty he called the house on Gwynn River Falls Drive, but the line was busy. He took down a dusty law volume and sat at his desk to read. There had been a case some years before . . . if he could but remember . . .

His fingers turned the pages over quietly. Sometimes he would pause a moment to scan a paragraph, but he did not find what he sought. Finally, with a sigh, he closed the book. While one hand pulled off his reading glasses, the other massaged the inner corners of his weary eyes, unconsciously rubbing dust into them.

Chapter 7

Nigger go home read the banner flapping above the head of the Exalted Cyclops, and it seemed indeed to be the entire burden of his speech.

'Because I'm telling yaw that while the whiteman was building the cathedrals of Europe and discovering America and I don't know what-all, them lazy nigras was living in grass huts and eating each other, yessir, that's what the anthro-*pol*-igists say. And now they're asking for Civil Rights! Civil Rights! Why, I bet they don't even know the difference between civil *rights* and civil *lefts*!'

The Exalted Cyclops paused for the laughter that was customary at this point, but there was none forthcoming. He scowled, and in the harsh glow of the automobile headlights his hawkish face resembled more than ever the rude handicraft of some benighted aborigine, hacked from a stump of wood, the abhorred and potent image to which the tribe would address its prayers.

For a moment it was so still that Owen Gann, at the edge of the crowd of Klansmen, could hear the hum of the insects and the wind rustling the young tobacco leaves out there in the blessed darkness. Darkness and quiet, an end to this drear, too-often-declaimed speech—that was all that Owen or any of them wanted now. And yet there was a part of him, he knew, that wanted to stay here with the others and listen—and not just for the sake of duty, but because that part of Owen Gann agreed with the Exalted Cyclops.

'We have just begun, brothers, we have just *begun* to show them the whip—the way you got to show the whip to a mean cur, and believe you me when he sees that we mean business *we* shall overcome.' The Exalted Cyclops laughed—a short, predatory *shree*, which, like the cry of a hawk swooping down upon its prey, was modelled upon the death-scream of his intended victims. This time his audience joined in his laughter.

They were, however, wearing. The declared purpose of the meeting had been to congratulate them on their performance of the afternoon, when they had driven up and down the streets of Norfolk in partial regalia—minus only their hoodwinks, or hoods with eyeholes. But that could have been accomplished in five minutes or less, and the Exalted Cyclops had been going on the better part of an hour. He was, doubt-less, electioneering.

'Now you all know who I am, and the office I'm running for, but just now I want you to think of me, not as Farron Stroud, then next sheriff of this great county, but as your Exalted Cyclops—and believe me when I say we've got our work cut out for us. We've got the whole damn Communist conspiracy to fight, because that's who's making the nigras rear up on their hindlegs and talk about Civil Rights. You don't think they'd git these notions on their own, no sir!—it's the Yankee agitators coming down here and stirring 'em to a fine froth. They say, "Hey boy, how'd you like to be just the same as white folks? How'd you like to git you some o' them white women, boy?" And let me tell you *this*—them black devils don't belong in this Land of the Free any more than do those Yankee Communists. The nigras was chained up and brung here and I say what's the matter with chainin' him up again and taking him *back* to Africa?'

The audience cheered quietly.

'That day is a-comin' but we got to do certain things first. We need iron-clad lawmen, who ain't afraid to stand up for the principles this nation was founded on—One Nation Under God, yes-sir!—with white supremacy and justice for all! Now, as you probably know, I'm running for the office of sheriff. I'm not gonna abuse the privilege of my position as Exalted Cyclops to make a campaign speech, no, but I'll tell you this: there'll be no more arrests of white citizens who do their God-given duty when and if I'm elected. So if you want law and order and your rights as a white citizen protected, you'll vote for Farron Stroud. But if you want a lily-livered, niggerlovin', mammyjammin' sheriff you'll vote for my opponent. And that's about all I've got to say to you fellas tonight.'

The Exalted Cyclops stepped down from the platform, and now the Klansmen—some ninety-four strong—joined hands and repeated the Oath of Allegiance, bringing the Klonclave to an end. Every man gave the password to the inner guard, the Klarogo, and then to the outer guard, the Klaxton. They went to their cars, which had been parked in a ring so that their headlights could be used to illuminate the meeting.

Passing by a ten-year-old, copper-coloured Buick, Owen heard the closely related sounds of a car stalling and a man cursing.

'Need a shove?' Owen inquired.

'That you, Owen Gann? That would be right friendly.'

Owen identified the nasal mountain voice as Peter Boggs's, a Kladd, or password boss, a recent recruit to the Den. Boggs was the only member of the Den, in fact, over whom Owen could claim seniority.

'I guess any battery could get wore down, what with ole Farron's speechifying,' Owen observed.

'Well, this one shouldn't. I haven't had it but twelve hours. Thought it was a real bargain at the time—seventy-five dollars, only. No fool like an old fool, is there?'

'Not unless he's a young one like me,' Owen said agreeably. He climbed the beer delivery truck he'd driven to the meeting and started it up. Coming up behind Boggs's Buick, he noticed that the old man had not yet bothered to get licence plates. For driving out in these country roads such things wouldn't so much matter. He pushed Boggs as far as the turnoff to County Road B, where he turned right, away from Norfolk instead of towards it.

Owen shook his head sadly. There was something about an old heap like that, the discrepancy between the wish and the fact, that made Owen Gann feel guilty, a traitor to his own people.

For that they were his people he could no longer doubt. He had grown up among them, worked at the same unrewarding jobs, known the same youthful, foolish hopes and the growing desperation of an adolescence leading nowhere, felt the acid of poverty nibbling at his character. Oh, he was one of them, there was no denying it.

That he was now an agent of the F.B.I. seemed, at times, quite beside the point.

And so the question arose whether he must resign. Could he conscientiously inform on these men, whose cause he was not entirely sure was not his own? His sympathy *did* run deeper than these vague stirrings of class loyalty; he *agreed* with them. He didn't, by and large, like niggers; they were all of them potential criminals in Gann's eyes, and their 'non-violent' demonstrations seemed to have proved it. No, he didn't like niggers, but even less did he like the Yankee agitators coming down South and stirring up all the trouble. Owen knew for a fact that the Communists were mixed up in the Civil Rights protests, and it upset him that he couldn't be set to investigating *them*. He just didn't understand why the niggers weren't content to leave well enough alone; *he* would have been.

And yet . . .

And yet he had worked for the Bureau faithfully for four years, ever since escaping from law school with his G.I. Bill-financed degree. To leave the Bureau now would be like losing a part of his own identity, perhaps the better part. He liked the work and did it well. He had received one commendation from the Chief for his bravery in capturing a convict escaped from Leavenworth. Most of all, there was a future there for Owen Gann—and almost nowhere else. A lawyer with the double liability of being honest and having no connections might as well resign himself to driving a beer delivery truck for the rest of his days; it pays better.

He would have liked to put off the decision (as he had twice before put off decisions about marrying, with the result that he was still single), but events seemed bent on not allowing him this easy way out. A massive Civil Rights demonstration was scheduled in Norfolk for the Fourth of July. Norfolk would seem the least likely city for a large protest: it was a large Navy base, and consequently the schools had been integrated in the early 'fifties, thanks to pressure from the base Command. The coloured population of Norfolk was allowed to vote in all elections, and they could go into any restaurant they wanted to and even expect good service in most of them. So what was all the fuss about?

Whatever it was, there promised to be a lot of fireworks that Fourth of July, because the Ku Klux Klan, not quite accidentally, was scheduling its own Norfolk rally that same day. Every Klansman in the Realm of Virginia was expected to attend what the newspapers had announced as 'a day of non-violent resistance and reprisals'. The least imaginative reader could read between those lines, but as yet Owen's knowledge of what was in fact intended in the way of 'non-violent reprisals' had not advanced beyond the stage of suspicion. Tomorrow, Tuesday, at half past four in the afternoon, he had been asked to attend a smaller meeting at the Norfolk Klavern, at which the Grand Dragon of the Realm was to be present. Then, possibly, Owen would be in a position to . . .

To be a Judas? Wasn't that it?

Next morning Owen Gann spent an unusually long time making the beer delivery to the bar and grill that occupied the ground floor of a three-story brick building with the rather grandiloquent title of Camelot Mansions. There, in a minimal office above the bar and grill, he handed his typed report to Agent Madding. As long as Owen remained on the Klan assignment he did not report to the official field office down town.

Madding was a slight, balding man with a professional attitude, which Owen envied him, of blithe anonymity. He seemed to approach his work as others would approach a crossword-puzzle—without any intention of intruding his own personality or concerns upon it. Owen admired the man's dispassion, but at times he could not help wondering what it had cost Madding—what fraction of his beliefs, his soul, his balls—to reach this present serenity. Was he as smooth within as without, all the thorny idiosyncrasies pared away so that there was nothing to snag against his duties? And if not, then was he no different from Owen? Wouldn't *he* perhaps strike Madding as the same sort of well-oiled automaton, rootless, ruthless, blank?

As a matter of fact, though Gann himself would never know it, such was not his superior's opinion. As he scanned the typed report, describing the uneventful week just past, Madding was engaged in his own speculation about Gann. The boy (though Gann was past thirty, he was still, by his style, a boy) wore a haggard, insomniac expression, not unsuitable for the role he played outside the walls of Camelot Mansions, but not at all the open, guileless face that had earned him, in law school and afterwards, the nickname 'Li'l Abner'. He was clothed in standard work clothes with the name of his employer stencilled on the back in a florid scrawl (not the F.B.I. but SPENGLER'S BEER). His arms and legs were too long for his overalls, but this did not make him seem gawky; rather it showed the ordinary dimensions of his uniform to be meagre. His nose was short and turned-up; his eyes, large, blue, and too close together; he could not speak without beginning to smile. Unless one had proof to the contrary, one would have supposed him to be very dumb. He was, like Madding, though in his own way, perfectly adapted to the role of an agent, but he was, in Madding's estimation, close to cracking. Madding didn't know why (motives didn't interest him); he just read the signs and thought it a pity—or, at least, a waste.

'Nothing more than this?' Madding asked, folding up the report.

'Later this afternoon I'm going to . . .'

'Yes, I read that. Do you think you can find time meanwhile to do a bit of routine inquiry for us?' Madding delivered his orders so that one might have thought he was really in doubt whether Gann could find time.

'Oh, I guess it's possible,' Owen allowed.

'Good enough. It's a kidnapping case in Baltimore. Little girl, eleven years old, name of Raleigh. Here's her picture. It was taken only two months ago at her school. St. Arnobia's. Over near Charlottesville.'

'Pretty little thing.'

'I suppose she is. She was grabbed Saturday morning, so the statutory three days are over and we're on the case officially now.'

'And they think she's down here?'

'Nothing as definite as that. But the girl's uncle is a lawyer—and incidentally he's in charge of her trust fund—and he showed up Sunday at the Baltimore field office with a lawbook under his arm. Seems as if there was another kidnapping, back in '49, that was done almost the same way: a little girl, a large inheritance, and kidnapping the governess along with the girl to use her as a messenger.'

'So she must have given you a description of the man.'

'Only of the Negro chauffeur that's in on it. The girl was transferred to another car, a Buick, copper-coloured, '57 or thereabouts. The governess didn't see the driver of that car. We showed her Dorman's latest prison photos but she couldn't say one way or another. At least we know she isn't suggestible.'

'Dorman, I take it, was the man who pulled the '49 kidnapping.'

'Mm-hm. He got life sentence, which was commuted, and he was released less than a year ago.'

'It sounds more and more like he's the man.'

'Except that Dorman isn't dumb. There's more than one way to get an eleven-year-old girl into a car. Why should he repeat himself—right down to the detail of the Negro chauffeur? It's almost as though he'd signed a letter and mailed it to us. As a matter of fact, he's done that too.'

'Oh, come on!'

'Well, the parents received a typed threatening letter yesterday with a Norfolk postmark. And Norfolk is where he used to operate from.'

'Well, if it *isn't* him, then . . .'

'Then someone is systematically laying a false trail. Whoever is doing it, even if it is Dorman, must know that we'll connect the two kidnappings. Even without the assistance of the girl's uncle. Though, admittedly, he got there first.'

'Could it be him, the uncle?'

'The man's seventy, and he already has control of the trust fund. What motive could he have?' Madding, as has been noted, was not one to interest himself in questions of motive.

'What about the governess then. Since so much of the information comes from her . . .'

'The Baltimore police have messed *that* up. Hauled her off to jail, gave her the third degree when she was damn near hysterical already. Now she won't talk unless she's got her lawyer sitting beside her. Not that she's been un-co-operative. *If* the story that she's telling is true, then she's been a model witness. She even drew a pretty good picture of the chauffeur from memory.' Madding showed him a photostat of the drawing.

Owen's lips tightened. 'A nigger.'

Madding laughed. 'You'd make a great Klansman.' Owen blushed. He had forgotten Madding was a Yankee.

'As a matter of fact, so is she. Negro, that is. She also had the presence of mind to plant a clue on the kid that *may* make it easier to trace her. She gave her a first edition of *Just-So Stories*, which looks like a piece of junk but which is worth a couple of hundred dollars. It was a gift from the uncle. We've put ads in the newspapers up and down the coast and phoned bookstores, offering $400 if they've got the edition we want. With Luck, it'll be tossed into a garbage can and some scavenger will notice it.'

'The threatening letter you mentioned—what was that about?'

'They'd found out somehow—or guessed—that the girl's father had gone to the police, and they were making noises to frighten him. Nothing to be learned from the letter except the postmark and that whoever wrote it wasn't illiterate.'

'Are the parents going to pay the ransom?'

'Yes and no. It's not the parents' money, you see. Comes from the trust fund that the girl's maternal grandfather set up when he cut the parents out of his will. But the ransom is being paid. In fact, the girl's father is giving it to them today. The Baltimore office is keeping its eye on that operation, of course.'

Madding smiled, the way a man will when he's itching to tell a very funny joke.

'How much?' Owen asked.

'A million dollars. Yes, I whistled too. But, to come back down to earth, your job will be to go around to these places . . .' Madding handed Owen a typed list, '. . . and find out the last time anyone there saw your good friend Harry Dorman.'

Owen looked at the names on the list—bars, cheap hotels, and . . . 'What in God's name did Dorman have to do with the Green Pastures Funeral Home?'

'I thought you'd ask that,' Madding said. 'As it happens, Green Pastures is no longer what it once was. It has become a cathouse, and Dorman used to pimp for it.'

Owen grinned boyishly and rose to leave. 'Well, I suppose that's all of it for now, eh?'

'Not quite, Owen. Sit down. Before you go, I'd like to tell you a dirty story . . .'

Chapter 8

'Here?' Alice asked, pointing at the sign nailed to the fluted wooden pillars of the porch, and, just perceptibly, cringing. 'Oh, surely not *here*!'

'You ain't going to make a scene *now*, are you, child?' Bessy tightened her grip on the girl's hand and began dragging her towards the swaybacked steps. It was five o'clock of a misty Sunday morning on North Tidewater Road, so that no matter what kind of fuss Alice put up at this point, it would make no difference.

'But the sign! Why do you want to come here? What are you going to *do*?'

'Oh—the sign!' Bessy had gone in and out the front door so many times that she wasn't even aware now of the weathered, but still distinct legend: *Green Pastures Funeral Home*—then, beneath, in larger, gilt letters *UNDERTAKING*. When she'd bought the place at auction, Bessy had decided to leave the sign up as a joke, and from a sense, besides, of the traditional; now the joke was grown so stale as to be, in Bessy's eyes, invisible. 'Don't take no account of that sign, honey. This here ain't no funeral home no more.' Then, though this joke too had lost most of its punch: 'Now it's a fun house, and we got *different* undertakings going on.'

Reassured but still dragging her feet, Alice let herself be led up the steps. Despite all the sleep she had had on the bus out of Baltimore, and then in the bus station in Richmond, and in the second bus, she was still groggy. Her back ached from having had to sit up all night, and her feet were raw from the long walk in shoes but no stockings. Worst of all, she was starving; since yesterday's breakfast she hadn't had anything but one ham-and-cheese sandwich on the bus. In a sense, she had been just as glad as Bessy to be here, to be anywhere so long as it marked an end, so long as she could take off these shoes and eat and take a shower to wash off all this brown ook . . .

Bessy rummaged through her carryall for her house-key, then, growing impatient, began pounding on the door. Within, Alice could hear running footsteps and a little girl's giggle (had someone else been kidnapped too?), and more footsteps . . .

'Christ Almighty, Clara,' Bessy called out, 'stop playing

footsy, and open this damn door.'

The lock rattled, and the door swung open, creakingly, upon a darkened foyer. There were more footsteps and whispers, but it was too dim to see anything but the indefinite, hulking silhouettes of furniture. Alice tiptoed through the foyer, straining to see and holding her breath. *This* was more like it! This was what kidnapping *should* be like—a strange, dark house, whispers, mysterious footsteps!

Behind her, Bessy closed and locked the door, then demolished the splendid suspense by throwing on the light switch and discovering, perched at opposite ends of a tawdry leatherette couch, in the centre of the most ordinary living-room, two grown-ups, a man and a woman. The man was black, the woman white.

'Clara, Fay, say Hello to Dinah.'

The white woman said, 'Hello, Dinah,' and broke into giggles. Alice realised with a pang of disappointment that it was her laughter that she had mistaken for another child's.

'What the hell!' said the black man, who was ugly and bucktoothed and not, after all, a man.

'You watch your language around Dinah, you hear, Clara?'

'My name isn't Dinah!' Alice said with exasperation. 'I tried to explain to you yesterday, but you wouldn't listen. My name is . . .'

'It's Dinah now, honey.' Bessy sighed gratefully as she began to ease off her shoes. 'Babydoll, why don't you go out in the kitchen and make us up some nice stiff drinks?'

'Okay!' said Fay brightly. 'With ice cubes!' Fay was, despite that she wore only a ratty seersucker bathrobe, as pretty as a movie star, and when she jumped up from the couch it was with a bouncy, lithe grace astonishing in a woman of mature years. Her hair was the same whitish blonde that Alice's had been only hours before.

'She gonna turn tricks?' Clara asked Bessy.

'Now what do you think? Good Lord, Clara, she ain't no more than ten years old, and she's littler than a cheese mite!'

'I'm eleven, going on twelve!' Alice protested. 'And my name is *Alice*!'

But Bessy and Clara continued their enigmatic conversation quite oblivious to what Alice had to say.

'So if she ain't here to work, what's she doing here? You sure as hell ain't gone and adopted her, for the love of sweet charity!'

Bessy's sigh expressed both resignation and pleasure—resignation at Clara's obstinacy and pleasure at being altogether out of her shoes. 'Since when does *anyone* work around here?' she inquired of her shoe. 'Ain't no one been working so's *I'd* notice it these last ten years.'

'Like hell!' said Clara. For a moment Alice wondered if maybe she *wasn't* a man. She was dressed like a man, in levis and a denim jacket. She had, as nearly as Alice could tell, a man's figure, albeit she was scrawny. She moved like a man. Her hair was cut short and shaped, with the aid of a pound or two of grease, into a spiky ducktail. Lastly, she had, if not a man's voice, a man's way of speaking.

'Clara honey, you are in pain, a real pain,' Bessy said good-humouredly.

'Shove it!' said Clara fiercely.

From the next room came a tinkling sound, like Japanese wind-chimes. Fay entered the living-room backwards through a swinging door, carrying a tray upon which four glasses of what Alice hoped without much conviction, might be cream soda were arrayed in a neat square. She served Bessy first.

Bessy sipped her drink. 'Why, that tastes very good, Fay. Thank you.'

Fay beamed. 'I made it myself.'

'It's real good—but why did you make *four*?'

Fay's blue eyes opened very wide. 'Because I counted! I didn't forget Fay this time. I counted one, two, three, four!'

'Crap!' said Clara. 'Don't you know nuthin? Dinah here can't drink this stuff. Fay. She's only ten years old.'

'Eleven,' Alice whispered to herself dismally. But no one was interested in the truth.

A puzzled finger strayed up to Fay's pouting lips, allowing the tray, upon which the glasses were no longer symmetrically disposed, to teeter portentously. Clara quickly took her own glass off the tray, and the tray righted itself.

Fay's smile, when it came, was dazzling. 'Why, then *I* get both of these! And...' (glancing mischievously at Alice) '... *you* don't get none!'

'I don't get *any*,' Alice corrected her. She knew it wasn't good manners, but then Fay herself was hardly a model of deportment.

With a little squeal of pleasure Fay plumped down on the couch, one glass in each hand. Seeing that abundance of rosy pink flesh before her, Alice felt more poignantly than ever how dirty and *black* she was. Fay looked as fresh as a baby, despite the cosmetic excesses spread over her pretty face. Her lips were so thickly frosted with lipstick that they looked like two pieces of pink fudge, and her eyes were like the glass eyes of a very expensive doll, the clearest sky-blue. They regarded the great world round about with a wide-open look of perpetual astonishment—an effect much heightened by the thin mascara arches that were inscribed upon her forehead fully half an inch above the probable line of her eyebrows. Her short, turned-up nose was very pink about the nostrils, as though she cried a lot, or had a cold, or was a bunny rabbit. She was, in short, very pretty, though it was not the sort of prettiness Alice would have wished for herself—under any other circumstances than the present.

Clara, by contrast, seemed to have set out to make herself ugly with the same deliberation with which Fay tried to look nice. Admittedly both of them had considerably native endowments. Clara's eyes protruded from a long, wedge-shaped face that was the hue of a charred pine log; beneath wide cheekbones her face tapered to a point at, unfortunately, her mouth, where one large white tooth overlapped a second, which in turn stood forth in proud independence from the lower lip. It was a weaselish face across which flitted a weaselish range of expressions: suspicion, calculation, a readiness either to pounce or to retreat, in equal measure, and when she glanced sideways at Fay, which she did not a little, something like hunger.

'Here comes Donald Duck,' Fay announced, raising one glass to her pink-frosting lips. 'Donald Duck wants to come in the door. Open the door for Donald Duck!' The door opened for Donald Duck and Fay took a delicate sip of her drink.

'Now here comes Micky Mouse. He wants to come in the door too.' She raised the second glass to her lips, and the door opened for Mickey Mouse.

Alice looked questioningly at Bessy, who stirred uneasily in her chair. You see, honey,' she explained, 'by the looks of her, Fay seems to be a grown-up woman, but inside she's just a little girl. Inside she ain't even as old as you are.'

'But I'm not a *baby*!' Fay announced in a concerned tone.

'No, you're not a baby,' Bessy agreed.

Clara pointed a warning finger at Alice. 'You keep outa my way, understand! Just keep outa my way, and I'll keep outa yours.'

'But I'm not *in* your way,' Alice protested. 'You're sitting down, for heaven's sake!'

'Just keep out of it, that's all I'll say. Kids don't have any business in a place like this. Christ, how I hate kids!'

'I love kids,' Fay said solemnly. I'm a mother, and I just adore babies. Would you like to see my baby?'

'Not if she's sleeping,' Alice replied.

'Oh, I can wake her.' Fay set her two glasses down on a three-legged end-table that was jammed into a corner of the room for support, then she got down on her hands and knees and felt beneath the sofa. 'Here she is,' she exclaimed at last. She held up a cheap, naked plastic doll by one leg. 'Isn't she just the sweetest?'

Fay sat back and began crooning over her baby and letting it drink from her glass of whiskey. 'I used to have a name for her, but I forget now what it was. Shall I call her Dinah now— for you?'

'My name isn't Dinah. If you want to name your baby after me, you should call her Alice.'

'Alice, my sweet little baby Alice,' Fay purred

'Your name is Dinah now, young lady, and you remember that. You say your name is Alice one more time, and I'm gonna let Clara give you a whipping with her strap. And believe you me, that won't be no fun.' Clara smiled weaselishly, in agreement. 'Now if someone asks you what your name is, what you going to tell them?'

'Dinah,' Alice answered sulkily.

'That's right. Because you *is* Dinah now, honey.'

'Can I take a shower?'

'Ain't no shower,' Clara declared flatly.

'A bath, then? I want to wash this ook off of me.'

Clara regarded Alice with curiosity, while Bessy laughed softly into her depleted whiskey glass. 'You go take a bath, Dinah honey, if that's what you want, but ain't nothing going to wash off you but a little dust from our bus ride. On account of you're coloured folks now, the same as Clara and me.'

'A Negro?'

'If that's what you want to call it, honey.'

Alice ran down the long hallway, opening doors to the bedrooms until she found the bath. It was a very queer bath indeed, with a tub fully eight feet long, but Alice could not spare a second thought for even the most anamalous tub now. She scrubbed her face and hands with soap and hot water, but the only result seemed to be that her face became *darker*.

A Negro! She thought of all the times this summer she had wished for a nice tan, of the times she had wanted to be like Miss Godwin. And now she was, if anything, darker than her governess—and it was awful, awful! She wanted desperately to be *herself* again. Instead, she was ... Dinah. Dinah had been a Negro, but on the other hand, Dinah had not been real. She'd been a fantasy—part of Alice's sickness. But she was over her sickness now, and she knew that Dinah had never been anything more than pretending. Pretending—and then, believing in it.

*Dinah didn't exist.*

But as she stared into the mirror of the medicine cabinet, she seemed to hear a teeny-tiny voice in her head, and it said: 'Oh yes I *do*!'

Bessy could hear Alice sobbing in the bathroom, but there wasn't very much she could do to comfort her. Besides, she thought, there were plenty enough little girls in this world crying their eyes out about the colour of their skin, and *they* was always going to be just one colour, black. Whereas Alice would start turning pale again in a week if she didn't take another pill. Maybe it wouldn't be a bad idea if all white folks took one of those every so often, just so they'd see what it was like to be coloured folk.

'Oh my dear little baby *Alice*,' crooned Fay over her doll. Clara gave her the raspberry and tramped upstairs to her bedroom.

*Alice:* Bessy had to stop thinking of her as Alice, or she'd let her tongue slip one of these days. She was Dinah now. Strange, that it had to be just *that* name, and not Georgia, for instance, or Mae Pearl. That would have been a better name for her: you don't hear of any white girls by the name of Mae Pearl. But Dinah was all right too. Bessy wasn't going to change the plans she'd been told, not a jot nor a tittle.

Not that she had any urge to. The more she thought the whole things over, the better she liked it. The idea of feeding them pills to the kid was a stroke of genius. Bessy hadn't even known there was such pills, but it turned out they was made of the same stuff that went into those special suntan lotions that people used in the winter instead of going to Florida—only about fifty times stronger. The beauty of it was that Bessy could take Alice anywhere, and she wouldn't be noticed. Because she wasn't Alice any more—she wasn't the little white girl who'd have her pictures in the newspapers—she was Dinah, a black little pickaninny, and the next best thing to invisible, as far as white folks was concerned.

Black or white, she was a nice little girl, Dinah was, polite and sharp as a tack. Also, Bessy thought guiltily, she was probably a very hungry little girl by now. She would have got up out of her chair and fixed her something to eat, except that her feet, her poor, aching feet, just wouldn't take her into that kitchen.

'Fay, honey?'

Fay's eyebrows lifted to their utmost extent, questioningly.

'Would you fix up Dinah a bite to eat and pour her a glass of milk, if there is some?'

'All by myself? What should I make?'

'Just a couple of sandwiches—and some potato chips, if you and Clara have left any.'

'I know how to make peanut butter sandwiches, or jelly sandwiches, or peanut butter *and* jelly sandwiches, or cheese sandwiches, or cheese and jelly sandwiches, or . . .'

'That'll do just fine, honey. You just go and fix them up and tell Dinah when they're ready.'

Bessy shook her head, as she watched Fay prance into the kitchen. If she weren't so damned soft-hearted she'd have thrown out the both of them years ago. They sure as hell didn't pay their way. That Clara was as ugly as sin, and as if that weren't enough, she hated men and always found a way to let them know it. Which didn't bring in many repeating customers to Green Pastures Funeral Home—except for the few men who *wanted* to be hated.

Fay didn't have many steady customers either, despite that she was the prettiest piece that Bessy had ever had working for her. The trouble with Fay was that after doing her business, she'd ask for a piece of bubble gum or do some fool thing that would let her john know he'd been making it with a five-year-old. Which most johns don't really like.

Two dead cats—that's what Bessy had on her hands. She would never have kept Green Pastures going if it hadn't been for the mortgages and an occasional windful from someone who needed a quiet rooming house till he could find a boat to go away on. This business with Alice . . .

Damn it, she had to remember to think of her as *Dinah*! This business with Dinah was the first piece of really big luck that had come Bessy's way since World War II, when she'd made her pile. Now, if only her luck *stayed* good. Three days —that's all she asked. Three days, and then the kid would be back in Baltimore and Bessy could move off to parts unknown, taking her bundle with her. She didn't expect to see Norfolk again till she was ready to be buried in Nansemond County.

Three days. Nothing could happen in three days. But, sweet Jesus, wouldn't there be the devil to pay if they caught her on *this*? A white kid kept prisoner in a coloured cathouse. There'd be a lynch party quicker than you could say Jackie Robinson. She chuckled, picturing old Farron Stroud, looking mean and trying to figure out some way to string her up. There wasn't a tree in Virginia big enough to string Elizabeth McKay up from.

But it wasn't really so funny when you stop to think. Because they *would* do for her, and for Fay and Clara too, and probably burn Green Pastures down afterwards, the sons of bitches. And then, even if there was a body left over to be buried, there'd be no money for a funeral, or for that pink marble stone, or for the plot. If she had the money, it would be different. Then she could go thumb her nose at the likes of Farron Stroud. Hell, she could even go around in one of those Civil Rights protests and sing about Freedom!

'Fay!' she called out.

'What *is* it! I'm terribly busy making these sandwiches.'

'Oh, it ain't nothing.' She wanted to ask for another glass, but she had to remember to cut down for these next three days. She'd promised, and in any case it was a good idea to go easy. She upended the glass and sucked at an ice cube to punish her tongue for still insisting on wanting another after she'd told it no.

Alice came in, wrapped in a towel, her black curls dripping water. 'Could I have some pyjamas, please?' she asked.

'Honey, ain't nothing here would fit you. You'll just have to sleep raw, or get along with that towel. Here, let me pin it up over your shoulder.'

Fay came out of the kitchen with a tray of sandwiches.

'Lord, Fay, what kind of stomach you think this child has got! How many sandwiches did you fix?'

Fay's eyes clouded from the effort of explaining: 'But I *asked* you what to make, peanut butter or jelly or peanut butter *and* jelly or . . .'

'All right, all right. You and Dinah go into the kitchen then and have your supper . . .'

'Breakfast,' Alice corrected, for it was quite six o'clock now, and the sun was creeping into the living-room through every crevice of the closed blinds.

'Your breakfast then, and wash the dishes when you're done.'

'I get first choice,' Fay insisted as she took Alice into the kitchen. 'I get the peanut butter sandwich. You can have the peanut butter and cheese, if you like.'

'No thank you,' said Alice politely.


It was a song in a foreign language, and the plaintive little voice would crack every time it tried to squeeze extra grace notes into the refrain. French?

Yes, French.

Bessy remembered—though she would have liked better to forget—the Creole girl. A pretty little piece, and always singing too. What had her name been? Something out of the way. She wondered what ever had become of her after that night back in '50. Some girls kept in touch, but not . . . what's-her-name. Couldn't much blame her for that. She had a better reason than Bessy to want not to remember. A hell of a thing to happen, and her only having come to Green Pastures a month before or so.

Bessy let her eyes close almost shut so that she could see the room not as it was now but as it had been then, in its moment of glory. Modern? Bessy had felt like a real pioneer when she'd fixed the place up like that. No velvet drapes and coloured glass for *her*. Those orange lamps she'd had on the end tables—what had ever become of them? Were they up in the attic? Or had they been busted in some sailors' brawl? And now just one poor end table left—and *it* was missing one wrought-iron leg And the *rug*: when she'd bought that the salesman had said it wasn't no trouble at all to keep a one hundred per cent nylon rug snowy white. Well, she'd have liked to have shown it to him *now*! It was so dark that you almost couldn't tell the stains apart from the rest of it.

Modern? Oh, it had been very modern—fifteen years ago. But the one piece of furniture in this room she could trust to last the week out was the rocker she was sitting in—and she'd taken that out of her mother's house, the time her mother had died. There was no telling how old it was. It seemed to Bessy she'd seen it around since she was a little girl no older than . . .

Dinah. The smooth gold oak showed through in patches where the varnish had rubbed off, but it looked none the worse for *that*. She wished she could have said as much for herself.

On the other hand, you take the very newest thing in the room—take that phonograph sitting on the three-legged end-table. The Creole girl had bought that the first week she'd worked at Bessy's, a tiny 45 record player with a thick red spindle and a stubby little arm that clicked and moved for all the world like a kitten's paw digging its claws into the records. All the records there used to be around the house—*Blue Moon, Tenderly, Garden in the Rain, Tell Me Why, The Little White Cloud That Cried*—all lost, all gone, all scattered to the winds or broken, and the phonograph broken too. Yes, you could take it—and throw it in the garbage!

Time, time, time! How it came sneaking up on a person! How it would trick a person into believing nothing would ever change, that life would always go on the same ... until there you were standing at the very edge of the grave and looking down into it and trying to pretend it wasn't yours but some-body else's ...

'Where do I sleep?' asked Alice, who had finished wiping the dishes.

'Can she sleep with me, Bessy, *please*?'

'No, babydoll—you know Clara wouldn't like that one little bit. Dinah here is going to sleep in Bessy's room.' Bessy heaved herself to her feet—and realised for the first time that she hadn't taken off her hat yet. She *was* tired.

Herding her little prisoner before her, she climbed the stairs with a sigh for each arduous step. Though it was quite bright outside now, Bessy's room was in semi-darkness. From under her own ruptured double bed she pulled out a trundle bed on squealing casters. She debated changing the sheets—they were anything but fresh—but Alice settled the matter by tumbling into it like she'd been chopped off at her ankles and pushed over. Those pills were still on the job.

Bessy undressed self-consciously, not quite sure that the child wasn't just playing possum, and got into a comfy night-gown—such a relief!—locked the door, pinned the key beneath her arm, and switched off the overhead light. She made absolutely sure that the girl was sound asleep (tickling the soles of her brown little feet), and then she knelt beside her bed and folded her hands.

'Lord?'

Surely there is nothing more dreadful than the darkness of a strange house—or, more dreadful yet, a funeral parlour; surely there is nothing more dangerous than to tiptoe right beneath the nose of the snoring giant; surely there is nothing quite so adventurous, once one is a little over the shock, as being kidnapped. Of course, in the strict sense Bessy's bedroom might not have qualified as *dark*, despite all that the curtains and the blinds could do; nor was it, as much as Alice might have liked, *strange* (imagine, though, if the walls had been stone! Imagine portraits of the ancestors; imagine a curse; imagine bloodstains on the tapestry, or, for that matter, imagine the tapestry!), nor yet a funeral parlour—any more. Bessy, however, came as close as one could fairly ask of a person to being a giant, and Alice *was* tiptoeing almost beneath her nose, and she was, beyond a quibble, kidnapped, which was, after all, the essential thing.

She raised a slat of the blind and peeked out . . .

. . . and there was nothing to see! Water—muddy brown water, much more than Alice could have swum across. Pressing herself against the window pane and looking straight down she could see tufts of marshy-looking grass. There must, she decided, be a better way to escape than climbing down from this window.

The door to the hall was locked, she had heard Bessy lock it, but there were two other doors that she hadn't locked. The first proved to be a closet, smelling of lilies-of-the-valley and mouldy shoes. The second opened on to a dreadfully messy bathroom—on the other side of which there was another door. Alice closed the door to Bessy's room behind her, and now the darkness *was* dark, since the bathroom was windowless and the transoms above the doors were shut tight. She moved barefoot across the chilly tiles with delicious stealth and felt for the knob of the other door. It opened . . . and there, near enough to reach out and touch, was Fay, asleep! What a strange house it was where everyone went to bed in the morning!

Sleeping in a twin bed across the room was Clara, also (and very audibly) asleep. And the door from their bedroom to the hall was ajar. She *would* escape!

Down the hall, down the stairs, then quickly across the living-room to the front door: ah, but of course *that* was locked. It should be a simple matter, then, to climb out of a window—but there was no way to open the living-room's big picture window, and the smaller window on the farther wall proved just as intractable, for the latch was sealed tight with layers and layers, years and years, of white enamel. The kitchen window was small and too high for Alice to reach without the help of a stepladder. But there were still all those other rooms along the hallway; one of them, *surely* . . .

But better than that there was another doorway at the end of the downstairs hallway, a back door, and Bessy hadn't thought to lock it.

From the ledge of the door to the ground was a sheer drop of three or four feet into marsh grass and mud of an uncertain consistency. Alice hated to get dirty, but people had dared worse fates: Jean Valjean, for instance, had escaped from that terrible police inspector by wading through the Paris sewers, compared to which a little *mud* . . .

'That's quicksand, you know,' came a voice from behind her. It was Clara, wearing a filmy nightgown and smiling in an ugly way—though perhaps that was the only way she knew to smile. 'You jump down into that crap, and it'll be the last we'll see of you. You'll just be swallowed up, *gobbled*.' She made a sound indicative of this process.

'But if it were quicksand, the whole house would sink!' Alice protested.

'Well, you just go ahead and jump into it, if you don't be-lieve me. Why do you think nobody bothers to lock that door? 'Cause no burglar's going to come in *that* way.'

'Then it's a dumb place to build a house.'

'The house was here before the quicksand. The quicksand came when the tidewater started backing up, and the tidewater started backing up when they built that big tunnel under the bay. And as a matter of fact, the house *is* sinking, but it just takes longer for a house to go down than for a person. You're a pretty little girl, did you know that? What'd you say your name was?'

'Oh no, I'm ugly,' Alice said with conviction. She wanted to add: 'And I'm not really black at all,' but she was afraid that would seem unkind, or even prejudiced, to Clara, who was so very black.

'Well, that makes two of us,' Clara said agreeably. 'But cheer up, kid—looks ain't everything.' She seemed in a much better temper now than she had only minutes before. 'How you come to be staying here?' she asked. 'Are you some relation of Bessy's?'

Alice lowered her eyes. Maybe Clara didn't *know* . . . Was it possible that she would be willing, then, to help her escape?

'How old did you say you was? Twelve? You look older'n that to me.' Clara rumped Alice's black curls in an almost affectionate way.

'Did Bessy tell you that I'm . . .'

'Mm-hmm? What's that, gingerbread?'

'. . . kidnapped? '

Obviously, Bessy had not told her, for her eyes became just that degree more protuberant than they had been.

'Yes, I'm kidnapped. Bessy and two other men kidnapped me, and I'm being held for ransom. I live in Baltimore, and my real name is Alice Raleigh. Dinah was my name when I was sick.'

'Sounds like you ain't got over it.'

'Oh, I'm quite well now, thanks to . . .' Alice's eyes clouded over, but only for a moment. 'But that's all over now, and in any case it's of no interest to *you*. You will help me to escape, won't you? You can boost me up to the kitchen window, I can't reach it myself, and Bessy need never know . . . need she?'

'How much ransom?'

'I don't know about that part. A lot, I suppose. I'm rather rich, you see, and I'm not . . . a Negro. Though of course there's nothing to be ashamed of. Being one, I mean.'

'You sure *look* black, honey,' Clara commented sceptically.

'It's because she made me take pills. I hope she has pills that will turn me white again.'

'I've been hoping that all my life, kid.'

'It's *true*. Look at my eyes, my eyes are blue.'

Clara looked into Alice's eyes, smiling that mean smile of hers. Alice felt herself blushing and wondered if it were noticeable. *Did* coloured people blush?

'Will you help me, Clara? If you do help me, I'm sure my uncle will give you a reward.'

Clara's eyelids tightened about her large eyes. 'You're *sure* of that, huh?'

'Oh, positive. After all, it will save him paying the ransom.'

'Well, *I* ain't so sure. I'm a lot surer of getting some of that ransom, now that I know what's going on. How much do you think it'll be? How much has your uncle got?'

'Then you *won't* help me?'

'I'll help you upstairs. That's where I'll help you. You must git yourself some sleep on that bed Bessy made up for you. And be quiet, understand. I don't want you waking her up.'

Clara locked the door between Bessy's bedroom and the bathroom. There was no escaping now, so Alice went quietly and quickly to sleep. She dreamt of a great snowball fight on a vast field of ice between the polar bears and the penguins. Every time that Dinah (for that is who she was in her dream) threw a snowball, big fat white hairy Mrs. Buckler would catch it and fry it and eat it, which became very frustrating in time, though it was not, exactly a nightmare.

The hardest part of being kidnapped, for a person of any intelligence, is the boredom, for kidnappers, however thorough their preparations may be in other areas, do not as a rule make provision for the entertainment of the kidnapee. There was nothing for Alice to *do*; there was nothing for Alice to *read*; there was nothing for Alice to *think*. Bessy had allowed her the run of the house, after securing her promise that she wouldn't try to get away (and warning her, once more, of the quicksand below the back door) or talk to anybody else that came in the house. She had to promise to go in to the bathroom or the kitchen, whichever was nearest, whenever the doorbell rang, and to stay there until the visitor had either gone away or up the stairs. It wasn't much of a bargain, since aside from the giant bathtub there were few interesting features to the house, one bedroom being very much like another, but at least it was better than being confined in Bessy's hot bedroom day and night, drenched in the cloying odour of her cologne.

She read through *Just-So Stories* once more, but she was a fast reader and finished it in under two hours. Bessy had tried to find her something about the house to read, but there wasn't anything, not a thing.

Clara, late in the afternoon, offered to play checkers with her. Alice asked if she wouldn't really rather play chess, and Clara used some of her filthiest language.

Bessy said, 'You watch that, Clara, or I'm going to have to wash your mouth out with soap.'

Clara said, 'Up yours!' Bessy just chuckled.

Clara proved to be a very poor checkers player. She never planned her moves ahead, and Alice trounced her three times running. They never did find all the checkers, after that.

There was no television set, but there was a staticky old radio. From nine till eleven on Sunday night, Alice sat with Bessy in the kitchen listening to the Top Forty and memorising the words of the songs. Or she would draw pictures with a ballpoint pen on Bessy's stationery (which smelled, like almost everything that belonged to Bessy, of lilies-of-the-valley), but she never had learned how to do good likenesses, and a ballpoint wasn't much good for anything else. For self-expression in the manner of Miss Braggs, she needed crayons or finger paints.

'I'm very bored,' Alice said. It was no longer a fresh observation, but it was more than ever true.

'Tell you what, Dinah,' said Bessy, 'why don't you and me make some rice pudding? You know how to do that?'

'My mother doesn't let me cook. She says it's beneath my station.'

'Lord! Eleven years old and can't cook.' Bessy shook her head.

'I'd love to *learn*,' Alice insisted, 'if you'll teach me.'

By two o'clock that night all the visitors had gone away, and while Bessy and Clara 'killed a pint', Fay and Alice ate the whole pot of rice pudding. Fay kept complaining that Alice had taken all the raisins for herself.

'I have not. I've had fewer raisins than *you*.'

'You *have*,' Fay insisted, on the verge of tears.

'Oh, for *heaven's* sake!' said Alice.

'You're a greedy old pig!'

'No I ain't! You're...' Alice caught her breath. She had said *ain't*, a word that she had *never* used in her life. But no one seemed to have noticed. Bessy was glassy-eyed from the liquor, and Clara had learned not to listen when Fay started to whine, as, after a night's work, she usually did.

'Yes you are,' Fay whined now. 'You're a pig, pig, *pig!*'

'No I ain't,' said the little black girl. 'I *ain't* a pig.'

'Come on, Dinah,' Bessy said. 'It's your bedtime.'

Bessy rocked back and forth in her rocker, humming a hymn. It was early—eleven o'clock on Monday morning, and things seemed to have settled into a comfortable routine. Little Dinah, now that she was over the shock of being turned black, had straightened herself out, and the only fuss she made now was the one fuss kids will make anywhere, any time—she fussed that she was bored. You'd think just being kidnapped would be enough for a child, but no, she had to *do* something.

Bessy did what she could. Yesterday she'd dug up a stack of Clara's old movie magazines that she'd tied up and stored in a spare bedroom to keep till the Boy Scouts came around on one of their paper drives. Wasn't a girl in the world that didn't like to read movie magazines. Not Dinah though. And Fay's comics, the same way—just turned up her nose at them. And *then* she'd holler because she didn't have anything to read! Well, try and reason with a child!

'There must be something,' Alice said. 'Don't you have any *books*?'

'Read that book you brought here.'

'I've *read* it. Twice.'

'I don't think all that reading's healthy for you. You'll ruin your eyes.'

'All right—then let me listen to the radio.'

'I told you—you can't turn the radio on when Clara's asleep. She don't sleep so good, and when she gets waked by noise she can make a real scene. Why don't you draw some pictures, like you did last night?' Bessy had been no little bit disturbed by Alice's scribbly, slashy drawings the evening before. She wondered if the girl might not be getting mentally. People that think and read too much, she was convinced, were in danger of getting mentally.

'Oh, I know I'm not any good at drawing. Don't you have *any* books?'

'You go look in my bedroom closet. There may be some books there that I never found to give to the Boy Scouts. But be quiet on those stairs!'

An hour later Bessy began to wonder what was keeping the girl so quiet, quietness being unnatural in a child, and went up to investigate. Even before she was in the room she could hear Alice giggling to herself. Trust a child to find mischief.

But when she opened the door, she was just sitting on the bed reading a big thick red book, which Bessy didn't remember having around the house.

'What you reading that's so amusing, child?'

Giggling, Alice lifted the book up so that Bessy could read the faded gilt letters on the cover: *Feminine Hygiene*, by L. T. Woodward, M.D.

'Lord, that ain't no fit book for young girls.' Bessy grabbed it and carried it downstairs to the kitchen, where she placed it on the top shelf of the cupboard, well out of Alice's reach. 'Books like that are for when you get my age,' she admonished.

'You mean I can't read anything I want to?' At home I can.'

'This ain't your home, and I don't want to send you back to Baltimore with no funny ideas. So while I'm at it I'd better check what other trash I got in that closet up there.' Bessy laboured back up the stairs, fumbling for the gold-rimmed glasses she kept in her purse. It mattered little that she couldn't find them, for their chief purpose had been ornamental and ritualistic rather than optical. She rummaged in the mouldy carton of books on the floor of her closet. Out came *Passion Fruit, Forever Amber, Mimi, Harlot of Babylon,* and a dozen other paperback novels, their spines split with many readings, their soiled covers depicting more or less the same full-bosomed redhead or blonde or brunette in a torn blouse with a gun in her hand, or a sword, or a whip. In the end Bessy had to carry the whole carton down to the kitchen, leaving Alice only a Gideon Bible, a copy of *The Little Engine That Could* (Fay's?), and Prescott's *The Conquest of Mexico.* After further deliberation Bessy returned and removed the last-named book as well.

'Well *gee,* what *am* I going to read?' Alice demanded.

'There's worse reading than the Bible. When I was a little girl, my Daddy read to us children every night from the Bible. Whatever else I may have to regret in my life, I ain't never regretted *that.*'

'Don't *you* ever read anything, Bessy? Even my mother read *something.*'

'No, I've never been much of a reader. 'Bout the only thing I ever look at any more is *Sunrise,* and a few magazines like that.'

'Could I look at those, then? Before you put them up on that shelf.'

'Oh, you can look at those all right. Ain't nothing in *them* to harm a young mind.'

'Bessy?' Alice asked a short time later, when they were both sitting in the living-room. 'Why do you read *undertaking* magazines?'

'Oh, I'm going to have me a nice big funeral one of these days, and I read through those magazines so I'll know what I'm putting my money into. There's more kinds of coffins and fancy trimmings these days than you'd believe possible, and each kind has got different advantages. Some coffins is got silk inside, and others is brocade, and I even read about one of Brussels lace. Wouldn't I like *that*! Costs a couple of hundred dollars more though. I didn't have any idea how complicated it all was till I moved in to this place. You see, I bought Green Pastures at auction, after the man who owned it, old Mr. Washburn, went and died, and after I moved in these magazines just kept right on coming to the address. I don't suppose they really belong to me, but the post office won't take them back, 'cause they're not first-class mail, so I always had 'em around the house. Then one day I got to looking at one. Well, you know how it says in Scripture—Vanity of vanities, the Preacher says, all is vanity. It's all just vanity and vexation, everything a person tries to do, and the wise man dieth even as the fool. And a bit farther on it says—there's a time to be born and a time to die. Well child, it's clear as day that this ain't my time to be *born*.'

It was Monday night, and Alice, sitting atop the kitchen table, was playing a game of chess with Dinah, who was winning. Since the chess pieces were only checkers and bottlecaps and medicine bottles, it sometimes was hard to remember just which pieces were which. Bessy, Clara, and Fay were sitting out in the living-room, waiting for a friend called John.

She was so tired of them, tired of Green Pastures and the unreasonable hours one had to keep here, tired of the Top Forty songs on the radio, and tired, especially, of her black skin. She vowed to herself, that when she got home, when the medicine wore off, she would never, never again wish for a suntan. Her skin would always be just as white as her mother's —a beautiful translucent sick-bed white.

'You're in check,' Dinah said. 'Why can't you keep your mind on the game?' She adjusted the position of the pink plastic doll (decently clad now in a handkerchief) so that it could concentrate better on the game.

Alice made a move.

'If you move there, I'll take your queen, stupid.'

Alice took back the move.

'You should have castled on your last turn. Now it's too late.'

'If you won't be quiet and let me *concentrate* . . .'

'Do you know what I think?' Dinah said meditatively—for

*her* mind was not really on the game either.

'. . . then I shall have to concede!' Alice concluded loftily.

'I think they must have had help, that's what I think.'

'Who?'

'The kidnappers. Bessy and Harry and the one who said he was the chauffeur. They had help from someone who knew you. How else *would* they know Miss Godwin's car was broken down? How else would they know about *me*?'

'*You* don't exist,' said Alice.

'I could say the same of you if I wanted,' Dinah pointed out to the pink plastic doll. 'I was only trying to help.'

'Who do you think helped them? Uncle Jason? Miss Godwin? Don't be silly!'

'What about . . . Mrs. Buckler?'

A rather frightened look came into Alice's eyes. 'I told you never to *mention* Mrs. Buckler! You *don't* suppose that . . . she. . . ?'

This conversation was interrupted by the ringing of the front door. Bessy peeked through the blinds in front of the picture window and announced, with some relief, that it was John. Alice pushed open the swinging door between the kitchen and the living-room just a crack to see him. He was a white man, and nearly as skinny as Clara, with a thin beak of a nose and pale, wary eyes.

'Well, if it ain't Farron Stroud!' said Bessy heartily. 'What a pleasure to see you, Farron, after all this time.'

Farron Stroud moistened his lips and cleared his throat but still found himself without a voice.

'We ain't seen you for so long we thought you must be spending every night making election speeches. Can't read a newspaper these days, without seeing your face in it.'

'Um, as a matter of fact, I was just this evening . . . Um, where is . . . Um, I hope she isn't already . . .'

'I'm right here, lover,' said Clara. 'If you'd look up from the floor a minute, you'd see me.'

Clara and Farron went upstairs together. Clara, who was wearing her usual levis, had removed the wide leather belt from them, and was *thwacking* it on her thigh energetically.

Bessy came into the kitchen and found Alice peeking out through the door, but she didn't seem put out by it. She turned on the radio, and for half an hour they listened to the Top Forty with the volume turned all the way up. That was how

Alice liked best to listen, but Bessy hadn't allowed it because of the neighbours. The neighbours—and here it was after midnight!

Try and reason with an adult!

# Chapter 10

'Don't you have any children of your own, Bessy?' Alice asked, early next morning, the morning of Tuesday the 3rd of July.

Bessy, who was still in bed, called upon the Lord in a tone of general, unspecific dissatisfaction.

'Because you said you *did*, and then, you know, you said you didn't.'

'Lord, child, ain't you starting off awful early in the day?'

'It's ten-thirty. I've been up for twenty minutes already, and I'm *hungry*.'

'I swear, that mother of yours must not have fed you *nuthin'*. If you lived with me a while, *I'd* fatten you up sure enough. Skin-and-bones!'

'You didn't answer my question.'

'Look here, child—I don't *have* to answer your questions!'

'But this *is* your husband in the picture, isn't it? You said so last night.' Alice held up a gilt-framed snapshot of Bessy (though it was hard to see many points of correspondence between the woman in the photo, just pleasantly buxom, and the so-much-larger woman in the bed) and of a Negro sailor in dress whites with an arm around her waist.

'I guess he'll have to pass for a husband. I'm not going to find anything better *now*.'

'Is he dead? Or what?'

'Yes, he's dead. Though it ain't no business of *yours*, and I'll thank you kindly to keep your little brown nose out of my business. Lord!' She was out of bed and had wrapped herself in a cotton housedress. She took the snapshot out of Alice's hands and put it back on the dresser. Then, with the key that had been pinned to her nightgown, she unlocked the door, and she and Alice went downstairs for a breakfast of fried mush, Alice having learned, as her latest lesson in cooking, how to prepare the mush itself in advance.

It seemed to Alice that she had seldom eaten a breakfast quite so good.

Upstairs there was a great clamour and a clattering, after which a door slammed and Fay came running down the stairs, half undressed, and giggling furiously. Inexplicable vapours

91

followed in her wake. The door slammed again and Clara, in her nightgown, came to the head of the stairs where she screamed terrible things at Fay who had by now locked herself into the downstairs bathroom.

'God *damn* it, Fay, who told you you could use my cologne? Birdbrain! Idiot! Moron!' And other epithets too, more terrible but less strictly relevant.

'What's the matter, Clara?' Bessy asked lazily, putting away the last dry dish into the cupboard and coming into the living-room.

'What's the matter! That idiot Fay spilled a whole bottle of my cologne, *that's* what's the matter! And woke me up when I've had about *two* hours of sleep, *that's* what's the matter! I can't keep a —— thing around here, without that —— idiot breaking it in —— pieces, *that's* what's the matter!'

'Tell you what, Clara—we'll get you a new bottle of that *expensive* cologne right the next time we're down by Wool-worth's. And for the time being, you better get yourself a long hot bath, and Fay too, 'cause the two of you don't exactly smell kissin'-sweet, if you know what I mean.'

Clara tried to make her receding chin jut forward aggressively but only managed to convey what she might have looked like without this defect. 'I've had just about enough out of you, Bessy McKay! You and your crazy kidnapping schemes. If I didn't know that...'

'Hush up about what you don't know, girl,' Bessy said, no longer lazily. 'Little pitchers got big ears.'

Clara's scrawny fist clenched about the cracked cologne bottle. For a moment Alice thought she would throw it at Bessy. Instead she stormed back to her bedroom.

Bessy settled down for a long day's rock (she could sit *hours* in that rocking chair, not doing a thing except rocking and humming), and Alice wandered over to the picture window to regard the weedy lawns and empty lots of North Tidewater Road. She imagined, rather listlessly, herself as a prisoner in a prison camp, where a beastly German officer threatened to torture her without ever quite getting around to it. She had to get back to her own lines with the secret of the German High Command, the secret that would win the war...

'Bessy,' she asked, 'do you want to buy some Spengler's Beer?'

'No thank you, child.'

A beer truck had stopped right in front of Green Pastures,

and a brawny, black-haired young man in a uniform with SPENGLER'S BEER embroidered on it in red was coming up the walk to the house. He stopped in his tracks and looked directly at Alice standing in the window.

'Because,' she went on, 'there's a man coming up to the house who's selling Splengler's Beer.'

'At *this* hour?' Bessy rocked forward, tilted herself to her feet, and joined Alice at the window. The Splengler's Beer man ground out the butt of a cigarette on Bessy's front steps, then came forward to knock on the door.

'You remember what you promised me, Dinah?'

'I'll go in the kitchen,' Alice promised meekly.

'It's too late for that now, he's seen you. Just put on your sunglasses and sit on the couch and no matter what happens you don't say a word. Just do whatever I say. Promise?'

'I promise.'

'If you don't, you may get me in a pile of trouble. You wouldn't want to do that, now would you? Aren't we good friends?'

Alice nodded. And it was true: she had come to like Bessy. Bessy might have, if she'd had a mind to, keep her asleep all the time with pills, but instead she'd been nice. She'd even been teaching her to cook.

Besides, a promise is a promise.

The man banged on the door impatiently. Bessy went into the foyer, where she was out of sight from the couch, and unlocked the door. 'The girls is both asleep, and you should know better'n to come knocking at this hour. Come back around six o'clock—even that's early—and . . .'

'You're Mrs. Elizabeth McKay?' the man asked, in the mumbly, uneducated accent of a poor white, an accent more offensive to Alice's ears that Bessy's own.

'That's who I is, but it ain't more than five minutes after eleven, and . . .'

'My name is Owen Gann,' he said. Then he said, 'Mumble, mumble, my credentials. Mumble, mumble, questions I'd like to mumble—inside, if I may.'

'Sure 'nough,' Bessy said, following him into the living-room. Her tone and manner had changed. Her shoulders were hunched up and she was bent forward at the waist, an attitude that made her look inches shorter. Beside the tall white man she seemed scarcely adult. Her face wore a wide, toothy grin, which was dismaying in its fixity and not like Bessy at all, not at all. 'The place ain't none too clean,' she complained in a whining tone. 'I try to make it look nice, the Lord knows, but what with one thing and another, one thing and another...' She ended with a sigh and a rolling of her eyes.

The man looked at Alice, incuriously, and looked away.

'Dinah honey, you run out to the kitchen and have yo'self a glass of milk, This gennulman and me's got a little business to discuss.'

As Alice was walking reluctantly into the kitchen, Bessy added: 'Dinah there is my sister's child. She only staying with me until Fanny can find herself a job.'

Before letting the door swing closed behind her, Alice took a last look at the Spengler's Beer man (who was, she was fairly sure, a policeman in disguise), but his attention was already directed back to Bessy.

After dutifully pouring out a glass of milk and taking one sip, Alice crept back to the door and pushed it open a crack, just enough to peek through. All she could see was the man's broad, muscly backside, and behind him the broader mass of Bessy. They spoke almost in whispers, and Alice could hear only a word now and then. One of those words was Dorman.

'Who's that, Captain?' Bessy said.

'You heard me—Harry Dorman.'

'Oh yes, Harry—bless his heart, I thought he was still in jail. If you find him I hope you remind him he owes me five hundred dollars. I just about done give up on seeing that money again. Been a long time.'

The man said something else, inaudibly, raising his voice at the end, as though in question.

'Why, Colonel, you know I wouldn't try to fool *you*! Why, if it wasn't for the police and the likes of you, I couldn't make a living. Bless you, Captain!'

Was he, Alice wondered, a captain or a colonel? Or neither perhaps, for Bessy seemed to be using both titles very freely. And why had she said: 'The police *and* the likes of you'? What was he, if not a policeman?

The man shifted his weight so that Bessy's face came into view, and Alice let the door close. The wood was as scarred with carving as a desk in a public school. There were names of people, and all the dirty words there are, and initials inside hearts. It seemed an awkward place to carve, since the door could swing freely in both directions and would have backed away under the pressure of a knifeblade unless held in place.

'Who?' Bessy said.

'Raleigh,' the man repeated impatiently.

Then he *is* looking for me, Alice assured herself. If only there were some way she could let him know she were here without breaking her promise to Bessy!

'Raleigh?' Bessy said, shaking her head. '*Wilbur* Raleigh?'

'Don't play dumb, lady. We've got it in the files.'

'I don't doubt you do, Captain. But there's just so many of them, and of course it's not always the same ones. Especially college boys. Soon's they graduate, most of 'em, they stop coming round to Green Pastures. Course I *do* remember that night you mention—Lord, I can't never forget *that*!—but not no Raleigh. You're talking about fifteen years ago.'

Alice hadn't quite followed the drift of this, but she had been amused to think that in a strictly grammatical sense Bessy might have been telling the truth, because to remember 'not no Raleigh' was a double negative and meant that she did in fact *remember* Raleigh.

'But what,' Dinah asked, 'did she mean by "fifteen years ago"?'

'You again!' Alice said angrily.

'It ain't nobody else!' Dinah declared.

'I won't talk to you!' Alice warned.

But Dinah, knowing better, lifted a coy finger and traced along the time-darkened crevices of the largest initials gouged into the door: D.B. Then, beneath that, by the same hand but smaller: K.K.K. 'What do you suppose D.B. stands for?' she asked of Alice. 'Dumbell Buckler, maybe?'

'I told you never to mention . . .'

'And K.K.K.? Would that be Kernel Karmel Korn? Or Karen at Kilkenny?'

Alice laughed and, doing so, surrendered to the black girl's charm. 'What about Krazy Kat Komics?'

'What about Ku Klux Klan?' the black girl suggested, not quite charmingly.

Apparently the policeman, if he was a policeman, was going to search the whole house, for he had gone down the downstairs hallway looking into all the bedrooms. There was a little shriek and much splashing about when he looked into the bathroom, where Fay was giving herself and her baby a bath in the long tub.

As he was going up the stairs, Alice heard him say, 'Mumble, mumble, member of Kappa Kappa Kappa. Still doesn't ring any bells?'

'Sorry, Captain,' Bessy said.

'Captain!' Dinah said scornfully. 'Kaptain Korny Krudd.'
Alice had no reply to make to this. She seemed to grow more
retiring in proportion to Dinah's outspokenness. That had
always been the way with them.

Upstairs Clara put up a big fuss before she let the policeman
look into the bathroom. When he came downstairs again, Bessy
was saying to him: 'I bet you think this is just the bathingest,
perfumiest house that ever was!' And she began telling him
the story of Clara's broken cologne bottle.

The Spengler's Beer man came into the kitchen. By that
time Dinah was already sitting at the formica-topped table,
sipping her milk, a perfect lamb. He looked about the room
with wan interest, only going through the motions of a search.
He opened the cupboard doors.

'Always keep your books here?' he asked.

Bessy laughed, and even her laughter seemed to be altered
for his benefit and implied that she only laughed by his
gracious permission. 'Not always, Captain. I just moved 'em
out here yesterday on account of little Dinah here coming for
a visit. Don't want her reading 'bout no feminine anatomy, do
we?'

The man laughed good-naturedly and took a book down. He
read the title aloud: 'School for Sinners.' He set it down on
top of the copy of *Just-So Stories* that was lying face up on the
kitchen counter.

He left the kitchen, and a moment later she could hear
Bessy letting him out through the front door. From under her
cheap sunglasses tears were streaming down her brown cheeks,
and though she stared at the swinging door she could no
longer see the initials carved there. When she heard the motor
of the truck starting up, she tore off the detested sunglasses
and, cradling her head in her arms, she began uncontrollably to
cry.

'There, there,' said Bessy. 'There, there, *there*! That's all
right, honey. That's all right. You're a good little actress, and
I'm proud of you. You saved my life, and don't think I ain't
grateful.'

'That's a double negative,' Alice wailed disconsolately.

'It sure enough was, honey, and I was scared every minute,
believe me.'

96

The phone rang.

'You gonna be all right now?' Bessy asked, stroking her curls. Alice nodded yes.

Bessy went to the phone, which was on a wall in the living-room. 'Hello,' she said, mildly enough, and then, with a quick flare of anger: 'You goddam stupid sonofabitch, what are you calling up here for?' There was a pause, after which she spoke more softly. Though she strained to listen, Alice could only catch her last words—'Are you *drunk*?'

She tiptoed to stand behind the swinging door again.

Bessy said, 'If you and Harry is having difficulties, you just leave *me* out of them. I ain't taking sides, understand? He don't take me into his confidence no more than you do, and I likes it that way. I'm just the baby-sitter—that's all I am.'

'She is undoubtedly,' Dinah noted, 'talking to one of your kidnappers. And *not* to Harry Dorman.'

Bessy said, 'Donald Bogan? What you expect me to know about *him* ...? Well, I don't love him either, honey, and you of *all* people should know that ... I don't see what difference it makes today, but I've got an idea he's dead ... About two years ago, but I can't remember who told me. Maybe I read it in the papers. Where you calling me from anyhow?'

There was a long pause, during which Alice could just barely hear the mouse-squeaks of Bessy's caller issuing from the receiver.

Donald Bogan, Alice thought. Donald Bogan—where had she heard that name before? That she *had* heard it somewhere, sometime, she was certain. If she could but recall the tone of voice in which she had first heard that name pronounced: her uncle's tinder-dry wisp of a voice? Or Miss Godwin's silken-smooth contralto? No, it was more a sort of ... *whining* voice.'

*If I'd married Donald Bogan, when I had the chance ...*

Her mother? *Her own mother?*

Bessy said, 'Don't hand me that! You're a damn fool, calling up this number. The F.B.I. was just here, and they was asking about *you*! Yes, they was ... and they looked right at little Goldilocks here three, four times. Funny? I thought I'd die. But what if they got somebody listening in on this phone? If they got suspicions enough to come calling ...' A long pause; then, 'It was about that night back in 'fifty. I told him one fraternity boy is just the same as another ... He never mentioned the kidnapping, but I don't think ...'

Dinah whispered: 'I know who it is on the phone.'

Alice said, 'No.' She backed away from the door. She went to the table and stared at the half-full glass of milk.

'Oh yes,' Dinah insisted. 'Oh yes.'

Reluctantly Alice lifted her eyes to the initials carved on the door.

'What do you suppose D.B. stands for?' Dinah insisted.

'Donald Bogan,' Alice admitted.

'And K.K.K.?'

'Ku Klux Klan?' Alice ventured weakly.

Dinah deigned no reply to that, but continued her interrogation. 'And *who* do you suppose is R.R.?'

'No,' said Alice.

'The Spengler Beer man said Raleigh, but Bessy said he didn't mention the kidnapping. He didn't mention *you*. He mentioned another Raleigh therefore, one that was here fifteen years ago.'

'Maybe the other kidnapper is Donald Bogan?' Alice said, shooting wild.

'Not if he's dead. Didn't you hear her say he was dead?'

'She said she didn't know for certain.'

'*I* know for certain.'

'No. No. No.'

'Your father was in Kappa Kappa Kappa fraternity. He still has the tie pin from those days with the three letters on it. K.K.K.'

'I won't ever talk to you again,' Alice warned. 'Ever, ever.'

'I didn't say anything,' said Dinah. 'I didn't name his name. And I won't.'

'But it can't be anybody else, can it?'

'No,' said Dinah sadly.

'It has to be my father.'

'Yes,' Dinah agreed, '... Roderick Raleigh.'

Roderick Raleigh first set out to drive his daughter insane shortly after that young lady's fifth birthday. It was not, admittedly, a course one entered upon with enthusiasm. Indeed, he had hesitated long and thought deeply before adopting it, and even then his initial efforts along these lines were half-hearted, bare, unserviceable gestures. Never could he escape feeling—if not regretful—poignant about the whole matter, for his Alice was such a bright little tyke and might have deserved so much better of him. But there had been—there was—there could be no alternative. It was certain beyond all doubt that Morgan Duquesne's will was never going to be broken.

That will had left almost the whole of the old man's estate to his grand-daughter Alice, passing over the intervening generation with scarcely a how-do-you-do—a fixed annuity of $10,000 a year. The residence in which Roderick and Delphinia were domiciled, the furniture in it, the servants who worked there: all these things were paid for out of Alice's trust fund and belonged to her. Even the food they ate was, so to speak, but the droppings from her high chair. It was degrading, it was intolerable, and it was (should such a thought ever occur to one or another of her parents) impossible to murder the child. Morgan Duquesne had maliciously seen to it that in the event of Alice's death before reaching her majority, the estate (including the house, the furniture, the servants, everything but the piddling annuity) trusted to Alice was to be divided among half a dozen irreproachable charities. Though it would have been inadvisable to contest too strongly this provision of the will (one's motive might be called into question), Roderick had received the same advice from all his lawyers: that this provision would stand up as well in court as all the rest had.

A man of ordinary resources and imagination might have desisted at this point, might have settled back ignobly in a borrowed armchair in his middle-middle-class house on Gwynn River Falls Drive (*his*, only in the sense that he lived there), and commenced his decay. Not Roderick Raleigh, for he was no ordinary man.

He set about his self-appointed task with no more exact knowledge of the science of psychology than was to be found laying around loose in the popular novels and movies of the time (though he considered himself a cultured man, he felt a rather donnish contempt for dry-as-dust science, a field of study he regarded as suitable only for garage mechanics), but he made quick progress through a number of paperbacks by Freud and his followers. On the subject of childhood psychoses he found Bruno Bettelheim and Anna Freud to be of immense utility—but really, if he had wanted to, he could have got along with nothing more than Dr. Spock.

The important thing to keep in mind when leading a child towards psychosis is that it should not feel loved. Nor should it feel, to any large degree, hated. It should feel, in general, as little as possible. Under the circumstances, it seemed to Roderick that this could be accomplished. Delphinia's feelings towards her daughter had never—at least since Morgan Duquesne's death—been other than ambivalent. She loved her daughter dutifully—but she envied her bitterly. She had, moreover, a natural talent for selfishness that Roderick had often envied, selfishness being a cardinal virtue in Roderick's rather utilitarian ethic. Had not his favourite philosopher (Roderick really did read philosophy) written: 'Selfishness is blessed—the wholesome, healthy selfishness that wells from a powerful soul'? He had, and Roderick's conduct was guided by that high principle.

The important thing was for the child to feel unloved, and so Roderick accordingly had set about not to love her. There are a hundred ways not-loving can be evidenced, but the underlying principles are too: unjust and arbitrary punishments and indifference. The first principle must be exercised with restraint to allow the second, and more important, principle to operate. Also, he was ingenious in inventing little ways to keep her 'off balance'. Thus, frequently when he was alone with her, he would praise her for doing things she had not done, call her by names not her own, and in general insist that what was not so, what she knew with a certainty was not so, was so, was so, was so. He was very mean to her but never, he prided himself, out of any native meanness on his part, only programmatically. His meanness was, in a sense, altruistic.

It was slow work—he had known from the first that it would be—and set-backs were not infrequent. She showed astonishing resilience. Blood, he had thought proudly, will tell.

His hardest problem was with the servants, for in proportion as Alice felt neglected by her parents she turned to the servants for friendship and a bit of consolation. They could not be expected to realise that this was not to be allowed, and it was sometimes hard to find cause for dismissing them. But eventually a suitable staff was assembled.

Roderick's hardest task had been to find the right governess for Alice, for governesses will, as a rule, show a certain interest in their charge, and even affection can creep in. This difficulty was aggravated by the fact that not Roderick but Jason, as executor of the will, hired the governesses. One after another, Roderick worked at eliminating these good women, usually by stage-managing a quarrel between the governess in question and his wife, which was settled, in the interests of family concord, by the dismissal of the former. At one time Roderick had hoped that Miss Stupp (or Stuck-Up, as Alice had nicknamed her) would work out, but alas, she tippled on such a scale and so brazenly that Delphinia, even she, had found it necessary to call her to account.

Then, with the advent of Mrs. Buckler, in 1960, Roderick knew that the search was over. Mrs. Buckler was in every sense a magnificent woman—fat, overbearing, crochety, secretly cruel, a congenital liar, a hypocrite, a snob, and a fake. She was everything that Roderick could have asked for in a governess.

Alice's response was immediate: she withdrew. But however far she might withdraw Mrs. Buckler would be there nagging at her to withdraw yet a little farther. There was no one she might turn to, no one who could listen to her little woes—and even if there had been, how was she, at age eight, to explain that for all Buckler's outward sweetness, the woman was a monster of cruelty? No one: she had no friends. When her grandfather had established the house on Gwynn River Falls Drive in her name, he had not taken into account that there would be few children in the neighbourhood. There was scarcely, this far out, any neighbourhood. The one child she had known best had been Dinah Watts, the daughter of Mrs. Watts, a former cook. Mrs. Watts had been fired shortly after Alice's fifth birthday, when it was discovered that she was stealing food from the Raleigh freezer for her own family. Mrs. Watts had denied this, but Delphinia had been able to prove it against her, and so Alice had seen no more of Dinah Watts.

Now Alice began to see Dinah Watts again. She would find her, at first, in the most unlikely places—under beds, inside closets, even, once, inside the automatic washer. Sometimes she was just the way she had always been, but sometimes she was a kitten—the kitten her Uncle Jason had given her for an unbirthday present. She was *always* sympathetic. She would say such things about Mrs. Buckler that Alice would be breaking into giggles over them the rest of the day—and Mrs. Buckler would never know that it was the grey kitten purring in Alice's lap that was causing the whole commotion.

Then, unaccountably (for the girl it was unaccountable; Roderick, who was torturing the kitten every night after Alice had gone to bed, could account for it very well), Dinah began to develop a mean streak. Her meanness progressed steadily until it was the equal of Buckler's, at which point Dinah bit Buckler (who had been pulling her tail), and she (Dinah) had to be sent off to the Humane Society. Her father explained to Alice what the Humane Society would do to Dinah. That was in September. From September to Christmas Roderick stepped up the pressure a little more each day. He was certain now of success. The child would spend entire hours talking to herself in corners. She had a very poor sense of what was going on around her. She grew indifferent to her lessons. She even stopped reading books. It was a matter, now that she stood at the brink of full psychosis, of waiting for the moment in which she would tip over into it and be lost from view.

Should Roderick achieve this goal, he had every reason to hope that Alice would not recover. Psychoses acquired between ages five and twelve are notoriously resistant to therapy. She would be committed to a good hospital, where her vegetable body could be kept in good health for decades. Jason was an old man and would soon die, and Roderick could then seek to be appointed trustee of his daughter's estate. Morgan Duquesne, oddly enough, had not provided explicitly against this possibility, and Roderick's lawyers had assured him that such an appointment was not without the bounds of probability. Entire fortunes have been squeezed through smaller loopholes.

He was, however, thwarted. On the Christmas before last, Jason had come snooping around, discovered his niece's condition, discharged Mrs. Buckler on the spot, and, in general, dashed Roderick's hopes. Miss Godwin was brought down from New York, and she stayed on with Alice despite Delphinia's and Roderick's most vehement protests. After eight months of therapy-*cum*-tutoring, Alice had wholly recovered the lost ground, and Miss Godwin recommended St. Arnobia's. From that day forth Alice was to be more than a transient guest at the house on Gwynn River Falls Drive.

Six years Roderick had laboured and planned; six years, with patient craft, he had spun his web, and then Fate, like a careless child playing in a meadow, had demolished it with a careless flick of her hand. Ah, there was no justice.

Last December, shortly before Alice had come home for the Christmas holiday, Miss Godwin had summoned her parents together to give them a few words of earnest counsel: 'I only wanted to suggest that the three of you spend as much time together as you can—talking, or playing games—whatever you think fit and will enjoy.'

'I don't think I need *you* to tell me how to raise my own child,' Delphinia said loftily.

'Of course not, Mrs. Raleigh. I'm sure that such a course of action is the one you had intended in any case. No doubt, I have been over-explicit, not to say over-obvious. Please accept my apologies.'

'I hope,' Roderick inquired delicately, 'there is no reason to fear . . . a relapse? She is no longer, I trust . . . in danger?'

'Unfortunately, Mr Raleigh, recovery from a mental breakdown does not provide immunity against a recurrence. There will always be *some* danger; there are scars, and though they have healed they are still tender. We should never forget, should we, that it *has* happened?'

'Oh, never,' Roderick agreed heartily.

So, following Miss Godwin's advice, a series of 'family evenings' were inaugurated. Conversation was ruled out by tacit agreement from the first, for the arts of speech as they were employed by Delphinia were not peaceful arts. Various games were tried, but Delphinia seldom had the patience to see them through to the end, and it was evident that both she and Roderick moved their counters about the board lackadaisically, with no very zestful sense of competition. Television was their usual recourse, for it demanded the least of them. Roderick, Delphinia, and Alice—the family—would sit whole hours before the television screen watching what purported to be comedies. (Delphinia had ruled out mysteries and westerns as being too violent.) Roderick tried hardest to have fun; he would say, 'Hey, will you look at that,' Or, 'Say, isn't *that* a crazy idea.' Delphinia was only moved to break the silence at the sight of opulence. A fur coat, appeals to come to Jamaica or buy a new Lincoln, swank interiors: any of these could move her to grudging approval—or to tears. Alice said nothing, and she was usually first to abandon these little *soirées*, pleading homework as an excuse. The only evening that was something of a success was the one that the family spent watching the servants decorate the giant Christmas tree; that, they all agreed, was a lot of fun.

It was on that evening, the 23rd of December, after the trimming of the tree, after both Alice and her mother had been put to bed, that Roderick went down town for a drink. He avoided the more central bars where he might meet acquaintances preferring, tonight, something dingier, where he might become maudlin if he chose. The holidays always set his *Weltschmertz* to aching. He found just the thing he needed on Willingly Street—a bar neither too shabby to be perilous or so tidy as to make him feel he needed to keep his collar buttoned, a bar he could condescend to, a bar he could be adequately miserable in. He ordered one of what the bartender was having, tossed it off neat, sipped the chaser, ordered a second. He regarded, with benevolent irony, the message soaped on the mirror—*Peace on Earth, Good Will to Men*.

'Good Will to you too,' Roderick toasted, raising the shotglass.

'Thanks,' said the bartender, 'I could use some.' He made a woeful gesture with his towel, encompassing the whole bar. With the exception of a man slouched over a whiskey at the other end, Roderick was the only customer.

'Christmas!' Roderick thought to himself, as the tides of whiskey and rhetoric began conjointly to swell about him. 'Season of renewed hope! Season of glad tidings! Where do you find me? In the stews of the city, alone, no longer young, illusions shattered . . .' The soliloquy broke down at this point, as Roderick groped for other misfortunes to enter on his debit. He might have mentioned the very real grievance of having an income of a bare ten thousand per annum, but he couldn't find any way to give this the metaphysical ring of the rest of it.

Infinite sadness! Roderick was overwhelmed by an infinite sadness. Everything around him was sad: the bald, paunchy bartender; the nondescript customer (who raised his glass to Roderick now in a pathetic parody of good cheer); the fly-specked mirror with its ironic message soaped on; the grained surface of the bar; the whiskey glass; the whiskey; the chaser. Sad, sad, infinitely sad!

Before Roderick had finished his second drink, the bartender had placed a third beside it. 'That's from him, if it's okay with you.'

Roderick lifted the drink and made a toast to his benefactor's health. His benefactor came sidling down the bar, a few stools at a time, and the first part of his address to Roderick was thus conducted across a gap of several barstools.

'Forget it, forget it! It's nothing. Hell, you may not believe this, but there was a time when I bought drinks all around for twenty, thirty people. Hell yes. "Bottoms up", I'd say and twenty, thirty glasses would go bottoms up.' He demonstrated this principle on a reduced scale. 'Another one,' he said. The bartender measured it out.

'That one's on me,' Roderick insisted.

'Thanks. And Merry Christmas to you, goddammit.' He was near enough now for Roderick to size him up, which was, at the moment, exactly what he stood in need of. A tall man, beginning to spread in his middle-age, he was wearing a sagging suit, short in the legs and tight about the middle, that he could only have obtained at the back door of a funeral parlour—or at the gate of a prison. His black, axle-greased hair was long as the veriest teenager's, a glaring anachronism above his seamed, anxious face. His eyes were green, disconcertingly green.

'You wouldn't believe it to look at me now,' the man said, 'but I was once worth half a million. Five hundred thousand dollars. Almost.'

No, I wouldn't believe it, Roderick thought. He smiled and said, 'As much as that! You must have been rolling in it.'

'Yeah. For all the good it did me.' He stared moodily into the empty shotglass.

'I see,' Roderick said, pointing to the black ring on his companion's right hand, 'that we are brothers.' He brought forward his own right hand for the man to see the identical ring there, and they exchanged the secret Masonic handclasp. 'My name is Roderick Raleigh,' Roderick volunteered.

'Mine's Harry Dorman. You ever heard of me before?' Roderick shook his head, but Harry seemed not to believe this. 'I'm not ashamed of anything I've done,' he insisted aggressively. 'I'd do it again, if I thought I'd stand a chance.'

'I don't doubt that you would—but I really haven't heard of you.'

Harry Dorman seemed, if anything, rather aggrieved than

cheered by this. 'It was in all the papers, as far as New York. It made the headlines for a whole week. I can't even go into a restaurant around here without some crumb comes up to me and asks, "Aren't you Harry Dorman?" You'd think they could forget in sixteen years.'

'That long?'

'I got life, but it was commuted for good behaviour.'

'Did you murder somebody?'

'Hell no—I was the guy that engineered the Larpenter snatch. You mean to say you never heard of that?'

'I'm sorry to confess my ignorance—but I would be most interested—yes, really most interested in hearing about it now. Bartender—two more, and can't you turn the radio up so we can *all* hear *Adeste Fidelis*?'


'. . . and that,' Harry concluded, 'is how I got sent up, and that's where I've been for the last sixteen years—the pen.'

'Stone walls,' Roderick began, after a judicious pause, 'do not a prison make, nor iron bars a cage. That is to say, they do, but the essentials of prison life can be found elsewhere as well. A family, for instance, can be every bit as confining as a prison. A stupid wife can be as stultifying to the intellect, and a child's hands can grasp your wrists as firmly as manacles. You were sentenced to life imprisonment, but your sentence was commuted and now you are free. I,' Roderick said, assuming as best the barstool would permit the attitude of a king enchained, 'can never be free. There is no power on earth that can commute *my* life sentence to Gwynn River Falls Drive!'

*Nicely done!* he told himself, *nicely done indeed!*

But Harry was no connoisseur. He went on worrying his own meatless bone after the barest assenting nod to the Prisoner of the Suburbs. '*My* mistake,' he said morosely, 'was not rubbing out that sonofabitch stool pigeon before he went to the police.'

'Yes, that was a mistake too.'

'A half million dollars,' Harry said, shaking his head. 'I had it in my hands. *These* hands,' he said, specifying the two that he now raised several inches above the bar, a dangerous manoeuvre in his condition. It made Roderick dizzy even to witness it.

'But what,' Roderick asked, 'determines the amount in these cases? The Lindberg's kidnapper only asked for $50,000 as I recall. You asked for ten times that much—and you say you got it. Why didn't you shoot the limit? What *is* the limit? Won't they be desperate enough to pay anything?'

Before Harry could assemble answers for these questions, a young woman stopped into the bar long enough to ask if either of the two gentlemen would like to buy her a drink.

'You should have been here an hour ago, beautiful,' Harry said regretfully.

'A cup of coffee will fix that, baby,' the young woman assured him.

'It's money I'm talking about—there ain't but a couple bucks left.'

The young lady left them.

'Damn it,' Harry said. 'It's been sixteen years, and I could use a piece. When I lived down in Norfolk it used to be I could knock off some any time I wanted to. I scouted up business there for this nigger madam, name of Bessy . . .'

'Bessy who?'

'Bessy McKay. You know of her?'

'Curiouser and curiouser,' said Roderick. 'I do.'

'She's a good ol' girl, but I hear she's come down in the world since then.'

'We've *all* come down in the world, brother,' Roderick assured Harry. 'But the question is—can they keep us down?'

'Hell no!'

'O my unconquerable soul!' Said Roderick.

'What's that?'

'Nothing—just a tag from Virgil. A question, my dear brother, a question: when you said earlier—correct me if I misquote you—that you would do it again (I need not, I hope, mention *what*), did you speak . . . in earnest?'

'You're goddam right!'

'How does a million dollars sound to you, brother? Shouldn't that about make up for the cost of living rise in the past sixteen years?'

Harry's expression was one of scornful incredulity.

'I am as serious,' Roderick assured him, 'as it is possible for a man in my present condition to be—which is rather more serious than I am at any other time. Consider, Harry, consider —a million dollars, and you will risk not sixteen years this time but five at the limit. I shall have to check that at the law library of course, but I think a conspiracy to commit fraud will involve not much more than that.'

'You're out of your head, mister.'

'Truly, if we are to continue this discussion, it were best we switched to coffee. Come, Harry, put your arm around my shoulder. To the cafeteria! Oh, Harry, if you only *knew* what divine ferment my mind is in now, the creative energies your tale has released within me! Do you know Nietzsche?'

'Who?' Harry asked tolerantly. They had left the bar and were stumbling arm in arm through the grimy midnight streets.

'The greatest of the philosophers, a profound man. He wrote: "Whoever must be a creator in good and evil, verily, he must first be an annihilator and break values. Thus the highest evil belongs to the highest goodness: but this is creative." '

'Sounds like Communism to me.'

Roderick took a deep breath of the sharp-edged wintry air. The stars, palely shining through the incandescent nimbus overspreading the metropolis, seemed to waver and spin like the stars of van Gogh, and Roderick began to laugh. 'Harry,' he shouted loudly, 'I'm an artist! I'm a goddam creative artist! I'm a genius!'

'You're some kind of nut, seems more like it.'

Roderick stopped laughing. He pulled Harry close to him so that their noses almost touched in an Eskimo kiss. Staring into those green eyes, Roderick whispered, 'Harry, how would you like to help me kidnap my own daughter?'

The morning of Monday, the 2nd of July, found Roderick on a bench in Baltimore's Carrol Park, where he was benignly feeding crumbs to pigeons. Roderick liked pigeons, they were so manipulable, and the noise of their squabbling provided a comfortable background for serious thought, a sort of environmental static.

Roderick's masterpiece was nearing its consummation. The ransom money was being assembled in banks all about the city; the police were keeping themselves busy with futile examinations of the Raleigh's servants; Roderick's only task for the day was to sit tight and to evidence just that degree of anxiety that a loving father should, under the circumstances, evidence, no more and no less.

There was no need to worry: the plan was thorough, the plan had foreseen all contingencies, the plan was working. It had all the scrupulous definition of a Flemish altarpiece, but the details were present without in any way obscuring its bold outlines. And it *was* bold! Its central feature, the notion of hiding Alice behind the colour of her own, metamorphosed skin, had come to Roderick in such a moment of ecstatic vision as Paul must have experienced going towards Damascus. Roderick had been passing by a movie theatre at the time, caught up in his planning, and the marquee of the theatre had announced as one of its features 'Black Like Me', the true story of a journalist who, to learn what it was like to be a Negro, had used chemicals to change his skin colouring. From that little mustard seed the whole great oak—or, in this case, mustard tree—had grown.

There was justice of a sort in it too. The money he was appropriating from Alice's trust was, in the larger view that Roderick took, his by right. A $10,000 annuity was not fair recompense for the labour of being married to such a woman as Delphinia; the million he was coming into now could, in this sense, be looked upon as back wages. Whether he would stay on with Delphinia in the future depended upon the outcome of his auxiliary plan—or, as he had dubbed it in a moment of whimsy, 'Operation Schizo'. If Operation Schizo were a success—that is to say, if Alice returned from her kidnapping in a very discomposed state—then Roderick might very well hang on, at least until Jason's death, when he would have a chance to be appointed executor of the poor mad girl's estate. But very likely Alice would not be given enough time to crack up, in which case—Good-bye, Baltimore! Good-bye, very probably, U.S.A.!

There was no need to worry: the plan would work, and it was working. Yet he was uneasy, distinctly uneasy. Perhaps all artists go through a similar period of misdoubting in the creation of their masterpieces. Small comfort, that!

Roderick crumpled the emptied bag of crumbs, tossed it at the pigeons, who scattered with an indignant protest, and walked out of the park along Baltimore-Washington Boulevard. Though he walked, as he thought, aimlessly, it was curious how quickly he arrived at the post office.

It could not hurt, he reasoned, if he just went in the door. He could buy a book of stamps at the stamp window. There was nothing unusual in that.

On the way to the stamp window he glanced at Box 445. There was, though this was quite unthinkable, a letter within the box. He stopped in his tracks to assure himself that this was not a trick of light on the window of the box. There *was* a letter there.

He bought a book of stamps and left the post office. He

dared not open the box, because he had every reason to suppose the police were trailing him. He had to suppose that they were. If they were to discover the postal box in which he had been receiving his mail from Dorman and Bessy ... no, it had been unwise even to go into the post office; he dare not open the box.

He had told them, a week before the kidnapping, to stop writing to him. And there was no one else who knew of the existence of that box. Only Dorman and Bessy. One of them had needlessly jeopardised an infallible plan—and for what reason?

Roderick went into a bar to consider this with greater care. If he were being followed, it would not be thought improbable for him to ease the tension with a whiskey or two.

The letter *had* to be from Harry Dorman. As he drank, Roderick became more and more convinced of it. Bessy could be trusted to obey orders, but Dorman had a rebellious streak. It was like him to risk the whole enterprise for a piece of foolishness. Assuming, always, that it was foolishness. What did the letter say? What could Harry Dorman possibly have to tell him that could not wait until tomorrow? Nothing. Unless...

'He wouldn't dare,' Roderick said aloud.

*Unless* the bastard was planning a double-cross. Unless he was asking for more money. Roderick could just imagine what the letter would be like. 'Dear Roderick,' it would begin—though Harry, who hadn't graduated grade school, would probably find some way to misspell his name. 'Dear Rodorik, I don't like getting only $150,000 for my share of the work, when it's me and Bessy and Bittle who do all the work. I think we should get haff. Yours truly, Harry.'

That son of a bitch! That greedy bastard! He thought he had Roderick in a position where he couldn't refuse. He knew that he couldn't go to the police. It was the same as blackmail. It *was* blackmail.

'Damn,' Roderick said aloud. *'Damn!'*

'Watch it, mister,' the bartender said. 'That's how you get heart attacks.'

His hands trembled as he lifted the water glass to his lips. He felt almost dizzy with the effort of repressing his righteous indignation.

Blackmail: the word brought back visions of pimply-faced Donald Bogan, that *other* son of a bitch, the king of them all.

110

Christ, how Roderick would have liked to get hold of him again! So long ago, so many years, and yet the hatred he bore him was still as tangible and immediately as a band of hot iron about his brow. Bogan had never been one to be satisfied with his share either. He had squeezed Roderick until he was bloodless: first, the bribe he'd demanded before he could get into Kappa Kappa Kappa; then the little rake-offs from Roderick's commissions from the bootleggers and cathouses he worked with; eventually Bogan even demanded a cut of his meagre allowance. In dollars and cents Bogan's squeeze had never amounted to much, not the way Roderick looked at things today, but then it had been the world.

And it had been Bogan, he must not forget that he would never forget, nobody but Bogan, who had ended Roderick's law career before it had had a proper chance to begin.

Yes, Bogan and Harry Dorman were two of a kind, but this time Roderick had his past experience to profit from. If Harry was now allowed a chance to double-cross him, if he were to meet an untimely end ... (Though whose end, really, could be timelier?) He had pronounced the words himself that sentenced him now: '*My* mistake was not rubbing out that sonofabitch stool pigeon before he went to the police.' Or, Roderick might amend, before he was caught by them.

There was, in the bottom of Roderick's dresser drawer, a gun, an unregistered war souvenir he'd bought as a young man. He had never had occasion to use it, though a few rounds of ammunition had come with it. Thinking about that gun helped to ease the tense muscles of his neck and shoulders, and his face assumed a more usual hue—a transformation that the bartender, observing it from the other end of the bar, regarded with approval.

Back at the post office on that same Monday, 2nd of July, the clerk was still busy filling out notices to box renters, reminding them that the rent for the third quarter of the year had come due. Box rental was something *nobody* seemed to remember—probably because it only came up four times a year. By noon almost every box in the building had a notice in it.

Chapter 12

It was misty but not chill that Tuesday morning. Roderick was again sitting in Carrol Park, he was again feeding the idiot pigeons from a bag of crumbs. A black attaché case was lying in his lap, and the hand that held the bag of crumbs lay upon this. Barring the pigeons, he was alone.

A man approached through the mist, wearing a hat and a tan trenchcoat. He took a seat beside Roderick. 'Mr. Raleigh?' Roderick nodded. 'I'm Agent Fields.' They shook hands.

'Excuse the crumbs,' Roderick apologised belatedly. He returned to his benevolent task.

'Quite all right. You're early, I see.'

'I couldn't sleep, thinking about ... And the house depresses me—without Alice in it.'

'You have the money?'

'I have the money. Jason Duquesne, my wife's brother, brought it to us last night.'

'And the case ...?'

'Is the one the kidnappers mailed to us.'

'We can go to the railway station now.'

'The instructions were to be there at eight o'clock. I don't suppose it would upset them if I appeared a few minutes early —they might not even know—but I should like to finish up this bag at least. To be candid, I'm afraid not to hold to the letter of the law, if one may speak of law in this case. And then too, once we get to the station you and I won't be able to talk. Talking helps. At least it is supposed, in theory, to help.'

Roderick and Agent Fields turned with one accord to watch the feeding pigeons, who seemed, in the absence of sunlight this morning, especially drab. Their thick red feet toddled and their heads bobbed with the abrupt and seemingly autonomous motions of a mechanical toy or a spastic. 'Do you like animals?' Roderick asked.

'Uh huh,' said Agent Fields.

'You may think it crochety of me, but I always judge a man by that. Is my daughter ... Is there any word ... ?'

'Nothing yet, Mr. Raleigh. We're checking out every possible lead.'

Roderick sighed. 'I pray to God ...' he whispered, but did not go on to tell Agent Fields the precise nature of his communications to the divinity.

'Are there,' Roderick asked, after another respectful viewing of the pigeons, 'many others at the terminal?'

'Each entrance is being watched. If either Dorman or the Negro that Miss Godwin identified come in, we'll be able to tail them.'

'But there won't be any arrests? Not, at least, until Alice is safe at home. You did promise that.'

'And we'll keep to the promise. Your daughter's safety is our paramount concern at this point too, Mr. Raleigh.'

'Thank you, thank you. If I could only tell you what these last days have been like for me ... Alice's mother has not borne up under the strain very well. She is an invalid, you know. As for myself, I'm afraid I owe you apologies ...'

'You're doing fine, Mr. Raleigh. We all admire your courage, and we realise what a strain you must be under. It won't be long now, sir.'

A Negro paperboy came by and flashed a headline at them, of which Roderick could catch only the word, VIOLENCE. He waved the boy on.

'I am not a religious man, Mr. Fields. I daresay I don't go to church above two times a year. However, in times like this a person realises how important his faith is. I wouldn't have been able to go through with this if I didn't feel that there was someone ... up there ... helping me. Perhaps this embarrasses you.' The bag of crumbs, empty now, was tossed aside.

'Not at all,' said Agent Fields with embarrassment. 'I'm a Catholic myself.'

'Then may I ask you to grant me a very important favour?'

'Please do, sir.'

Roderick gripped the detective's hand between his own, rubbing off crumbs. 'Would you pray for me, Agent Fields?'

Agent Fields blushed. 'Of course, sir. We're *all* praying for you.'

Roderick made no effort to wipe away the tears rolling down his cheeks. 'Thank you, oh thank you.'

The Baltimore railway terminal had been built along the ample, Roman-baths model of the era of the robber barons; beneath its vast barrel-vault the modern blazonry of advertisers seemed to be scaled to almost human proportions, though the presence of some few hundred actual humans was sufficient to contradict this false seeming. Both this cathedral, and the writing upon its walls, had been fashioned for another and more heroic order of beings than the puny things that scurried through it this Tuesday morning whom it tolerated only until the Olympians, for whom it had been intended, should arrive and take possession.

Even as a child Roderick Raleigh had not been able to enter this building without feeling himself inflated, transformed into something a little larger than life, something Wagnerian, and now ... now the old feeling came over him with such force that he was obliged to stop at the threshold to catch his breath. Today this usual afflatus was merely the illusion of art, for now he was transcending the bounds of the merely human, all-too-human; now by his cunning and his courage his spirit was grown large enough to fill the high vault comfortably.

The large Bulova clock on the west wall gave the time as 7.58. Roderick proceeded directly to the bank of telephone booths beneath the clock, following the instructions that had been brought back by Miss Godwin. Thanks to the police, the end booth was blocked by a conspicuous OUT OF ORDER sign. Roderick took the sign off the door and entered the booth, which fitted him snug as a coffin. He tried to get through the time by examining the graffiti smutched on the metal walls or cut into the wood of the door, an alphabet soup of initials and obscenities. He enjoyed a momentary, high pleasurable quiver of indignation at the oafs who had defaced the phone booth this way. What did they think to gain by deeding to the world these meaningless, unbeautiful scrawls?

He twisted about impatiently in the booth. On the hook the plastic receiver was growing sticky in his hand. He opened the glass-panelled door to let in fresh air and saw, spread out on a bench, an out-of-town newspaper. On the left side of the front page was the two-column headline: KLAN VIOLENCE PREDICTED FOR THE FOURTH. Beneath this, in smaller type: *Second Day's Civil Rights Agitation Sees Twelve More Arrests*. He was unable to make out the small type of the news story.

The phone rang. 'Yes?' he said into the receiver.

'Raleigh?' It was unmistakably Harry Dorman's voice.

'Yes.'

'You go over to the other side of the station, understand? The east side, where there's another bunch of phone booths. You go into the right-hand booth and wait till I call you there.'

'Would you repeat that?'

Harry Dorman hung up. Roderick, his face turned to the

back wall of the booth, smiled. He imagined the chagrin that the policeman eavesdropping over the tapped line must be feeling now. There would not be time to tap the line to 782-8840, where Harry would call now.

Roderick left the booth and walked across the expanse of granite floor to the other side of the terminal. Agent Fields caught his eye, and he pantomimed dismay.

It was quite genuine dismay, for he had seen, at the same moment, that the booth Dorman had designated was occupied already—by a Negro so fat that he had not been able to close the door of the booth behind him. Roderick was thereby afforded the added agony of overhearing the man's assinine small talk, a monologue as unsignificant as the initials that had been scrawled in the other phone booth: 'Uh-huh ... Uh-huh ... He is, and Mae-Pearl is too, uh-huh ... Uh-huh. I don't know... I said to her that I'd stay with the kids on Saturday night, but I don't know if they can go now. Did you talk to her afterwards?... Uh-huh, uh-huh ...'

Roderick ground his heels against the granite in a fury of impatience, but the man in the phone booth had no sense of his causing an inconvenience, for the entire row of phone booths stood empty. Ordinary Roderick prided himself on his attitude towards coloured people, which was almost Northern in its liberality, but at times like this he realised that the Negro race was, after all, essentially inferior.

'That buzzing sounds like we're gonna be cut off, Nitty. Lemme see if I got another dime.' He dug into his pockets: no dimes. He held out a quarter to Roderick. 'Hey mister, would you be able to change this quarter for me?'

'No!'

The fat Negro gave Roderick a peculiar look. 'Listen, Nitty, before they cut us off, whyn't I give you my number here? I'll wait inside the booth till you call back, okay? The number here's 782–8840.'

Roderick wanted to tear the phone out of the man's fat fingers. When he'd hung up, he came forward and addressed him very earnestly: 'Please, I'm waiting for a very important call on this line.'

The Negro smiled and shrugged. 'Sorry, mister, I didn't know I was in your place of business. I'll be off in just a minute now.'

The phone rang and both their hands reached for it. The Negro pushed Roderick very firmly back from the booth before

115

he lifted the receiver off the hook. 'Hello. Hello, Nitty? ... Who?' He turned to Roderick. 'Your name Raleigh?' Roderick nodded. He held his breath. The Negro seemed to be debating whether or not to hang up.

With a wry smile he handed the phone to Roderick. 'It's for you.'

'Who was that, Raleigh?' Dorman's voice asked. 'You haven't called the police in on this, have you?'

'For ...' Roderick bit his lip. (He had been about to say: *For Christ's sake, Harry, of course not!*) 'No. Please, what are my instructions?'

'If you came to the station with any fuzz you tell them that you're going to take the local train to Norfolk. And that you should take a seat on the left-hand side of the train and watch for a red convertible with a big Freedom Now sign on it. Understand? Buy your ticket, and *then* you excuse yourself to go to the bathroom. Understand? The men's room is one level down on the west side. Bring your satchel with you. Go into the last pay toilet in the row. Unwind the toilet paper and you'll find your next instructions.' Harry hung up.

Roderick crossed to the ticket window and bought a ticket for Norfolk on the 9.30 local. Agent Fields was now waiting on the bench beneath the Bulova, reading the discarded newspaper whose headline Roderick had been studying. They conversed with each other through the paper. Roderick explained about the red convertible. Then he excused himself to go to the toilet.

As Roderick neared the men's room, his throat tightened and his stomach seemed to sing. He was carrying on such a good masquerade that half the time he found himself taken in by it. He strode across the gleaming, disinfected tiles, his dime already pinched between thumb and forefingers. All the pay toilets were occupied. He waited. It was the fat Negro who had been in the phone booth who came out of the last toilet in the row. He smiled at Roderick peculiarly. Roderick, blushing hurried into the stall and pulled the door shut behind him.

· Roderick and Fields were the last ones to mount the Norfolk-bound local. During the tedious quarter-hour that it took the train to escape the cindery yards of Baltimore, Roderick asked to borrow the paper that Fields had picked off the bench, and he read about the Klan violence expected in Norfolk. There was little more to be learned from the story than what had been said in the headline. Someone with the improbable name of Exalted Cyclops Stroud had made the apocalyptic promise that the Grand Dragon of Virginia would be present at the threatened Fourth of July demonstration outside the African church. Roderick knew a moment of soothing contempt for the poor trash who needed such cant and Boy Scout mysticism to give their hollow lives a sense of importance.

Once out of the city, they began to watch for the red convertible.

'Don't look so worried, Mr. Raleigh,' Fields said. 'I know this is a hell of an ordeal, but it'll be over soon.'

Roderick tried to look a bit more worried at these words, but inwardly he had to chuckle. Because he knew it was already over.

Not until the train had left Maryland, crossing the trestle bridge over the Potomac, did Roderick take the crumpled piece of paper out of his coat pocket and hand it to Fields. 'The man on the phone told me to go to the men's room,' he explained. 'Into the last pay toilet. This note was rolled up in the tissues there.'

Fields read the typewritten note to himself: 'Shove your briefcase under the partition to the next stall, take the briefcase that the man in that stall pushes back. Flush these instructions down the toilet. When you return to the waiting-room, act as if nothing has happened. Get on the train to Norfolk and pretend to watch out for the red convertible. Don't open the new briefcase till you get to Norfolk. Your daughter's life depends on you! If you want to see her alive, obey these instructions!' Agent Fields swore.

'I had to do what was written there,' Roderick said earnestly. 'For Alice's sake. You understand that, don't you? I disobeyed when I thought it would be safe—I didn't flush the note down the toilet, and I didn't wait until Norfolk . . .'

'You waited long enough. Whoever took the money has had a good long time to get out of the railway station. Let me look at that briefcase.' Roderick handed it to him. 'It *looks* the same.'

'They probably bought them at the same time,' Roderick offered weakly.

After a bit of trifling the locks sprang open, and wadded newspapers spilled out.

The train was pulling into a station. The sign said DAHLGREN. 'I'd better get off here, Mr. Raleigh, and phone back to Baltimore. Do you want to give me that case and the note? Thank you. And you can catch a lift back to Baltimore with me, if you like.'

'Thank you, but I think I'd best go all the way to Norfolk. Someone may be watching for me there. I don't want to take any chances. Alice's life may depend on the slightest little thing. I'll call your office as soon as I get there. And will you call my wife and tell her everything seems to be turning out for the best?'

The train began pulling out of Dahlgren, and Agent Fields had to walk alongside the churning iron wheels.

'It *is*, isn't it?' Roderick asked loudly. 'It *is* turning out all right?'

Agent Fields (who was running now) shouted something that could not be heard above the roar and commotion. He was smiling. He waved at Roderick. Roderick waved back, smiling bravely. 'Good-bye,' he shouted. 'Good-bye, suckers! Good-bye!'

Roderick left the train at Ordinary, an infinitesimally small town twenty-five miles outside of Norfolk. There was no one on the platform, no one in the station waiting-room, no one at the ticket window. When the train had pulled away Roderick very carefully peeled off his toupee and put it in a cellophane bag in his coat pocket. The absence of the toupee added ten years to his face; unless one knew him very well one would not have been able to recognise him now.

Outside in the small parking area adjacent to the station the tan Chevrolet that Bittle had rented in Hampton two weeks before was waiting for him. Still no one had seen him. He unlocked the car door and slid in behind the wheel. The engine started faultlessly, and in a moment he was sailing down the asphalt-topped state road, watching for the Dr. Pepper sign that marked the turn-off to Bittle's cabin.

'Wonderful,' he whispered to himself. 'Just wonderful.'

It was past noon, and if there had been any mist this far from Baltimore the heat of the midday sun had quite dissipated it. Roderick stopped the car, took off his jacket, rolled up his sleeves, rolled down the windows. He had forgotten what a joy it could be driving through the countryside on a fine summer day like this.

'Perfect,' he whispered. 'Oh, flawless.'

He chuckled, as he imagined the F.B.I. men examining the washroom attendant, trying to get a description from him of the man who had occupied the stall next to the end stall at 9.10 that morning. And even if the attendant had an eidetic memory, it would make no difference. Because there had been no man in the next stall—at least, there need not have been. Ever since Roderick had seen Fields that morning the briefcase he had had with him had been filled with newspapers. The actual transfer of the cases had been effected in Carrol Park.

Roderick had arrived at the park with the money at 7.15. Beneath a designated bench lay an attaché case identical to the one he was carrying, which contained the ransom money. Roderick had exchanged the cases and walked on. A turning to the right and then a few benches on Roderick had passed a delivery boy with a bag of newspapers. The boy rose from the bench and walked off in the direction from which Roderick had come. He would put the case of money into his delivery bag and bring it to young Bittle, who was waiting some few blocks away in the car that Roderick was driving now. (Bittle's old Buick was useless now, since Miss Godwin had given the police its description.) When Bittle had the money, the newsboy (now ten dollars richer) was instructed to return to the park and walk past the bench where Roderick was feeding the pigeons. Nothing more than that. And so he had, and so, all the while that he had performed his pantomime at the railway station, Roderick had known that the essential task had been accomplished. By now, the money would be in Bittle's cabin, spread out probably in four piles—the largest pile being Roderick's, naturally. And the three others would be for Bittle, for Bessy, and for Harry Dorman.

That son of a bitch. That greedy bastard.

Roderick felt a sudden sweat prickle his brow. Would he do it—the thing that he had to do? Wasn't there room yet to turn back—not from Bittle's cabin, of course, but from this thing that had to be done? *May not this cup pass away from me, except I drink it?* he wondered.

If only he had been able to *talk* to somebody... (If only there had been somebody to talk to!)... but he had not dared, once the plan had been set in motion, to telephone or meet with any of the others. Now, briefly, while he could be sure he was not under surveillance, he might.

He pulled the car up to the pump of a lonely gas station and set the attendant to filling the tank and checking the oil and air pressure, while he went inside the station and used the pay-phone.

'Hello?'

'Bessy,' he blurted out, 'I've got to talk to you. It's important . . .'

She flared up. 'You goddam stupid sonofabitch, what are you calling up here for?'

The receiver was trembling in his hand. He had to sit down on the grease-stained chair behind the cash register. He knew now that Bessy would not be able to help, nor could anyone else take the cup away. How could she answer a question that he would not ask? He tried to approach the matter indirectly. Bessy refused to listen. 'Are you drunk?' she asked scornfully. He didn't listen to the rest of her scolding chatter.

*If I do do it now (and I must, I must), and if she remembers this call, then she will know it was me.*

Therefore he would have to convince her that he had made the call for another reason than he had (which reason was, indeed, anything but clear to himself).

The question with which he hoped to cover his tracks came unbidden to his lips, from what buried association of ideas he would never know: 'Do you know, Bessy, whether Donald Bogan is still alive?'

'Beer, Owen?' Farron Stroud asked, when Owen Gann had emerged from the cooler into which he had just trundled two steel barrels of Spengler's. Farron had promised (an election promise, perhaps?) to stand treat to all the Klansmen returning from their first day of non-violence. Not to overdo it he was laying in extra quantities of the cheapest beer he could get.

'Make it a Spengler's. We ain't supposed to go round drinking the competition's stuff. Leastways, not with our uniform on.'

'Aw hell, Owen, one's just the same as the other.' Farron drew a beer at the tap and slid the glass down the bar to Owen, spilling foam. 'Some of 'em advertise more, that's the only difference. You know, I even heard they ship all of it in the same tank cars, then just fill up the barrels and bottles with whatever they got handy.'

Owen grinned. 'I heard some people say the same thing about cars. They say that, dollar for dollar, Fords and Chevies are just the same.'

Farron thrust his narrow, hawkbeak face close to Owen's. 'And what do *you* say?'

'I ain't never had a new one so's I could find out, Farron. I just got to take other people's word for it.'

'Well, I've had plenty of new cars. I get me a new Ford every other year, and you know why?' His eyes darted to the right and the left, a gesture more of theatrical than of practical value, for the only other customer in Stroud's Bar and Grill was a plumber's apprentice who worked across the street whenever there was work across the street to be had. He sat upon his bar stool, swaying slightly and regarding his face amicably in the mirror, while at his elbow a transistor radio was stomping out the week's number-ten hit.

'I'll *tell* you why. Because General Motors is all owned by kikes! It's a fact—they're all a bunch of damn Jews! Ford is the only hundred-per-cent American car.'

'That's a funny thing, Farron,' Owen said, 'because I always heard just the opposite. I always heard it was Ford that was all Jews and G.M. that was white folk.'

'Naw!'

'S'what I heard.'

'Say, Owen, if you don't mind my asking, what's that funny smell you got all over you? Smells like perfume.'

'That, oh yeah. That must of been when I made a delivery to this-here cathouse down along the tidewater. Somebody'd broken a bottle of perfume there, and the place was reeking with it. Must have got some on me.'

*Have a safe and sane Fourth!* the radio bade all of them.

'Safe insane Fourth!' the apprentice plumber echoed, toasting the radio. He gestured to Farron for another whiskey.

When Farron returned to Owen he said in a grave, conspiratorial tone: 'You know what, Owen? I just thought of something—what if we was *both* right! What if both Ford and General Motors was Jew-dominated?'

Owen grinned his L'il Abner grin. 'Don't know, Farron. Guess we'd all have to go out and get ourselves Volkswagens.'

'I don't think that's so funny,' Farron said stiffly. 'VW is a rotten foreign car that comes into this country just to take bread from honest American mouths. There oughta be a tariff against things like that. I say that anybody that drives a foreign-made product isn't any better than a kike himself.'

*... and drive carefully. Alcohol and gasoline don't mix.* The plumber's apprentice nodded sombrely. 'True, very true.'

'I hear our Kladd, O'l Boggs, has got a car he wants to sell,' said Owen, sliding gracefully into the subject that (aside from the delivery) had brought him to Stroud's Bar and Grill.

'Yeah, he got himself a real pig. You pay nothing and you get nothing—that's what I say. I hear tell he bought it from some nigger. Them niggers will drive the guts out of a car.'

'Still, I'd like to have a look at it,' said Owen carefully. 'I know a little about cars. If it's only a valve job, I can take it down myself.'

'You wouldn't want an oil-burning pig like that. Believe me, Owen, that car is with its last owner right now.'

'Can't hurt to look at it though. Thought I'd run over to Pete's place this afternoon if it ain't too far. Where does he live?'

Farron looked miffed that his advice should be valued so slightly. 'Well, if you really want to waste your time... He lives in this tumbledown cabin, used to be part of a motel, but nobody ever stopped there. Go across to Hampton, then take Route 17 out past this town, name of Ordinary. Motel's called by the same name. You can't miss it, there's still a big sign.'

122

'Thanks. I think I'll go there now. Don't you go calling up Pete and telling him I'm interested, hear?'

'Can't. He ain't got a phone. Hey, before you go there you should take a bath. You smell like some goddamn fairy with that perfume all over you.'

But Owen Gann was already out the door. The plumber's apprentice waved at the departed figure benignly and bade him, loudly, a safe insane Fourth.

Within fifty feet of Bittle's cabin, the wheels of the rented car slewed and settled into the red-brown mud. 'Everything is going *wrong*!' Roderick's tone was shrill, especially for a man speaking only to himself.

No—if he could keep himself calm, calm and courageous, but above all *calm*, then everything would be all right. Truly great men meet setbacks with a glad heart, for these are the best yardsticks by which their greatness may be measured.

He raced the engine, but the back wheels only dug in deeper. 'He!' he called out the window. 'Can't you bastards come out and give me a push? I'm stuck in your damn slough.'

Bittle, looking unhappy in a business suit, came out on to the wooden platform of the porch. '*Leave* it. I'm not going out in that muck with this suit on. Besides, Harry's going crazy, waiting to divide up the cash.'

'I'll bet he is.'

The cabin was far cleaner than Roderick, judging by its exterior, had expected. The plasterboard walls, though violently warped, were recently whitewashed, and the boards of the floor had been scrubbed to ashy whiteness. The room achieved a sort of spaciousness by admitting only the barest bones of furnishing: a pallet covered with an army blanket, a home-made table and three wooden chairs, a metal wall locker, and, at the foot of the pallet, a black trunk with *M/Sgt J. Bittle* stencilled on it in white.

'You were in the Army, Jim?' Roderick asked, in a fatherly way.

'No, sir, that was my Daddy's footlocker. I haven't been in ... yet.'

'You shouldn't have any trouble with it, by the looks of this room. It could pass inspection this minute.'

The attaché case lay atop the table, unopened, and lying on the attaché case was Harry Dorman's hand. Harry looked briefly towards Roderick, flicker of green eyes, and away.

*Clever of him,* Roderick thought, *not to mention the letter he sent me with young Bittle present. Clever, but his eyes give him away.*

'Shall we?' Harry asked, holding up a small chrome-plated key. Roderick nodded. Harry unlocked the case and solemnly, slowly opened it. Bittle, who had lived through this same moment in numberless movies, knew his part: he whistled.

'There's so much,' said Harry.

'There's enough,' Roderick replied coldly. He kept his hands in his trouser pockets. It would have looked odd to be wearing gloves on a hot July afternoon.

Bittle whistled.

Harry removed the packages from the case. There were a hundred banded bundles each containing a hundred hundred-dollar bills.

'I suppose,' Roderick said off-handedly, 'that you'd like half of that.'

Harry opened and shut his mouth in the manner of a fish considering bait. 'Half?' he managed at last to say. 'You think I ought to have half?'

'It's only fair, isn't it, Harry, considering how hard you've worked for this? You've certainly done *half* the work, haven't you? What can I do to *prevent* your taking half, if you want it? Go to the police?' Roderick laughed mirthlessly and, mirthlessly, Harry joined in. All the while Roderick had been talking. Harry had been putting the bundles in stacks of five, each worth fifty thousand dollars. Now there were twenty such stacks.

Roderick carefully pushed one of these stacks to the side of the table. 'That's Jim's.' Another stack to the other side of the table. 'And that's for Bessy. Now the rest must be for us.'

Dorman's upper lip tic-ed. 'You're sure in a generous mood, Roderick, old pal.'

'I can afford to be! But I'll leave it up to you, Harry—what do you *want*? There it is on the table. Take what you think is your fair share.'

With no uncertainty Harry scooped up three bundles, the agreed-upon $150,000. His green eyes lifted then to regard Roderick curiously. Tentatively, his eyes not moving from Roderick's, he stretched a hand forward to take another bundle, two more. He stuffed the money into his coat pockets. Soon there was no more room in his pockets.

'Are you sure you don't want more, Harry? Go ahead, take

a few more.'

Harry's eyes narrowed. 'Say, what kind of game is this? Are you making fun of me, or what?'

'It's not like that at all, Harry. I'm just trying to be fair. Fair's fair, isn't it? I know what a lot you've gone through for this, Harry. How many years were you in jail? Go ahead— take a few more. If you need something to carry it in, why don't you use the case?'

Harry surrendered to an unconsidering greed. He emptied out his pockets into the attaché case, then took more bundles from the stacks on the table. When he'd finished, he had taken fully two-thirds of the ransom money. 'There,' he said weakly, 'the rest of it is yours. No matter what you say.' He took up the case and cradled it in his two arms like an infant.

Roderick let the silence grow hollower and hollower until Harry would look up at him. Bittle, meanwhile, had retired to the corner of the room to sit on the pallet.

'Harry, Harry, Harry!' Roderick said, giving each repetition a slow, sad shake of his head. 'I'm really surprised at you. I would have thought you'd had more sense than that. Not to mention *honour*. Haven't you ever heard of honour among thieves? You have to ruin a wonderful crime like this because you just can't get enough.'

'I—but you said . . .'

'You know what you are, Harry? You're an avaricious son of a bitch, and like many another avaricious son of a bitch, Harry, your greed has been your undoing.' Roderick took the pistol out of his pocket and aimed it at a point between Harry Dorman's wide-open, ivy-green eyes.

'You should be ashamed of yourself, Harry,' Roderick said, and pulled the trigger. Harry, in his last conscious moment, reached for his own gun, and he was quick enough so that before he fell to the floor he had it in his hand.

'Sorry I had to mess up your place,' Roderick said to Bittle, who had risen from the pallet, though remaining in the farthest corner of the cabin.

'*You* don't want more than your fair share of the money, I hope?' He asked, stooping to take the gun, a ·45, from Dorman's hand.

'No . . . I . . . no. I don't want *any* money.'

'None? Nothing at all? Oh, don't be silly!' Roderick stooped again to pick up the briefcase and set it on the table. 'How old are you?' he asked.

'Me? I'm nineteen.'

'Nineteen. Then you'll be needing some money for college, or dates or something, won't you. You can't get anywhere these days without a college diploma.'

Recognising the mocking tone that had preceded Harry's murder, Bittle began to weep. 'No, please—take the money and just leave me be. I won't ever talk, I swear to God. You don't have to kill me.'

'It's a pity. I know.' Roderick was quite astonished at the kick that the ·45 had. His first shot ploughed into one of the whitewashed rafters overhead.

The youth rushed at him, but the second shot did not go wild. 'God!' Bittle screamed, and his body convulsed about the belly wound. He assumed a curled-up attitude on the floor that put Roderick distinctly in mind of a photograph in that morning's newspaper of a civil-rights demonstrator.

Was he quite dead? To fire another bullet to make sure would not advance the impression he'd hoped to create of the two men having fallen out over their spoils and killed each other. On the other hand, it was better to be on the safe side, so he fired a third bullet, into Bittle's head. He replaced the ·45 in Dorman's hand, and his own gun in Bittle's.

He congratulated himself on his self-control, but now that the deed had been done he could feel the panic swelling up in him, like a wolf standing outside the cabin door and demanding to be let in.

He reopened the case and packed a full amount of the money back inside it. He checked his clothing to make certain he had not splattered himself with blood; he had not. He took a tranquilliser, and while he waited for it to take effect he recited the poem that was reputed to be Franklin Delano Roosevelt's favourite, *Invictus* by William Ernest Henley.

'I'm Averill Hotchkiss of KHGG-TV's *Hotline News*. And what's your name, sweety-pie?'

'Mmankf,' said the little black girl.

'Look into the camera now. There, that's more like it. And speak into the mike. Now, what was that name again?'

'MMNKF!'

'Alice!'(Hotchkiss made an adjustment in the audio level of the microphone.) 'Well, Alice, what do you think of all this trouble?'

'I don't know what to think. I *don't* think that man should be kicking the poor old . . .'

'A terrible thing, yes. What about *school*, Alice? Do you want to go to the same school as little white girls?'

After a brief pause, the girl said: 'I don't see why not. *Shouldn't* I want to?'

'Wellthankyouverymuchyounglady,' Averill Hotchkiss said, hurrying on to his next hotline interview. 'Now *here's* a man who looks as though he might have something to say . . .'

'You bet I have,' said the bedsheeted but unmasked Klansman. 'First, let me say this to every nigger in this town—stay in your houses. Ya hear? Because tomorrow . . .'

'Now that's what I mean,' said Peter Boggs, turning down the sound on the television set. 'It just ain't *right*! I swear, sometimes a person's ashamed to be white, some of the things the Klan does. It wasn't like this where I come from. We always treated the niggers *nice*, and they was nice right back. Course, there weren't so damned many of them in Booneburg. I ain't no nigger-lover, the Lord God knows, and I say there's a place for the Klan, but did you see him there, just *kicking* that old woman. That just ain't a Christian thing to do.'

'Why don't you quit, if that's the way you feel, Pete?' Owen asked.

'I reckon I ought to, but the truth is I'm scared to. And maybe I always keep hoping that things'll get the way they used to be, back when I was your age. I can still remember the day I joined up. I'd just seen Mae Marsh in *Birth of a Nation*, a movie about the Civil War and afterwards. She was about as pretty and sweet a girl as ever walked this earth, more like an angel than anything else, and there was this nigger—he was wearing a Yankee uniform—that chased her up this mountain, and there she was, standing right on the edge of the cliff, with that black beast slavering after her. Of course, there was only one thing she could do—she jumped. Now, *that's* the sort of thing the Klan *should* be looking after.'

Owen had arrived at the Ordinary Motel fifteen minutes before, and he still hadn't been able to get around to inquiring after the Buick sitting outside in the drive. He had first made the association between Peter Bogg's newly-purchased (and un-licenced) car and the description of the kidnappers' car when he had been at Bessy's, and he had somewhat abbreviated his investigations there in order to follow out his hunch. He was obliged, finally, just to blur it out: 'Pete, what are you asking for that old copper-coloured Buick of yours?'

'I paid seventy-five for it, and to tell you the truth, Owen, it ain't worth any more. It's been drove to death.'

'Where'd you get it? Somebody around here?'

'Ol' Jim Bittle, a nigger that lives up the turnoff by the Dr. Pepper sign. But I don't think Jim had it very long before he sold it to me. He didn't even know what kind of tyres he had on it. Nylon cord tyres, almost brand new. For seventy-five dollars I figure it'd be worth it just for the tyres almost. Anyhow, that's what I said to Jim, and he didn't say *boo* back. Seemed glad to be rid of it. I wouldn't be surprised to find out it was stole.'

'Yeah? I noticed the licence plates was gone. I'd hate to buy it off you and find out it was stolen, so I think I'd better wait a while. See you at the meeting tomorrow.'

'Sure enough.' Puzzled, Pete watched the young man drive away. He couldn't figure Owen Gann, generally or in particular. Generally he just didn't seem like the right type for the Klan, and in particular it didn't make sense to drive twenty-five miles into the country to look at a broken-down heap that he could have seen the next time Pete came into town. Now Gann was driving off in the wrong direction.

'Not that way!' Pete shouted. 'There ain't nothing that way but . . .' The beer truck turned off on to the side road, scraping its sides against the scrub pines. 'But Ol' Jim Bittle's place,' he finished, rubbing the stubble on his jaw.

Meticulously Roderick wiped the car free of prints: steering wheel, door handles, shift, keys. It would have been better, he realised with hind-sight, to have put on the gloves at the Ordinary railway station instead of the moment before entering the cabin.

He broke up evergreen branches and mashed into his footprints in the mud. Suitcase tucked under his arm, he headed back towards the main road, walking on the grassy strip between the clay ruts. There had been a cabin of sorts a short distance down the road, with a car parked in front. The owner could probably be persuaded to give it up. As soon as he got to Norfolk, Roderick could rent a car.

Ahead along the rutty road there was the sound of a motor accompanied by a clashing and banging, like a marching band of muffled cymbals. Roderick ducked into the stand of evergreens siding the road. A truck hove into view; painted on the red surface in silvery letters was the trademark: SPENGLER'S

BEER. Had that dumb Jim Bittle been planning a beer-blast to celebrate the kidnapping, or what? Incredible ill luck!

Once the truck had passed it took all his will power to leave his covert and return to the track. There was not yet, he assured himself, any need for panic. A man of reason has, has he not, infinite resources? He is never at a loss for the right response. Step by inexorable step, he proceeds towards the conclusion that he has willed. But the wolf, the hairy wolf, was pounding on that door, threatening to blow the house down.

What had Bessy said over the phone? 'The F.B.I. was just here, and they was asking about *you*!' And there had been that fat Negro who had twice anticipated Roderick's movements at the terminal, that surely exceeded the limits of simple happenstance. And now *this*!

Sweat pouring down from the bald crown of his head, Roderick began to run. Just when he reached the main road and stood in view of the Ordinary Motel, he had to duck back into the greenery along the road as the beer truck rocketed past once more, hell-bent for Ordinary.

Nothing could surprise Peter Boggs any more. First Owen going off like a madman down the road to Bittle's cabin, like to breaking an axle, and then his coming back like two madmen with the devil after him. Now this stranger, in his city clothes and out of breath, coming up from nowhere with his big black satchel.

'I'm, in a manner of speaking, lost,' the stranger explained with a sweet-sick smile. Pete nodded. 'And my car got stuck in the mud.'

'You want a push?'

'No! No, actually I wondered if I might buy this car from you. If it runs.'

'It runs—barely. But it should get you back to where you come from, if that's all you need. You come from around here?'

'How much would you say it's worth?'

Pete shrugged.

'Two hundred dollars?'

'I guess so,' said Pete, permitting himself a smile.

The stranger extended two bills of a denomination Pete had never seen before and took the ignition key in exchange. 'Just a second. I'll go in the house and root up the bill of sale.' Once inside, he held the bills up to the light in trembling, tobacco-stained fingers. How was he going to know if this money was the real McCoy? Outside the stranger had started up the engine. Pete wished he'd had a chance to take off the nylon cord tyres first. But two hundred dollars! He hoped Owen wouldn't be too mad when he found out the car was sold. What a piece of luck!

Roderick drove along Route 17 till he reached the outskirts of Hampton. Then he found a pay-phone in a bar and dialled Bessy's number. Bessy answered after just two rings. 'It's all over, Bessy. I'll bring you your money to the place we agreed to meet and you can hand back my darling daughter.'

'Guess again,' Bessy said mournfully.

'Don't tell me something *else* has gone wrong!'

'It's Alice. She's escaped.'

It was as clear as clear could be, it was certain past all doubt, that Green Pastures Funeral Home was nowhere to be but then was her own home on Gwynns River Falls Drive anywhere to go? Besides, there was the matter of her promise to Bessy.

'And what sort of promise is *that*?' Dinah scoffed. 'A promise made to a desperate criminal!'

'Nevertheless,' Alice returned smugly, 'a promise is a promise.' (It may be that the notion of attempting an escape was also a little scary, but somehow this aspect of the subject was never openly discussed.)

'A prisoner of *war* is honour-bound to try and escape.'

'Where should I escape *to*? Answer me that! Home? Maybe Daddy would just bring me right back here. Or to the police? *They*'ll just treat me like those people on the bus treated me, like the man with the beer truck treated me, because they only see my black skin.'

'What about Uncle Jason?' Dinah asked reasonably.

There was no denying that her uncle had always been nice to her, so Alice veered off on a new tangent: 'It's all very well to say "Go to Uncle Jason"—I suppose it seems a very simple matter for *you*—but have you thought where Uncle Jason *is*? He's in Baltimore, and *you* don't even know where you are.'

'We're in Norfolk,' Dinah said, though not quite confidently, since her source of information had been Fay.

'And *how* do you intend to get to Baltimore from a city that may or may not be Norfolk? You can't very well ride a bus without money for a ticket.'

'Oh, will you *can* it!' said Clara, coming into the kitchen, where this dialogue had been going on. 'I may have to be a goddamned baby-sitter, but I sure as hell don't have to put up with your crazy jabber.'

'I'm *very* sorry, I'm sure,' Alice said with an etiquette as lofty as the ineffable Miss Boyd's. Then, seeing that she'd offended Clara, she quickly went on: 'I can recite *Jabberwocky*. Would you like to hear it?'

'Yeah,' said Clara, though by the way she said it you would have thought she didn't really mean it. Alice was uncertain therefore whether to recite or not. She began, in a tiny voice:

> *'Twas brillig and the slithy toves*
> *Did gyre and gimble in the wabe:*
> *All mimsy . . .'*

'I'll mimsy you, Miss Uppity!' Clara growled in her manliest manner. She was wearing her usual off-duty ensemble of denim trousers and jacket, which contrasted strangely with the cloying smell of the spilt cologne. Half an hour's bathing had not been able to efface the smell.

'You wouldn't talk like that if Bessy were here.'

Shortly after the phone call from Roderick, Bessy had had an attack of trembling for which, she claimed, the only cure was a good stiff one and then a bit of a nap. Alice couldn't understand how anyone could go back to bed within three hours of getting up and had protested violently when Bessy had wanted to take her upstairs with her. She'd promised then to be very, very good and mind Clara in every respect.

'I'll Bessy you!' Clara said, not at all reasonably. 'Come here, smarty-pants!' Alice moved towards her reluctantly. 'C'mon, c'mon! Godammit.' A scrawny hand, all bumpy with purple veins, seized the soft flesh of Alice's upper arm.

'Ow! don't do that! *Ow!*' Then her head jerked back till the bones of her neck grated and she was looking at the cracks in the ceiling. Clara had *hit* her! Hit her across the face with her other hand. It was so incredible (grown-ups don't hit children, do they?) that Alice didn't make a sound. She was simply thunderstruck.

'You'll learn to put on your uppity manners around me, little black girl! You think just because you're white you gotta be treated like some goddam princess? Well, you ain't going to be, not here. No, you're black as I am now, and you're gonna get treated black.' Clara was pulling her out through the swinging doors into the living-room, where Fay was nursing her 'baby' at her breast. She looked up from this tender task reprovingly.

'Fay, pull down the shades. I'm going to teach this here piccaninny a lesson or two.' Fay's full, pink-swathed figure bounced about the room, and presently they were in semi-darkness. Alice was made to sit on the sofa between the two women. The scent of their cologne was so strong that Alice felt like vomiting.

'Why?' she asked, forcing herself to sound calm, and imitating (though she did not know it) Miss Godwin. 'Why do you want to pick on me? I never did anything to you, did I? Did I?'

Clara laughed roughly. 'To me? No. No, you never did a thing to me, baby. But let me tell you some facts of life. I been living in this world for more years than I care to remember, and it's a white man's world, and I been living by the white man's rules, and did I ask *them* why? But now you are in *my* world, babydoll, and I make the rules here. Fay, take her arms.'

Fay, though in other ways still a child, had a grown-up's strength; it did no good to struggle against her.

'I hate you,' Clara whispered, but though her previous tone had communicated just this sentiment, she pronounced these three words with something like affection. With one hand she began unbuttoning Alice's dress at the back; with the other she held a doubled-up extension cord.

'I've never given you any reason to hate me,' Alice pointed out, still striving after calmness.

'I hate you because you're white. That's reason enough, and more.'

'But she ain't white, Clara,' Fay protested. 'She's almost as black as you.'

'Shut up, stupid. She only *looks* black. Inside, she's all white.'

Alice had braced herself against the expected blow, but the extension cord came down not on her back but across her bare thighs, left exposed by the too-young dress. She yelped with pain.

'Now, don't you make any noise, or you'll only get it worse.' But of course her only hope lay in waking Bessy, so she screamed again, louder. Clara's thin hand clamped down across Alice's face, not just silencing her but—since it pinched her nostrils shut—smothering her as well. Alice tried to struggle free, but Clara seemed to be on top of her, she couldn't move, she felt herself grow faint ... The doorbell rang. 'Damn!' said Clara.

She began buttoning up Alice's dress. 'Fay, you go answer that.'

'I hope it's not a john,' Fay whined. 'Because I haven't finished feeding my little Alice yet.'

It was indeed a john, the same hawk-faced man who had been here just last night.

'Well, hello again,' said Clara. 'We can't hardly keep you away these days, can we?'

'Hello, um, Clara.' Farron was scarcely audible. He lifted his

133

·eyes from the floor, before they had lifted quite to Clara's face he eyes encountered Alice. A thin tip of tongue licked across his thin lips. 'Is, um, is she ...?'

Clara's hand came down to play in Alice's kinky hair. 'You asking after my little cousin Dinah here? Naw, Farron, forget about it. You could never get that much money.'

Farron had come to stand over Clara and Alice. Alice snuggled back into the sofa, obscurely frightened. 'What's that smell?' Farron asked.

'It's that goddamned Fay,' said Clara. 'She broke my cologne bottle.' They started talking about the cologne bottle and forgot about Alice. They were halfway up the stairs when Clara called back: 'Fay, you look after little Dinah good and proper now, understand? She isn't supposed to go outdoors. Otherwise ...' There was a slap of leather against wood, and Alice saw Farron's legs tremble.

When they were alone, Alice asked, 'Does Clara ever hit *you*, Fay?'

'Oh, lots of times.'

'Why don't you tell Bessy about it?'

'Can't. If I do that, Clara says she'll kill me *dead*.' Fay stuck her thumb in her mouth and made a popping sound, either by way of demonstration or simply to punctuate her remark.

'How?'

'With a poison stick. She has a poison stick that she hides in her closet, and if I don't do just what she says she'll touch me with it, and anywhere she touches me, even my littlest toe, then I'll *die*!'

Fay, Alice decided, was surely the stupidest, most gullible grown-up that Alice had ever met, and she had met some very stupid grown-ups.

'I know a fun game,' said Alice.

Fay began to chew on a strand of loose blonde hair with anticipation. 'What is it? Do I know how to play?'

'Hide-and-go-seek. I hide somewhere, and you have to find me. You want to play that?'

Fay bit into the pink fudge that was her lower lip. 'I'd *like* to, but I don't think I'd better. Clara wouldn't like it, if you ran away.' There were, it seemed, limits to Fay's credulity.

'Then I know another fun game. It's called Don't-Peek. We both close our eyes, and the first person who peeks is the loser.'

After a few games of Don't-Peek, Alice realised that this idea had been no better than the first. By the clock on the wall she measured the time it took Fay to peek, and it was always less than a minute. Not nearly time to do what she had in mind. The episode with Clara had resolved all her hesitancies about escape.

'I know an even better game,' she said determinedly. 'But we'll need some bottles and plates.' She dragged Fay and her baby into the kitchen. There were two cartons of empty Coke bottles under the sink, and Fay took down a stack of saucers from the cupboard. Alice showed her how to stack them: a bottle, a plate, a bottle . . .

Fay squealed with delighted expectation: 'If you put another one on top of those now, it's going to fall down for sure.'

'Now, this game is called Tower-of-Babel, and here's how we play it. I get the kitchen and you get the living-room. Whoever makes his stack first'—she handed Fay a carton of bottles and six saucers; Fay left her doll lying on the counter—'has to run and catch the other one. For instance, if I get my stack done then I run in and tag you and say, "You're it!" and then *I've* won. But if you get all your bottles and saucers piled first, then you run and tag me, and then *you're* the winner.'

'What does the winner get?'

'The winner gets to be Queen of Babylon. Okay?' She led Fay back out into the living-room, to a spot that afforded no view into the kitchen, and started her building her Tower. 'Now, in case any of your saucers should break, here's an extra supply.'

Back in the kitchen, she quietly pulled the linoleum-topped table in place underneath the high half-window. Standing on the table she was tall enough to pry open the window halfways but still too short to climb out through it. From the living-room there was a sound of crashing and shattering, followed by a fit of giggling. Alice pulled out three drawers from the kitchen counter (the first held cooking utensils, the second pot-holders and dish-towels, the third two bottles of Bessy's cheap gin) and stacked them criss-cross on top of the table.

'Are you building your tower?' Fay called into the kitchen.

'Oh yes,' Alice said. 'And I'm almost finished.' In testimony she kicked the carton of coke bottles and threw a saucer on the floor. 'Ohhh, it fell down!'

She took a medium-sized paper bag from the niche beside the icebox and put in a quart carton of milk and a loaf of bread. Unfortunately, there was no lunch meat left. This way she would have something to eat during the day, and it would look, to a casual observer, as though she were just carrying home groceries. She found her copy of *Just-So Stories* underneath *School for Sinners* and put that in her grocery bag. Then, just out of mischief, she stuffed in Fay's baby.

She peeked into the living-room where Fay sat discouraged, picking her nose. 'I'm almost done,' she screamed, frightening Fay into a second flurry of building.

Grocery bag in hand, she mounted to the table top, then climbed up the makeshift, unsteady steps. Raised as far as it would go, the window was just wide enough to crawl through. With a prayer that the carton would not split, she threw the bag down into the weeds. She climbed through the window head first, then realised she would have to go back and try it the other way. She didn't fancy dropping six feet—more than six feet—on to her head! There was a crashing sound behind her—Fay's second tower crashing down. Her toe reached back for a foothold on the topmost drawer, she felt the drawer teeter and slip away. Closing her eyes, she pushed herself through the window and off the sill. She landed with a clatter of kitchen utensils. She was free. She picked up the grocery bag and started to run.

The milk was so warm and ooky it was like yogurt, and the spout hadn't opened out the way it should have, so that she'd spilled milk all down the front of her dress. And her feet! Her feet were *raw* in these wretched, toe-crimping saddle shoes. But she couldn't very well go barefoot over the blistering, July-afternoon pavements. When she'd sat down on the kerbstone to have her lunch, she'd taken off the shoes and put them in the grocery bag, but as soon as she started walking again ...

She was tired, terribly tired, so tired she wouldn't think in a straight line. She'd walked and walked for *hours*, and she simply couldn't find a way out of the city. Norfolk was a trap for pedestrians: it was bounded on every side by water. The only road going north went through the big bridge-and-tunnel across the Bay, but it was closed to foot traffic. If only she could get a map of the city, but when she'd gone into a filling station to ask for one, the attendant had treated her with unimaginable rudeness. Really, it was *most* perplexing and impossible.

Discouraging too, perhaps? No, she wouldn't let herself

become discouraged, and this brave resolve she strengthened by reciting to herself a verse from a poem that her father used once to read to her:

> *In the fell clutch of circumstance,*
> *I have not winced nor cried aloud:*
> *Under the bludgeonings of chance*
> *My head is bloody, but unbowed.*

But the poem made her think of her father... Her *own* father... A tear plopped into the warm milk.

Almost a block away, where the other people had been sitting down along the street, a car stopped and four men in red and white silk gowns, like Episcopal choir members at Christmas, got out. Similarly-gowned men were appearing from other directions, and there were policemen, in two different kinds of uniforms. Alice reasoned, from these many evidences, that a parade was about to begin, or perhaps it had just ended. Ordinarily she would have enjoyed seeing a parade.

'And just what do you think you're doing?'

For the first time Alice noticed the boots in front of her. Her gaze travelled up the gabardine-clad legs, past the gunbelt, the khaki shirt (with silver numbers on the collars), to the large, red, and extremely foreshortened face. The face wobbled atop its tower of flesh, as the policeman (whose face it was) rocked back and forth on the balls of his feet.

'I'm having my lunch,' Alice said. 'Sir,' she added, for he looked angry enough to be called 'sir'.

'Come on,' he sighed. 'Move along.'

'Couldn't I finish my lunch first? I'm not in anybody's *way* here, am I?'

He grabbed her up so suddenly that the bottle of milk was knocked over. 'Oh *dear*!' The accumulated sorrows of the day seemed to reach the threshold of the intolerable, and Alice would have broken out into a flood of tears if she hadn't reminded herself that she would be crying literally over spilt milk. This was such a droll idea that instead of tears she burst into giggles.

'Where you come from? You don't talk like any piccaninny from around here.'

'Baltimore,' she replied, watching the last of the spilt milk trickling down a gutter grating.

The policeman said, 'Uh-huh.' He took her hand and led her into the crowd of people that had gathered about the other people who had sat down (and who were now singing hymns).

There was evidently not to be a parade, after all; in fact, there was something like a traffic jam going on. Car horns honked festively.

'Now I want you to point out your mammy and pappy to me, hear?'

To please the policeman, she looked over all the hymn singers carefully, though it seemed highly improbable that she would find either of her parents *here*. There were Negroes of all ages, and a number of white teenagers, and a very old white woman who was the loudest of them all, though she sang off-key. 'I don't see my mother or father anywhere,' she said, truthfully.'

'Uh-huh.' He didn't seem to believe her.

At the periphery of the crowd the general uproar came to a sudden, sharp focus. The people at the edge of the crowd were pushed forward, right into the laps of the people sitting down. In the ensuing mêlée, one of the gowned men began to kick the old woman who sang off-key. Alice could scarcely believe her eyes. The old woman hadn't done a *thing* to provoke him; besides, grown-up men just don't kick old ladies, no matter what old ladies may do! Others of the red-robed men cheered him on: 'That's it, Lem!' or 'Kick her goddam ass off!' And that kind of language. Nobody tried to help the poor old woman. Her friends just sat there singing sad hymns. Perhaps the two groups belonged to different religions.

'Uh-huh,' the policeman said again, faintly. He let go of Alice's hand and pushed his way through the crowd to the man in red, who stopped kicking to talk with him. His compatriots made a disappointed noise, but the group sitting down kept on singing so that Alice couldn't hear what the policeman said to him. Even the old woman was singing again, though not so loudly. An approaching police siren or fire klaxon tried to drown out the hymn.

A man in a grey suit, with slicked-back hair that made Alice think of a seal, appeared beside her and thrust a microphone at her. 'I'm Averill Hotchkiss of KHGG–TV's *Hotline News*. And what's your name, sweety-pie?'

'Alice,' she said after a moment's indecision. 'Alice Raleigh.'

'Look into the camera now.' Talking all the while, he turned her about so that she was staring into what appeared to be the window of a mobile and highly-elaborate automatic washing-machine. 'Now, what's that name again?'

'ALICE!'

'Alice! Well, Alice, what do you think of all this trouble?'

'I don't know what to think. I *don't* think that man should be kicking the poor old...'

'A terrible thing, yes. What about *school*, Alice? Do you want to go to the same school as little white girls?'

Alice looked perplexed. Away from a mirror, it was hard for her to bear in mind that she was no longer a little white girl herself. 'I don't see why not. *Shouldn't* I want to?'

Averill Hotchkiss disappeared into the crowd, trailing behind frail, inaudible burblings and the cord of the microphone. Awkwardly, the mobile washing-machine lumbered after him. It wasn't till that moment that Alice realised she'd just appeared on television.

There was the problem now of food, a problem she had never been confronted with before. Never, at least, with any urgency. It was after six o'clock and she hadn't had anything to eat since breakfast. It was all very well to be free, but did it have to mean starving to death? At least at Bessy's she'd always had enough to eat.

It was a pity about her loaf of bread. She'd taken it out of the grocery bag, and when the policeman had taken her into the crowd, she'd had to leave both behind. When she'd gone back for them, the grocery bag with the book and the doll (and her ragtag shoe) were still there, but not the loaf of bread. She would have traded everything else to get that bread back now. It was ridiculous: here she was, an *heiress* for pity's sake, and she didn't have the price of a Salted Nut Roll!

It was then she chanced to look up (her eyes seldom left the endless plain of the pavement now; she was numb with weariness) and to see the gilt letters in the dusty window. Because of the narrowness of the storefront the letters were bowed upward in an arch:

STAN'S USED BOOKS AND MAGAZINES

Covers of used magazines were Scotch-taped to the glass: sunbleached *Playboy*'s, *Rogue*'s and *Knight*'s, their nudes and demi-nudes changed to various sickly shades of blue and yellow. A few dead flies had somehow managed to wedge themselves down between the magazines and the window.

'Why, that's it!' Dinah said aloud. (For Alice had better manners than to talk to herself on the street.) 'You can sell your book!'

'Sell my book?' Alice asked incredulously. 'Sell the book

139

that Uncle Jason gave to me? A first edition of *Kipling*?'

'All the more reason, my dear. If it sells for a lot of money, you may have enough left over after you eat to buy a bus ticket. At least to the other side of the Bay. In any case, what else *can* you do?'

Dinah, in her usual utilitarian way, was absolutely right, so she pushed open the heavy door, triggering a bell in the farthest reaches of the shop, dark as another Africa. Alice waited demurely before the main counter of the bookstore and passing the time (as the owner seemed to be in no hurry) by looking over the titles: *The Kama Sutra* (with an introduction by L. T. Woodward, M.D.), *The Perfumed Garden* (with an Introduction by L. T. Woodward, M.D.), *Lady Chatterley's Lover* by D. H. Lawrence, *Song of the Whip* (no author mentioned on the cover), *City of Night*, by John Rechy, and *Psychopathia Sexualis* (with an Introduction by L. T. Woodward, M.D.).

'Hello?' Alice called back into the obscurer depths. 'Is anybody home?'

'Aak? Unx? Mmp!' Then he appeared, a squat balding man with a funny hobbling walk like a chimpanzee's. His dirty white shirt was open to reveal a dirty white tee-shirt, the neck of which had been so badly stretched out of shape that an unseemly amount of his pink, fuzzy chest was exposed to common view. His face was sprinkled with more than one day's growth of salt-and-pepper beard, and his eyes, like the recesses of the shop out of which he had just emerged, were deeply, darkly shadowed.

'I'd like to sell this book to you, sir,' Alice said, taking *Just-So Stories* out of the grocery bag.

'What? Yaa?' He snatched the book out of her hand. 'Wha! Whaziss?' He looked at Alice intently, then back at the book. He opened it to the title page, snorting still more fiercely.

'Is something the matter?' Alice asked concernedly.

'Where you steal it, kid?'

'It's *mine*! It's my own book. It was a present to me from my uncle.'

'Ya'spect me to believe a story like that?' He punctuated this question with a very rhinoceros of a snort.

Tears came into her eyes. 'But it *is*! Really, really, it is!'

'Fifty cents,' he murmured, as though to himself. 'I can give you fifty cents. It's more than you'll get anywhere else in town, but I've got a soft heart.' He touched his soft heart, where his lank tee-shirt hung down to reveal it. 'Look, this is

my price sheet. I can't pay any more than what it says here.'
He waved a sheaf of typed papers, dirty as his shirt, in her
face.

'Are you sure that's all? Because it's a first edition, you
know. A first edition of *Kipling*.'

'So? So, who reads Kipling? This is what people read
nowadays . . .' He waved a dirty hand at the dirty books spread
out on the dirty counter. With his other hand he held out a
fifty-cent piece of not more than usual dirtiness. Alice only
hesitated a moment before accepting it. Only half a block
away, she remembered, there was a restaurant where fifty cents
would buy a hamburger and french fries.

When the little nigger girl had left his shop, Stan hobbled
back into the darkness, holding the tattered old book with
sacramental respect. He looked at the gin bottle, then at the
telephone. He decided to make the phone call first.

A different woman answered than the woman who had
called him that morning.

'About that book you were asking after?' Stan wheezed.
'Those *Just-So Stories*? Well, I got the edition you want. So
you can bring your money—I can't take no cheques, sorry—to
Stan's Books on 47 Truslove Street. When can you be here by?
I'll stay open late if you'll send someone tonight.'

'I'm afraid, sir, that a rather urgent matter has come up
that's taken everyone but myself out of the office. I'm just
answering the phone here, and I really can't tell you anything
about that book. And I can't say for certain when anyone will
be coming back. So maybe the best thing would be for you to
call back sometime in the morning.'

'In the morning?'

'Yes, in the morning. After nine o'clock. That would be best.
Thank you, sir.'

Stan held the receiver to his ear long after she'd hung up.
Then he began to swear. Fifty cents! Fifty cents down the
drain! He poured himself a glass of gin and stared at the
traitorous phone until the half-light of the July afternoon had
become a quarter-light and finally none at all. It never rang
again that night.

Chapter 15

A million million cars had passed her by, and now it was dark. Would the drivers be able to see her in the dark? The cars swooshed by in sequence, dazzling her with their headlights, deadening her with their utter and unanimous lack of charity. One could understand a driver being reluctant to pick up the usual sort of hitch-hiker (Miss Godwin, for instance, had always refused to) but what sort of threat could an eleven-year-old girl pose? True, this wasn't the ideal spot to be standing (a hundred feet short of the cloverleaf that fed into the tunnel beneath the Bay), but there *was* room for a car to pull over to the side, and the traffic wasn't so dense now that the drivers couldn't see her in time to stop. It was just another example of Prejudice.

It had been Prejudice likewise, she realised now, that had been at the root of the trouble she'd witnessed earlier that day. The men in the silk robes had been Klansmen. She hadn't recognised them then, because they hadn't been wearing their pointy hats, but when she'd seen the headlines on one of the morning newspapers (KLAN VIOLENCE PREDICTED FOR THE FOURTH), she'd realised why the man had kicked the poor old woman (because of Prejudice) and why none of the old woman's friends had helped her (Civil Rights). Of course, it was illegal to sit in the streets and sing hymns, or even eat lunch (as she'd discovered), but it seemed probable that if the Klan had been the ones sitting in the street, *they* wouldn't have been arrested, much less kicked.

Another and another and another car whizzed by in the nearer lane, and out of the last of them, a convertible, somebody threw a beer bottle. It shattered on the gravelled siding inches from Alice's feet. Had they meant to *hit* her with it? No, it was scarcely credible.

And yet—it was equally incredible that anyone would deliberately try to run over her, and some teenagers had tried to do just that only an hour before. She'd had to throw herself into the ditch beside the road to avoid being hit. Kids were certainly different here in Norfolk from kids in Baltimore. She remembered, with an ache of sadness, the busload of butterfly-bright teenagers on the way to the beach, their radios blaring, their blonde hair streaming in the wind. It all seemed worlds away and years ago, and yet she knew that Baltimore wasn't terribly far off and that she'd been on that bus only last Saturday morning, not four full days before.

A truck approached thunderously. It hardly seemed worthwhile, but she dusted off her dress and put out her thumb. A giant tanker of MILK roared past at sixty miles an hour. It had Maryland licences. She sighed. Milk and Maryland—Good Lord, she would never see either again at this rate! Maybe she should start looking for a place to spend the night.

The next vehicle began slowing before it reached her. Alice was at first uncertain whether she had a ride at last—or if it was another dirty trick. The car stopped and the right-hand door flew open. She ran towards the headlights, which had already attracted a cloud of insects, up to the open door. 'Are you going to B . . .'

A hand grabbed each of her shoulders and pulled her into the car. 'Alice, my darling girl!' His lips kissed her forehead perfunctorily. 'We going home now. The nightmare is over. You're safe.'

It was her father.

At ten o'clock, after six hours of futile searching in the streets of Norfolk, Roderick had given up. He paid off Bessy and started back for Baltimore. Alice would have to turn up somewhere, sometime. And if not . . . Well, it wouldn't be his fault.

Alice's escape had jeopardised Bessy's position more than his own, but now Bessy and her ménage were packing their bags. His own twelve-hours' absence was an embarrassment, but not unaccountable, since he had thought to establish the precedent that morning of receiving and acting under 'secret' instructions from the kidnappers. He had not performed a single action (excepting, of course, the murders) that could not be accounted for in this way, if need be.

So that when he saw the little Negro girl hitch-hiking on the highway leading into the tunnel, it was a bit of luck too good to be believed. Aside from her first astonished shriek, she hadn't said a word to him. As they drove through the neon whiteness of the tunnel, he would glance at her from time to time, curious about this well-nigh autistic silence. With her hair dyed and curled, with her so dark, he had difficulty believing she really was his daughter. Her manner had changed as much as her appearance. She, who had been so lively and full of giggling nonsense, sat immobile, eyebrows drawn together in a half-frown, pale eyes staring dully ahead at the yellow dashes flicking past down the centre of the road, the very picture of a sullen piccaninny. Bessy had certainly done her job.

'I bet you're anxious to be getting home, eh, kid?'

Silence.

'If you don't want to talk about it, I understand. It must have been pretty bad, back there. You're safe now, thank God, but I suppose it will take a little getting used to.'

Silence.

'Your mother has been terribly upset by all this.'

Alice turned to look at him. Was it a trick of the shifting light or some effect caused by the darker pigmentation of her skin—or was there in those eyes an expression of ... what? He could not be quite sure: contempt? fear? accusation?

*Hold on there, Raleigh,* he told himself. *Pretty soon you'll be seeing accusations in stop-lights.*

'Daddy,' she said quietly (he realised that he'd been expecting her voice to have changed, to have become a piccaninny voice), 'how did you know where to find me?'

'Well, you see, my pet, the kidnappers told me to get on the train to Norfolk. I gave them the money in Baltimore, and they were going to hand you back over to me down here. But when I got here they told me you'd escaped. I was frantic. I didn't know whether or not to believe them. I was afraid that they might have ... done something to you. When I saw you out on the highway, I'd already given up searching for you; I was going back to Baltimore.'

She smiled a curious, lopsided smile, her brows still pinched together in a frown. 'How did you know that it was me on the highway? It was so dark, and I'm ... disguised.'

Roderick laughed nervously. She had an attorney's mind, the brat! 'Actually, sweetheart, I didn't know it was you until I'd stopped. I surely was surprised. As soon as we get home, we'll wash that brown stuff off you.'

'Yes, I'll bet you were surprised. I was surprised too.' Her laughter was harsh and humourless. Roderick began to wonder whether the stay at Green Pastures, brief as it had been, might not have accomplished what all the years of Mrs. Buckler had not been able to—to wit, driven his little darling mad.

'I certainly am glad to see you, Alice. You're my darlingest daughter.'

144

'Don't call me that. Don't call me Alice.'

What *was* going on in her mind? She was staring out through the windshield again, though there was nothing to be seen but the hypnotic flicker of lane markings. She had put on a pair of cheap plastic sunglasses, and with that token she resumed her former, impervious silence.

An hour passed. They left the junk architecture of drive-ins and filling stations behind. They crossed the York and Rappahanock Rivers. Roderick almost came to forget that Alice was in the car with him. She had fallen asleep curled up at the other end of the seat. He would have liked to be asleep now. He'd got scarcely two hours' sleep the night before. Twice he stopped the car so that he might walk about in the cool evening air and revive himself. He reviewed his alibi and tried to discover loopholes in it.

Another hour. They had crossed the Potomac on Route 301 and were in Maryland now. He had to have a coffee. He pulled over into the parking lot of Midge's All-Nite Truck-Stop Eateria. Alice woke groggily, making little animal noises of discomfort. 'Let's get something to eat, honeybunch. Okay?' He leaned over and kissed her on the cheek. All these charades of father affection! Soon, perhaps, he would leave the country; then there would be no need for such hypocrisies.

'I wish you wouldn't do that, Mr Raleigh,' she said sleepily. (It was surely Dinah who spoke; Alice would have had better sense.) 'That was a very mean trick you played on Alice. You should be ashamed.'

'What trick?'

'Having her kidnapped.'

Roderick had been about to step out of the car. Instead he pulled his feet back in and closed the door quietly. 'Now then, what's this? What kind of foolish, foolish story have you been listening to? Hm, my love?'

'I'm not your love! And I think you were a perfect *beast*!' She refused to look into his eyes. Now that she was wider awake, she seemed to regret having spoken.

'Whenever did you get this strange notion, darling?'

'It's not strange at all. I figured it out myself. Though it didn't take much intelligence. I heard you talking to Bessy on the phone. I knew it was you because of some things Bessy said. You talked about Donald Bogan. And how else did Bessy know to call me Dinah, if you hadn't told her to? Answer me that!'

'It's true,' Roderick said carefully, 'that I called that woman. I had to arrange your return with her. But that's surely no proof, my dear darling'—Alice's lip curled scornfully at this—'that I *assisted* them.'

'Proof? There's one proof that you can't very well deny, my dear Daddy. If you aren't helping the kidnappers, how come you're driving their car?'

'But . . .'

He calculated rapidly what the probability of this was. Bittle had assured him that the car would be scrapped after the kidnapping. But it *was* a Buick, of the same vintage and colour as Bittle's.

'What a strange coincidence,' he said chillily. 'It does somewhat resemble the car that Miss Godwin described. Though it didn't occur to me till just this minute.'

'It resembles it more than I resemble Alice Raleigh. If you want more *proof*, I've proof right here.'

Proof, proof, proof: it was as though he had moved backwards in time, back through eons on that breakfast table where his daughter had chirruped on about the new mathematics.

Alice dug into the crevice formed by the two cushions of the seat and withdrew a crumpled wad of paper. 'That should be proof enough. When that man called Harry took me into this car, I thought I'd better leave a clue behind so that the police could trail me.' She pronounced 'clue' to rhyme with 'yew'. 'So I tore a page from my book—and stuffed it behind the cushion. And that's the page.'

He took the paper out of her hand and smoothed it flat. Even in the poor light he could recognise the Kipling illustration—the Elephant's child trying to pull away from the crocodile who had caught him by the nose. He took his cigarette lighter from his coat pocket and set fire to the paper.

'*That* won't do you any good, you know,' Alice counselled.

Roderick looked down at his daughter consideringly. 'You really are a clever little bitch,' he admitted. She stuck out her tongue at him. He started the motor.

'You turned the wrong way,' Alice said, when the car was back on Route 301. 'Baltimore is the other direction.'

This time it was Roderick who was obstinately silent the whole trip. They arrived back in Norfolk at 2.15 a.m. the morning of July 4. All the lights in the Green Pastures Funeral Home were blazing.

Chapter 16

Roderick catapulted Alice into the room with an underhand slap across her backside. Bessy was lying flat on her back on the couch, Fay and Clara stood over her in attendance. The three women turned to gape at Roderick.

'What are you two doing here?' Bessy brought out at last, though weakly. Her face glistened with sweat. She seemed to be ill.

'I could ask you the same question,' Roderick said. 'I thought you were going away on the midnight bus? What happened?'

Bessy moaned and shook her head.

'We tried to,' Clara said, while she patted Bessy's brow with a washcloth. 'But when we got to the damned bus station, ole Bessy came down with some kind of fit and said we had to come back here. In any case, she wasn't fit to be taking no trip then. She's better now than she was, though, and the taxi's coming to take us to the station again. There's a 3.30 bus. But *you* still ain't said what you're doing here—and where you found our little Dinah. Welcome home, Dinah.'

'She was hitch-hiking on the highway out of town. It's a good thing *I* found her there, because the damn brat knows everything. One of you has got some explaining to do.'

'What you know?' Bessy asked in a sorrowful voice, turning her head sideways on the armrest of the sofa. Alice bit her lip and made no reply. 'Well, with you carrying on this way and bringing her round here, she sure enough knows everything *now*.'

'I tell you I'd practically got her back to Baltimore, when it all spilled out. One of you told her I was in on her kidnapping.'

'Don't look at me, mister,' Clara growled. 'I don't know nothing of what this is all about, and I don't want to know nothing. You two kidnappers talk this over by yourselves and leave me and Fay out of it. First minute I saw that little piece, I knew she was gonna be bad luck.'

Roderick's eyes locked with Clara's in a communion of hatred. There was something about the girl's ugly, angular face, something about the way she stabbed out her cigarette, as though it were no ashtray she used, but the palm of his hand

... something ...

'I told you before,' Alice explained in a small voice, 'that *nobody* told me. I figured it out by myself. Actually, Daddy, there were all *sorts* of clues.'

He slapped her across the face. He couldn't stand the way she pronounced 'clues'.

'You'd better take her upstairs and lock her up,' he commanded, pushing her across the room to Bessy. 'Then we can discuss what we're going to do.'

Bessy seemed to welcome the opportunity to leave the room. 'Come along, Dinah,' she said, taking Alice by the hand. She was more than usually slow up the stairs, and her breath wheezed and whistled like a toy accordion.

Clara kept on regarding Roderick with the same disquieting fixity, as though she hoped, by staring hard enough, to nail him to the wall. He avoided her gaze now.

'Trying to remember who I am?' she asked, jutting her teeth forward like a belligerent weasel. 'Can't place me?'

'No, I'm afraid ... not ...'

'I know!' Fay said, with a dazzling, whiter-than-white smile. 'You're *Clara*!'

Roderick had backed into a corner, where he toyed with the broken forty-five phonograph, spinning the little turntable with one finger.

'I 'spect I've changed some since the last time you saw me. But then I 'spect all niggers probably look just the same to you, don't they? *Don't* they?' Her eyes narrowed. She walked to within a few inches of him and whispered: 'I held her down. *Now* do you remember?'

'Shut up! For the love of ... for the love of ...' The three-legged end-table rocked away from the wall that had been supporting it. Waving its single arm, the phonograph crashed to the floor.

'I guess you do,' Clara said.

'No!' said Roderick emphatically. He walked into the kitchen. It was strange how after all this time the kitchen still seemed familiar, not to say homey. Though it was seedier than he'd remembered.

No. He *didn't* remember.

When Bessy came into the kitchen he was draining a carton of milk, in gargantuan swallows. The milk trickled down from the corners of his mouth.

'I remember,' he said, when the milk was gone, 'that you used to serve coffee in here. You made me drink it black.'

'You all right, Roderick?'

'I thought they'd killed her. I thought she was dead.' He sounded disappointed.

'Clara? They damn near did. They came round in white robes, so I suppose they must of been Klansmen. Though I would guess college boys, more likely, judging by their voices. After all, why should the Klan be concerned? She wasn't no white girl. Police never did a thing, of course. Took Clara to the hospital and fixed up the bones that were broken. She's got a silver plate in her head to this day. She can't sleep on account of it, that's what she says. So when she gets mean, I try and take into account what she's been through.'

'You're a fool, keeping her on after what happened. No wonder this dump has gone downhill and you don't have any more business.'

'It ain't Clara that's to blame,' Bessy said, sighing and sitting. 'She brings in more than her share of regular customers. Klansmen, especially. We got them cutting their meetings short some nights just to come here and be with Clara. Kladds and Kludds and Kleagles. She's become sort of famous. They call her Ku Klux Klara.'

'I don't think it's funny.'

Bessy shrugged. After an awkward silence, she asked, 'What you meaning to do with little Dinah?'

'Maybe you should take her away with you and keep her.' He began to collapse the empty milk carton. 'For a while.'

'How long a while?'

'Till I can get good and lost. Of course, I'll give you some more money.'

'It ain't the money I care about. It's the trouble I'm getting into. When she escaped I thought, "Well, that's it, Bessy McKay. You've had it." If you hadn't found her, I might be in jail now—and *you* would be, sure enough.'

'Then why did you come back here? Why didn't you leave on the bus when you had the chance?'

Bessy shook her head slowly. Tears trembled at the corners of her eyes. 'Oh, you whitened sepulchre! You old Pharisee! How can you sit there cold as stone and talk to me after what you been doing?'

'What have I been doing?'

'It's on the front page of the newspaper. The morning paper

comes out at eleven o'clock. I saw it at the bus station. You damn fool!' She went into the living-room and returned with the paper. News about the Civil Rights protests and the Klan had squeezed the headline—KIDNAP SUSPECTS FOUND MURDERED—into the two columns on the left side of the front page. Beneath the headline were two photos: a prison portrait of Dorman and a picture of Alice in her St. Arnobia's pinafore. He skimmed the text:

'*Ordinary, Va.* Two men believed to have abducted Alice Raleigh of Baltimore, the eleven-year-old heiress to the Duquesne fortune, were discovered dead yesterday in a cabin a few miles outside of town. They were identified tentatively as Harry Dorman, white, and James Bittle, Negro. Dorman, who was implicated in the famous Larpenter kidnapping case, was recently released from a Federal penitentiary after serving sixteen years . . .'

The article had little to say about the actual kidnapping, and nothing concerning Roderick himself. The F.B.I. (who had taken the credit for the discovery) were evidently doing their best to keep the newspapers out of the case as long as possible.

'It says here,' Roderick pointed out, 'that they may have killed each other.'

'And it says that it don't seem very likely. And it don't.'

'Well, if I killed Harry—and mind you, I'm not saying I did—I would have had a good reason. He sent me a letter asking for more money. He wanted *half* for himself. Otherwise he was going to let the police know about my share in the kidnapping. That's blackmail, Bessy. If I'd given him what he asked for, do you think he would have been content with half? Not on your life!'

'There was *two* of them.'

'The boy, you mean? Yes, it was too bad about young Bittle. But he was in with Dorman. They were both going to blackmail me. But that's no reason for you to cry your eyes out, is it? Harry Dorman was a rat, and Jim Bittle was another. The two of us are a lot safer with them out of the way.'

'Jim Bittle was my son, Roderick.'

'Christ Almighty, Bessy, why didn't you ever say so? I didn't *know!*'

'Don't make no difference *now*.' But this explicit stoicism was belied by her tears.

'Bessy, I'm sorry. I'm *sincerely* sorry.' This, somehow, did not seem quite adequate, and he expressed his sincere compassion directly by pouring her out a glass of gin from the bottle for which she'd been reaching. Then he poured a glass for himself.

'I don't blame *you*, Roderick. It's my own goddamned fault. My fault for letting him get mixed up in this business. I thought I'd be doing him a good turn, making up to him for never having been a mother to him. He grew up in an orphanage, you know, my Jimmy. I was glad to get him off my hands then. It was the war, and the money was rolling in. His Daddy died on one of those islands out there. We was married, but I never told that to the people at the orphanage. I tried to get an abortion at first, but I wouldn't go through with it. I did get an abortion the next time. That's why I couldn't ever have a baby after that. Funny thing—it's like that's what I done, after all. It's like he was an abortion too, but I just had to wait all this time to do it.'

Roderick had stopped listening to her drunken croaking. Bessy, for her part, was not really narrating for his benefit, but more as a sort of elegy. He was thinking about the first time he had ever held his own daughter in his arms. The bundle of pink blankets about the tiny pink face. The two-month-old blue eyes. The tiny hands clasping at air. Looking at those little eyes he'd wished his wife had had an abortion, a course to which he had often urged her. Delphinia had never agreed that he'd been right until after the reading of her father's will. Then it had been too late.

The sun was just coming up before Roderick was drunk enough to be able to suggest what he had in mind, and even then it was Bessy who had to take the initiative: 'How come, Roderick, that you come back *here*? Seeing as how you say you thought we'd be gone away on the bus already.'

Roderick didn't reply directly. Instead, after allowing time for her question to dissolve into the hazy morning light of the tide-water, he said, 'I've got a bargain, Bessy. I've got a deal to make with you.'

'Don't want to make no more deals. They don't get me nothing but misery.'

'I'm sorry about Jim, Bessy. Really I am. If there was some way I could make it up to you, I would. I can see that the money doesn't mean anything to you. You can't put a price-tag on a human life. No, there's only one fair exchange for what I took from you. How does the Good Book put it? An eye for an eye, and a tooth for a tooth? If you understand me.'

Bessy looked at him with revulsion: 'Then *that's* why you came back here! You was going to kill her, and then make it look like it was me!'

'I might have had such an idea, but I realise now that I would never have had the heart to carry it out. Basically, I'm too much of a sentimentalist. I could never have lifted a hand to hurt my own dear little Alice. But you ...'

'You want me to ...'

Roderick smiled an inveigling, Erroll-Flynn smile (the smile his wife had fallen in love with). 'If you would, I'd appreciate it very much.'

In the 'forties the room at the back of Stroud's Bar and Grill had been fitted with blackout curtains, which were immediately drawn shut, nevermore to be opened. In the centre of this room stood a table covered with a crimson cloth, upon which a white cross was embroidered. At the extremities of the cross stood four white candles that shed the only light in the room. Six men stood around the table—five in red hoodwinks and robes, and a portly stranger in lime green—the Grand Dragon of the Realm of Virginia.

Exalted Cyclops Stroud spoke: 'The reason I called us here together, despite all the hard work we done already today and the further hard work we got before us tomorrow, is that I've learned something concerning a member of this Den—I refer to Owen Gann—that couldn't wait even so much as one night to be told. You wouldn't have an idea what I found out—would you, Pete?'

Peter Boggs stirred uneasily, remembering Gann's strange behaviour of that afternoon. But no—he shook his head inside the loosely fitted hoodwink—he had no idea, no, nothing to say. But he was glad the hoodwink prevented the other men from seeing the worried look on his face.

'Because he seemed particularly interested in talking to *you*.'

'He came round today asking after my car, but I sold it to someone else, meantime. I was going to tell him tonight out at the big Klonclave, and then you made me come away with the bunch of you. What's Owen done?'

'Maybe he was only pretending to be interested in your car. Just like he pretends to be a Klansman.'

'Come to the point, Cyclops,' the figure in green said with a portentous rustle of silk.

'The point is just this—that Owen Gann is an agent of the Federal Bureau of *In*-vestigation.' Farron paused to savour the sensation he had caused. It wasn't every Exalted Cyclops that could expose a traitor like Gann in the presence of an officer of the Grand Realm. 'So, I guess we ought to form a *tri*-bunal. The Kleron's here. The Klexter and Klailiff's here. And I swear on this Bible, by the Lord God Almighty, that what I'm about to say is the truth, so help me. And Pete, since you're a friend of Owen's'—Pete shook his head in violent disagreement—'since you're the nearest thing he's *got* to a friend, I thought you could defend him. After all, this is a democracy and we got to do things fair and legal.' Farron throughout his testimony affected to ignore the Grand Dragon, whose presence was, in theory, of no moment at the trial of a Den member.

'Today, about noontime this Owen Gann came around to the Bar asking after our Kladd Boggs here, and I observed at that time that this Gann sort of *stunk*. He had some kind of perfume all over him, and I ast him how he got perfume on him that way, and he said he'd made a delivery—that's what he does for a cover, he delivers Spengler's Beer—to this cathouse, only he never said what cathouse, and it didn't occur to me at that time to ask him. But later on I started getting suspicious, something didn't seem quite right, so I did some detective work, the F.B.I. ain't the only ones that can . . .'

'Yes, yes,' the Grand Dragon said impatiently. 'You're a goddamn Sherlock Holmes. Get on with it.'

'The long and the short of it was that I went over to Bessy's . . .'

'Bessy's?'

'That's a cathouse here. You probably wouldn't know about it. It's in an undertaker's, or used to be.'

The green silk rustled affirmatively. 'I *have* heard of it.'

'Anyhow the place was all stunk up with the same kind of perfume, so I ast the nigger-girl there, casual-like, if they'd had a big beer delivery that morning. She says no, and I says, like I'm joking, then how come I smelled your perfume all over the Spengler's Beer delivery men this morning? And *she* says, "Ha! He ain't no more a Spengler's Beer delivery man than I am." And *I* said, "What do you mean by that?" And *she* says, "He's a federal agent, that's what!" He'd come around there that morning asking after some ex-convict or somebody that used to hang around with Bessy. He searched the place upstairs and down looking for this guy, which he wouldn't of done if he was just a beer delivery man. So you couldn't have clearer proof than that.'

'What does the Defence have to say?' asked the Klailiff.

The Defence had very little to say, since the Defence, though it tended to like the defendant personally, had its own reasons for supposing Farron's accusations to be true. Pete had heard of Bittle's and the other man's murders, and he'd been all day wondering if he should go to the police and tell them about Owen's visit. Now, it seemed, Owen *was* the police. So the defence could only suggest weakly that Gann be given a chance to defend himself before his accuser, the nigger whore. He was a white man, after all, and white men were entitled to a fair trial.

'What you say is true,' said the Grand Dragon in a weighty (if unofficial) manner. 'However, we should consider that if he lives to see what we got lined up tomorrow night, and then lives to tell about it in a Federal court, we may find ourselves on trial instead of him. Of course, I don't have any business speaking out. It's your affair, handle it your way.'

'Nevertheless, boys, the Grand Dragon's got a point worth considering,' Farron said with an obsequious smile, invisible behind his hoodwink.

The judges did not spend very much time considering the Grand Dragon's point.

'Death,' said the Kleron, snuffing out one of the candles between his thumb and forefinger.

'Death,' echoed the Klexter, extinguishing a second candle.

'Death,' said the Klailiff cheerfully, putting out the third. 'I think we can trust Farron to look after the details. The important thing is to get rid of Gann without bringing the whole damned F.B.I. down on our necks.'

Farron pulled off his hoodwink with a short predatory laugh. 'I've got it all figured out. Gann's going to have to trail along behind us all day tomorrow, so's he can spy on us, right? It wouldn't surprise me at all, knowing how these niggers have been riled up and agitated by Northerners, if one of them niggers was to shoot his head off. On account of his being in the Klan. Them niggers can be pretty vicious when they get the opportunity.'

He winked broadly, becoming for a moment truly a Cyclops. Then he snuffed out the last candle. The meeting was adjourned.

He lay upon the bed as he had fallen into it, fully dressed. The overalls were soaked with sweat, his hair matted wetly to his brow. He had been dreaming. There had been chains in the dream, but he remembered no more than that. A nightmare, surely. He needed a cigarette. His head felt as though the sutures of the skull were being forced apart by a knife blade, the way an oyster is opened.

It was a hangover, but not from drinking. From guilt. He sat

155

up in the creaking bed to fumble on the table-top for a pack of cigarettes. Inadvertently he caught sight of himself in the dresser mirror. It was not a pleasant sight.

Smile, you sonofabitch, he thought. You deserve every nightmare you get. Obligingly the face smiled. He hated himself. Christ, how he hated himself.

Could it have been only a part of the nightmare perhaps? No, the old Negro man that had been half whipped to death last night had been as solidly flesh and blood as the hand that held the match to the cigarette now, that trembled. The only difference was that this hand was white.

The dream came back then, brief as a flash of lightning. The Klan had been a part of it, except their robes were black instead of white. They wore black hoods, like medieval executioners. The air was perfumed with evil, and the wooden floor was slimed with the blood of their earlier victims, the white man and the coloured man. He was their victim now. He was black. His face, his arms, his fingertips, his bleeding torso, all black, and this metamorphosis was more painful to him than the actual pain that the black-robed Klansmen inflicted on him. And then the memory of the dream, evanescent as the memory of a perfume, slipped out of mind.

The phone rang. He glanced at his alarm clock. It was half past nine. 'Gann here,' he said into the receiver.

'There may be a break in the Raleigh case, Gann.' It was Madding. 'A call came in yesterday from Stan's bookshop on Truslove Street. You probably know the place. The owner's gone to jail a couple of time on pornography charges. He found the copy of *Just-So Stories* that we advertised for. He called in yesterday when everyone was out at Bittle's cabin, and again this morning. Shrewd fellow—wouldn't give us any idea of how he got hold of it until we'd brought the money over to him.'

'And then—when he'd been paid?'

'His story is that a little girl brought it in. She fits Alice Raleigh's description pretty well except for one small detail. The kid was black as sin. She was wearing a dirty red check dress, and that is the only thing we know besides her colour. It looks like four hundred dollars down the drain. The kid probably found the book in a garbage can, but we're not likely now to find out where that garbage can was. Except we know the Raleigh kid must be in Norfolk. Just thought you should know.'

156

'I should. Thanks. Any word yet on the girl's father? Is he still missing?'

'Yes, the last I heard. I also heard the meeting last night was pretty rough. That old Negro is in the hospital.'

'I'll write up the report this morning and mail it to you.'

'Do. And cheer up, Gann. This should be the last day of this nightmare.' Madding hung up.

The enlightenment and the horror came upon him in the same instant, as if, this time, the lightning had flickered over the interior landscape of his mind long enough for him to make out the features. He remembered how, in the dream, he had pleaded with his executioners, trying to persuade them that it was only dirt that made his hands black. But it was dirt that would not wash away.

He knew there were pills that would turn a white man dark temporarily. He knew that Alice Raleigh had been made to take such a pill, and that she had been the little coloured girl that had sold *Just-So Stories* to Stan's bookshop, *the same little coloured girl whom he had seen yesterday at Green Pastures Funeral Home.* He tried to remember her features, but in his memory the girl's face was only a dark blur, a composite of all the faces of all the coloured children he had ever seen. He realised what a perfect disguise her black skin had been. It made her well nigh invisible to a man like himself.

But she had worn, he recalled a red check dress, and she had worn sunglasses inside the house. To conceal her blue eyes?

It was, of course, entirely improbable. He knew better than to suggest his theory (though it was already, for himself, a certainty) to Madding. Not till he had proof. And the proof was no farther away than Green Pastures. He could be there by 9.45 if he didn't take time to shave.

Chapter 18

Mrs. Elizabeth McKay was aware of a peculiar sensation, or rather the absence of usual sensations, somewhere in her abdomen. Her heart still beat, her lungs pumped breath, and yet there was a sort of pause, a suspension of some vital inner motion. Had she been forced to find words to describe it, she might have compared it to a drop of water on the end of a faucet, drooping, lengthening, threatening to drop, and still not dropping.

'Yes,' Roderick repeated. 'I would appreciate it very much indeed. I was thinking you might drown her in a bath, but do it in whatever manner suits you best. I'll wait here downstairs in the meantime. Naturally, I'll pay you for this—any reasonable price.'

'What do you think, Roderick—that I'm some hired murderer?'

'How about that abortion you were just carrying on about? Don't you call that murder?'

'Maybe it was, maybe it was—the Lord will be my judge. God knows, I've regretted it many a time. But I'm not about to risk my soul—and my life—on any murder charge.'

'Bessy, you already *have*,' Roderick said, in a tone of wheedling reasonableness. 'As far as the law is concerned—and I should know because I was almost a lawyer once—you're as guilty as I am of Harry Dorman's murder—and of your son's. Once a person has entered a conspiracy, he becomes responsible for whatever anyone else in the conspiracy does. You're as guilty as I am, Bessy—before the law.'

'No!'

The drop of water finally fell, silently into a pool of silence, and silent concentric rings rushed outwards from the point of impact and threatened to engulf the room—and her mind. Her son was dead: it would not be believed, it could not be borne.

'I killed your son, Bessy. That's perfectly true, and nothing can be done about it now. In return, I'm asking you to kill my daughter.'

Had he actually said that, or had she just imagined it? It was hardly credible that any living soul could ever say anything so foolish and terrible, and yet by the way he seemed to be waiting for an answer, he must have said it. The only answer she could make to him were tears. The tears rolled down her cheeks, but inside she felt that same strange cessation. It was not pain. It was something deeper than pain.

*My heart*, she thought. *My heart is breaking.*

'Are you all right? You don't look well.'

'Fine. I'm just fine, I . . .' Her vision steadied, and she wiped her eyes dry. You just couldn't afford to let your emotions run away with you when you were dealing with a son of a bitch like this.

'You wouldn't by any chance,' Roderick asked, 'have a firearm around here?'

'Why, as a matter of fact . . . yes!' She marvelled at the irony of it—the little pistol in her dresser drawer, with its mother-of-pearl inlaid handle, had been a gift from Jim Bittle's daddy. Was that the answer then? It did seem that the hand of Providence was guiding her. She sent Clara up to the bedroom to fetch it. (She just couldn't go up those stairs again herself.)

'Is it loaded?' Roderick asked.

'Yes, it's loaded,' she said wearily. She considered Roderick, whose outmoded and strained nattiness seemed so much in keeping with everything else at Green Pastures—the Latin moustache, the black pompadour set on his head askew, the beginnings of a second chin. No, she couldn't do it. However much he might deserve it, she couldn't shoot him down in cold blood.

She laid the gun down on the table.

'Well? Are you going to do what I asked or not?'

'I'll do it.' She raised herself wearily out of the wooden chair. She'd had too much liquor and not enough sleep. 'I'll take care of Alice, but not with that. That'll make too much noise.'

'Strangle her then, or smother her. Do what you like, but don't . . .' Briefly his composure deserted him. He glanced about, as though he might find the wanting words suspended in the air or scrawled on the wall. 'Don't tell me, afterwards, what you had to do. She *is* my daughter, after all, and I can't help feeling a little . . . sentimental. You know how it is.'

·'While I'm taking care of her, you'd better get away from here, don't you think? The police must be wondering what's become of you.'

'Fifteen minutes one way or another aren't very important. You won't want to leave her body here. The police have come

159

around asking after Harry once; they're bound to come again. I've got a car outside, and we can wrap her up in blankets with a cement block and dump her at another point further along the tidewater. So you take care of what *you* have to do, and I'll just wait downstairs.'

Reluctantly Bessy followed Roderick into the living-room. She shooed Fay and Clara up to their bedroom. Roderick lay back on the sofa, yawning loudly. Bessy felt heartburn rising up in her throat.

'Well, you just have yourself a good nap, hon,' she said. 'I'll be as quick as I can.'

Roderick nodded, smiling abstractedly.

There was no question of killing anybody, least of all the child, but Lord, what *was* she doing to do? *Lord*, she thought, *Lord, deliver me from the unjust and deceitful man*. A spasm of giddiness overtook her then, and she rested her head on the hand that gripped the banister. She felt as if she had been left all alone, as if the Lord had hidden himself from her. *But be of good courage, and he shall strengthen your heart, all ye that hope in the Lord*. It was a comfort to know that.

As soon as Roderick heard Bessy locking her bedroom door, he went back into the kitchen. After putting one of the gloves back on, he pocketed the pearl-handled revolver. He had a presentiment that he would have occasion to use it.

'I don't like it, I don't like it a damned bit,' Clara whispered fiercely. 'If it don't work just exactly *so*, what you think is going to happen? He ain't playing games down there, you know.'

'Then what you got to suggest better, Clara?' Bessy asked. 'That we go ahead and do what he wants? You think he don't mean to do the same with you and me and Fay as he did with Harry and Jim Bittle? Like hell he don't!'

Alice's fingers shook as she buttoned up the back of Fay's pink organdie party dress. Though Bessy had been careful that she should not overhear her and Clara discussing their plight, she could not help but have suspicions concerning her father's intentions.

'We're going to look like a goddamned circus parade,' Clara complained.

'We'd look less like one, if you'd change out of those denim overalls,' Bessy suggested. Clara made a suggestion of her own in reply.

'Are we going to the circus?' Fay asked eagerly, all buttoned at last.

'You remember everything I told you to do?' Bessy asked of Alice. She nodded. 'And you're not afraid?'

'Only a little.'

'I'm not *at all* afraid,' Fay assured Bessy. 'The animals will all be inside cages, so there isn't anything to be afraid of.' But no one seemed to pay any attention to her today. She began to chew on her hair fretfully.

Bessy began to tie Alice up in one of the sheets from the bed, while Clara began knotting another sheet to this one, then to the second sheet a third.

'What if she runs off and leaves us stuck up here?' Clara asked. 'Then what will *we* do? Jesus Christ, who would have thought yesterday that I'd be *helping* the kid escape today!'

'You won't do that, will you, Dinah? Promise me.'

Alice criss-crossed her heart and pointed to God. Bessy helped her sit on the window sill. The ground was a fearful distance down, but this time she wouldn't have to jump.

'Don't be afraid,' Bessy said. 'We'll be holding on tight.'

'Are we going to the *circus*?' Fay asked loudly.

'Sssh, child. Clara, can't you keep Fay quiet? Clara, where'd you go?'

Clara came out of the bath that adjoined her own bedroom. She was holding a boot. 'I got this for her to knock on the door with. If she only uses her hand, it won't sound like no F.B.I. man.'

'What a clever idea,' Alice said, smiling uncertainly at Clara, who frowned back at her fiercely.

'Ready?' Bessy asked.

Alice nodded her head. Clara caught her up under her armpits and lowered her outside the window until the sheet pulled taut. Then she and Bessy together began lowering Alice by the rope of sheets to the marshy ground fifteen feet below.

Roderick walked to the foot of the stairs. 'What are you *doing* up there?' he called out. 'You've been half an hour!'

'We won't be long now,' Bessy answered.

He returned to the sofa, but the minute he sat down he found himself dropping off to sleep again. That would be a hell of a note: to let the police come by and find him asleep on the sofa—with his daughter's dead body upstairs! He went into the kitchen and threw some cold water on his face.

161

There was knocking at the front door, a sound portentous and heavy with authority. He was about to call and ask Bessy if it had been her making the noise, then checked himself. If it *weren't* she, if it were someone at the front door . . .

Clara came charging down the steps, wearing her denim pants and jacket and a single boot. 'Stay away from that window,' she hissed at Roderick, who had been about to peek through the venetian blinds to see who was at the door. 'You want people to see you *here*?' She pushed him away from the window and lifted a single slat of the blinds. 'Jesus Christ,' she whispered.

'What is it?' Roderick asked.

'The F.B.I. The man who was here yesterday asking after you. You'd better hide.'

He looked about the room helplessly. 'Where?'

'You can't go out the back way 'cause you might get caught in the mud. It's happened before. You better get into that closet.' She pointed to a door opening on to the brief foyer.

Reluctantly he went to the closet door and opened it. It was crammed with raincoats and heavier, wintry clothes. 'There's no room,' he protested.

The knocking came again. It seemed incredibly loud—as though, Roderick thought, someone were pounding on the door with Clara's missing boot. But its loudness was probably due entirely to his own fear.

'Of course there's room,' Clara said, pushing him inside. 'Now, don't for Christ's sake move around in there or make the least noise. Get yourself comfortable *now*.'

'But suppose he *looks* in here?' Roderick whispered urgently, as she pushed the door closed.

'I'll lock the door and tell him the key is lost.'

'No!'

But Clara paid him no heed, and he did not dare protest any louder. In the stifling, woollen-musty darkness he listened to the key moving the tumblers of the lock. Clara opened the front door then, but he couldn't hear what she said to the man who'd been knocking, because the sound of Bessy coming down the stairs drowned it out. Shadows passed back and forth in front of the key-hole, but putting his eye up to it Roderick could see nothing but the forty-five phonograph laying smashed on the floor on the other side of the living-room. The front door slammed shut, and all was silence. 'Clara,' he whispered. 'Clara, let me out of here. Do you hear?'

But how could he expect her to hear him if he only whispered?

He woke up all in a sweat. Someone was moving around the house. He had not wanted to sleep, but the air in the closet was so close, he was so tired, his bed of overcoats so comfy. Had he slept long? It was too dark in the closet to read the face of his watch. He pressed his eye, gummy with sleep, to the key-hole. The living-room was strident with daylight. He blinked, seeing that phonograph collapsed upon the floor, remembering, and wanting not to remember.

He had been putting the finishing touches to his initials, carved on the kitchen door, when the screams began coming from upstairs. Bessy, who had just then been putting another stack of records on the brand-new phonograph (*Tenderly* had just finished playing) stood up suddenly, jarring the end table and sending the record player crashing to the floor. Automatically (record players are expensive) she bent down to recover it, and so it had been Roderick who got up the stairs first. The screams continued to come out of the bedroom, shrill soprano agonisings that must have torn blood from the girl's lungs. The door was unlocked.

It was the Creole girl. She was naked, her ankles tied to the lower bed-posts, while Clara, the black homely girl that no one really cared for, stood at the head of the bed holding her wrists. Clara's face was a mask of indifference. When she saw Roderick come into the room the Creole girl stopped screaming. Her skin was so light, with her hair dyed and straightened, she might have passed for white—north of Norfolk, at least.

Bogan folded up his bloody penknife and pocketed it. Roderick's gaze returned again to the girl's smooth belly, where dark blood welled from the cuts. It was just possible, through the mess of blood, to make out the letters that Bogan had carved there: KKK.

'It was an accident,' Bogan said. 'Honest. My hand slipped.' He pouted.

'My God!' Roderick said, holding to the door frame for support (and, incidentally, to bar the others who had followed him up the stairs from the room). 'You beast! Bogan, you beast!'

'It was an accident,' Bogan repeated idiotically. 'I'll pay for any damage I done, but it was an accident. You'll back me up on that, won't you, Hot Rod? You'll say it was an accident?'

'You better get out of here before Bessy comes up and sees what you done. Damn it all, Bogan, you must be a raving lunatic to think you can pull off a stunt like this.'

'It was an accident. You'll back me up. You'll stand by your brother.' Bogan prepared to leave the room, but stopped, consideringly, before the dresser. He picked the ashtray from the glass top with drunken over-preciseness. 'We'd better cauterise that wound, or it'll get infected.' He turned the ashtray upside down over her belly. She began to scream again, though not with the same hysterical intensity. Roderick hit Bogan a glancing blow on the back of his head, and then Bogan was out of the door and into the hall, doubled with laughter.

'Get him out of here,' Roderick commanded the other fraternity brothers. 'Take him out to the car. This year's Howl is over, as of now. And keep Bessy calmed down till I can get things straightened with this girl in here.'

He returned to the Creole girl. Clara was still holding her wrists as though she sensed that all was not over.

'Are you conscious? Can you understand me?' he asked the girl. She nodded. Her face was wet with tears and sweat.

Awkwardly he began to wipe away the filth of butts and ashes from the still bleeding wound. He was uncomfortably aware of the warmth growing in his loins. 'Does it still hurt?' he asked.

She nodded and began sobbing with relief.

Roderick looked into Clara's eyes, and there was a spark of mutual understanding before she resumed her customary mask of inexpressivity. He did not even need to tell her to continue holding the girl's wrists.

Roderick was still making love to the unconscious girl when the police arrived. They took her to the coloured hospital, where she was two days coming out of a coma. For those two days Roderick and Bogan were held in prison. When they were released, Roderick learned that he had been expelled from the University. He had been just *days* short of graduation! Bogan, whose father was in the Virginia State Judiciary, received his degree though he was barred from graduation ceremonies. Roderick knew then that if such things could happen, there was no justice in this world, and thereafter he had planned his life accordingly.

Again there was a knocking at the front door, and thirty

heartbeats later it was repeated. Bessy must have left the house, for no one came to answer the door. The question was —had Alice left with her? Or was she up in the bath, or under a bed, dead? Whichever were the case, Roderick could think of no better strategy than silence, and he eased back into his nest of winter coats. He could hear the front door opening, and a man's voice called out: 'Bessy? Bessy McKay, are you here?'

A client perhaps? No, it was too early for that sort of thing. This time it probably was, as Clara had pretended before, the F.B.I. agent.

Roderick followed him about the house in his imagination: up the stairs, in and out of each bedroom. Downstairs: in the kitchen; along the corridor out-of-use rooms; then, across to the living-room window. Roderick, kneeling at the keyhole again, saw him stoop to pick up the phonograph from the floor. Across his back, in red script, was scrawled the trademark, SPENGLER'S BEER.

Again! The shock he felt exceeded simple fear and passed almost into the realm of the supernatural, a sort of terrorised reverence or reverential terror. His fists, his guts, his glands, all were suffused by it.

The Spengler's Beer insignia left Roderick's small range of vision. The man wearing the overalls (if only Roderick could have seen his *face*!) came and stood in front of the closet. He jiggled the door handle. Roderick reached into his pocket and gripped the handle of the revolver.

His faceless antagonist muttered an obscenity and strode out of the front door, slamming it behind him. A moment later Roderick heard him start up his truck and drive off.

He was afraid to shoot through the lock, and he had no idea how to set about picking it. He braced his back against the upper wood panel of the door and pushed with the full force of his arms and legs against the wall of the closet. He ripped the back of his suit and strained a shoulder muscle, but he got out. He lay on the floor of the foyer, crying and drinking in the cool, delicious morning air. It was so good to be alive!

He would have to kill Bessy now, of course. Probably the two whores as well. He could see now that this had always been the most logical plan of action, but he had not had the courage, or the honesty, till now to admit it to himself.

Before he left Green Pastures, he ran upstairs just to make sure that Alice's body wasn't somewhere about. He found her dirty red check dress lying beside the clothes hamper in the bathroom. She must have been changed into the turquoise-blue dress she'd been kidnapped in.

Somehow the cast-off dress made him feel sad.

He smiled, remembering his Nietzsche: *Your killing, O judges, shall be pity and not revenge. And as you kill, be sure that you yourselves justify life! It is not enough to make peace with the man you kill. Your sadness shall be love of the overman: Thus you shall justify your living on.*

And Roderick did definitely feel sad.

And justified.

Chapter 19

'Hold on tight,' Bessy said, gripping Alice by her right and Fay by her left hand, while she tried to forge a path through the jostling crowd around the news-and-tobacco counter at the front of the station. 'Did you ever see such a crowd! Where they all going on the 4th July?'

'Where's my baby?' Fay demanded petulantly.

'Dinah's got your baby, honey. You ain't got no cause to fret.'

'*I* want it!'

'Soon as we sit down you can have it, but Dinah ain't big enough to carry that suitcase, and you are.'

'Why can't Clara carry the old suitcase?'

''Cause Clara's already carrying three suitcases, honey-bunch. Now *try* and behave.'

In the crowd of grown-ups Alice could see very little but midriffs and behinds. Even so, it seemed to her that there were a lot more coloured people here than one usually found in a crowd this size. And it wasn't like the crowd on the street yesterday. That crowd, with its hymn-singing and bright costumes, had had something of a holiday mood about it, while today everyone, white and black, wore tense expressions and talked in whispers. At the back of the station, in front of a glass door with a plastic number 1 above it, was someone she recognised—the policeman who had made her spill her milk into the gutter. In the press of bodies she was quite unnoticeable, so she stuck her tongue out at him.

There were long lines in front of the ticket windows. Even so, no one was being waited on. Behind the counter, the ticket sellers—three middle-aged men in shirt sleeves—were discussing something with a younger man in a black suit. The man in the black suit said something very loud and definite, and the three ticket sellers returned to their windows, and each of them hung a small plastic sign across the round speaking-hole in the glass: THIS WINDOW CLOSED. PLEASE USE NEXT WINDOW. The people waiting in line groaned.

The man in the black suit (the manager of the station?) came forward and very earnestly requested that everyone go home. They would all be much happier at home. The bus station was nowhere to carry on violent quarrels, and in any case all bus services were cancelled for the day. The effect of his speech was vitiated somewhat by the arrival at just that moment of a bus. The heavy engine sputtered to silence, followed by the hiss and thud of its door opening. The policeman standing at number 1 entrance twirled his night stick nervously.

A few people, blacks and whites, straggled in through the door, looking up in surprise at the mob. (Actually, Alice could see now, there were two mobs: one almost entirely black; the other unexceptionably white.) And the mobs, in turn, looked surprised and, almost in unison, sighed. Everyone stayed where they were, except those who'd just dismounted from the bus, who bore their children and luggage out of the station through the side doors.

'What's everybody waiting around here for?' Bessy asked of the man ahead of her in the line.

'You mean to say you ain't heard! Them ministers and all them other CORE people are coming down here from Washington, just like they said they was.'

Outside the station Alice could see the bus driver changing the sign on the bus. NORFOLK was wound back till it became BALTIMORE. She tugged at Bessy's hand.

'What is it now, child?'

'Where are you getting tickets *to*, Bessy? Have you decided yet?'

'Lord knows. I got some friends in Atlanta that should put us up for a few days. Leastways, they'll take Fay and Clara off my hands. After that, I just don't know. But don't you worry, sweety-pie—I'm going to look after you.'

'Because, you see, that bus is returning to Baltimore.'

'Dear God, I ain't taking you up *North*! I might just as well go hand myself over to that policeman there. You don't want Bessy going to prison, do you, darling? Course not.'

'But you don't have to go with me. Just get me a ticket and put me on the bus and when I get there I can call up my uncle, and it's all perfectly safe and sure, and I promise that no matter what I won't tell on you. Criss-cross my heart. But as for Daddy...'

Bessy nodded grimly. On that subject nothing more needed to be said between them. 'I'd feel safer if you was with me, but I s'pose that don't necessarily mean you'd *be* safer. So if that man'll open the ticket window, I'll just get you a ticket to Baltimore, but it looks like we picked just about the worst time we could to come here.'

'Oh, look!' said Fay, beside herself with excitement. 'Here's some of the clowns from the circus!'

It was the Klan. They pushed in through the side doors (the front of the station was one solid wall of waiting mob now), the majority in white robes with red crosses, a few in red, and a single Klansman in lime green. This last figure, as though to make up for the general scarcity of green, was far and away the largest of them all. For sheer bulk he rivalled Bessy.

None wore masks, though they did have on their pointy witch-hats.

The green Klansman walked to Gate 1 and talked to the policeman there, who seemed almost to be relieved at their arrival, though he should have known that they would bring nothing but trouble. After all, he'd seen what they'd done yesterday. After they'd talked, the policeman left the bus station through the door the Klansmen had come in at.

The green Klansman was helped to stand on one of the benches, from which he addressed everyone in the bus station. 'All right! Shut up and listen to me. We warned you dumb niggers—Shut up, I said!—yesterday, and we've been warning you right along, to stay home today. Some of you have got pretty thick heads, and don't remember so well. Well, that's a damned shame. Because now it's too late. *Nobody*'s leaving this bus station now until we've welcomed the nigger ministers to our fair city. Is that understood?'

Somebody from the crowd shouted out, 'No!'

'Then this will make it understood,' the Klansman said, puckering fat lips into a smile that looked like a cluster of grapes. From underneath his green robes he took a shotgun; several of the attendant Klansmen took out shotguns or rifles as well.

There had been something about the green Klansman's voice, or his manner, that made Alice think of her father. On those rare occasions when he had undertaken to punish her he had spoken in just that way.

'Come on, children,' Bessy said, grabbing hold of Alice's and Fay's hands. 'We better get out of here. We'll get us a bus later on.'

But the Klansmen had moved in front of all the side doors. The mob at the front of the station was a mob of white men, who blocked the way to any coloured person trying to push through it.

Clara chuckled and set down the three suitcases. 'Well, that's that. At least we can be sure Ole Roderick is gonna have just as much trouble getting in here as we'll have getting out.'

'If we're going to wait, we might as well wait sitting down,' Bessy said, heaving a sigh. She led her three charges to a bench at the periphery of the crowd of Negroes.

'Just a minute!' exploded the Klansman in green. 'Just a god-damned *minute*! Is that a white woman sitting down there in the middle of all those niggers? Is she going to let them niggers feel her up? What is this?'

A Klansman in candy-apple red pushed his way forward to speak to the lime-green Klansman. Alice recognised him: it was Farron Stroud. 'No cause to be alarmed, Grand Dragon, sir,' Farron said. 'She's just a hoor, and sort of simple besides. She don't know no better.'

But the Grand Dragon paid Farron no heed. 'You! White woman! Come here! Yes, *you*!'

Trembling but smiling prettily (Hadn't Bessy always told her she had to smile no matter *what* the men told her to do?) Fay stepped forward.

'Just what the hell do you think you're doing here with all these niggers?'

'I don't know,' Fay confessed. 'But I think *you're* nice.'

The Grand Dragon blushed brilliantly. As he regarded Fay in her snug, peppermint-stripe party-dress, sucking on a strand of her own blonde hair, he seemed to be choking on something. At least, he found speech difficult.

'Can I go now?' Fay asked, when his colour seemed to have subsided.

'Back to them niggers? A pretty girl like you shouldn't be running with a bunch of dirty niggers and Commies and I don't know what-all!'

'But I *have* to! I have to get my baby and feed her, and it's time for her nap. Oh, it's way past time for her nap already, and she's *very* sleepy.'

The green Klansman looked from Fay to the person he supposed to be her baby—Alice, black Alice. 'She's your *baby*?' he gasped. Then, with full explosive force: '*Your baby?*'

The colour returned to his face more richly than before. Like a ripening plum, it seemed to be passing from red to the violet band of the spectrum. With his shimmering regalia and funny hat, he had taken on an altogether clownish appearance.

Fay giggled. 'Are you one of the clowns?' she asked, believing sincerely that he was.

The Grand Dragon snorted wrathfully, and raised an arm to strike Fay but the blow was never to fall. A thin black shadow materialised suddenly into the air before him, slammed into his fat body, toppling him. It was Ku Klux Klara. Her knee came up against the Grand Dragon's groin, her nails raked his face, her voice whispered obscene endearments.

White silk robes closed in around Clara, and Alice could see nothing then but a rush and tumble of midriffs and behinds, as the crowd broke for the unguarded doors. A bus was pulling into the station, and somewhere a policeman was blowing his whistle.

Owen Gann was getting into his truck having searched the house on North Tidewater Road to no purpose, when someone hailed his name, and a car pulled over to the opposite kerb.

'Gann, it's a damned good thing I found you.' It was Jenks, the Knight-Hawk, a pox-faced man with bad teeth and extreme halitosis. Even at a distance of several feet Owen was sure he could catch a whiff of him. 'I been at your rooming house. I been at the Spengler's loading docks but they was shut down for the 4th. And where do I find you? In Niggertown! You ain't forgotten where we're all supposed to be this morning, have you?'

'We're going to the African Church *tonight*,' Owen protested, feigning not to understand.

'I'm talking about the bus station, not the church. Jesus Keerist, you got a head as thick as ...' He looked up and down North Tidewater Road for a metaphor. '... as thick as thieves. You drive this truck to somewhere you can park it—behind Farron's Bar would be a good idea—and then you can drive on to the bus station with me.'

Gann would have demurred, but he could think of no convincing reason for not doing as Jenks said. Today of all days he should not miss out on the Klan's activities. He began to wonder if it were possible that his whole brainstorm about the Negro girl he'd seen yesterday being Alice Raleigh might not have been a devious tactic of his subconscious seeking to avoid an unwelcome task.

He drove behind Jenks for the three miles to Stroud's Bar and Grill, where a Klansman (though not in regalia) stopped him as he pulled the truck into the driveway.

'Ayak?' asked Owen.

'Akia,' responded the man, ritually. 'What is the Oath of

Allegiance?'

'Obedience, Secrecy, Fidelity, and Nishness,' said Owen, completing the time-honoured formula. The man waved him past.

Peter Boggs, wearing a white robe, was alone in the parking lot. He explained to Jenks that everyone else had left already for the bus station: could he come along in Jenks' car? For some reason Jenks seemed reluctant, but it was impossible to refuse so reasonable a request.

'Where's your own car?' Jenks asked.

'Sold it,' Boggs said laconically. He darted a look at Gann, as though there were something he was about to say to himself —but then, why *didn't* he?

*Probably*, Gann thought, *he wants to apologise for having sold the car without giving me another chance at it.*

The nearest parking space to the bus station that they could find was four blocks off. While Boggs rolled down the car windows, Jenks took out a sawed-off shotgun and a bundle wrapped in newspapers from under the car's front seat. The bundle contained two robes. Jenks tossed one of them to Gann.

In the brief instant when Jenks was slipping his robe over his head, Boggs sidled up to Gann and whispered something, of which Gann caught only the two words, *they know*. Who were 'they', and what did they know? It was something to do, most likely, with the bodies that had been discovered in Bittle's cabin. Boggs, not knowing Gann's reason for visiting the cabin, must have been wondering what the connection was between his visit and the two murders. But Gann was hardly in a position to explain to him that it was not a sinister connection.

When all three men were in their robes, they started off towards the bus station. Whenever Jenks could not see him, Boggs would make exaggerated faces and point at him—or at the gun that was now concealed beneath his robes. Gann didn't know what to make of his behaviour. They arrived at the bus station just as the Grand Dragon was saying, 'You! White woman! Come here!' 'Jesus Christ,' Boggs said, in a tone more reverent than profane. 'Will you *look* at that?'

'What?' Gann's view was blocked by another Klansman's tall hat.

'At that angel from heaven! I'd swear it was *her*, except that I know she must be an old woman by now. But, glory, she's the spit-and-image of her!'

'Of who?'

172

'Of that girl I told you about in *Birth of a Nation*, the one who threw herself off a cliff to escape being raped by that nigger. Mae Marsh, her name was, and she was an angel of . . .' Pete gasped. 'No, he can't *do* that!'

It was then that Clara, being of the same opinion, actively prevented the Grand Dragon from striking the lovely angel from heaven, after which, as we know, was pure pandemonium. Pete fought his way to the front of the crowd of Klansmen, who seemed to be in some confusion whether to remove Clara from on top of their leader or to kick her to death then and there. It was then, too, that the busload of ministers and leaders of CORE arrived from Washington. The thirty of them, blacks and whites in nearly equal proportions, filed in through Gate 1, singing *We shall Overcome*. At first weak, the song grew in volume as the Negroes already in the station picked up the strain. Soon it quite dominated the room. Caught by surprise the shouters and screamers, the brawlers and kickers, stopped shouting, screaming, bawling, kicking.

When the song was ended, a Negro Minister (his face seemed strangely familiar to Gann; had he seen it in newspapers?) walked forward in silence till he was stopped by the main body of the crowd of whites. 'May I pass through, please?' he said softly.

'Pass back to Washington, you black sonofabitch,' someone shouted, though it was no one standing immediately in his path. Gann could feel the violence in the air, as tangible as rain. The other Klansmen, all but himself and Peter Boggs, had lowered their hoodwinks.

A group of Klansmen in red approached the Negro minister, encircling him. A boot flashed out from under a silk robe, aimed at the minister's crotch, but he sidestepped it neatly. Then, as if on signal, the entire group of Civil Rights workers sat down, huddling themselves in the familiar protective positions of foetuses. They took up their song once more with even greater emphasis and volume. In a moment the other Negroes in the station had joined in. The Caucasian mob, not to be outdone, began chanting: 'Two, four, six, eight! We don't want to integrate!' But their chant followed the rhythm set by the singers and served rather to accompany than to disrupt the hymn.

Peter Boggs approached Gann. 'It ain't right, Gann! Did you see him, did you see the Grand Dragon? He was going to hurt that sweet little thing! I couldn't believe my eyes. And these folks: what have they done that's so awful wrong? I don't understand what the Klan is for any more. Honest I don't. It ain't *right*! I guess I don't have to tell *you* though, do I?'

'Why?' Owen asked, bewildered by Boggs's outpouring.

'Well, 'cause you've known it was wrong all along.'

'I don't understand what you're talking about, Boggs.'

'Jesus Christ, what do I have to do to make you understand? *You*, of all people!' A light dawned in Peter Boggs's eyes: he had just realised what he had to do to make *everyone* understand.

Solemnly, with a full sense of the significance of the gesture, the old man pushed his way to the front of the crowd of Klansmen. Then, hiking up his white robe, he sat down alongside the Negro minister and joined in the singing.

Farron Stroud and a few others who knew Pete, laughed as if in anticipation of the punch-line of a joke, but when the song had droned on a while longer and they were still waiting they began to grow uneasy.

'Kladd Boggs!' Farron shouted. 'What do you think you're doing? Get on your feet, you son of a bitch, and shut your mouth with that singing.'

Negroes and whites were crowding around Boggs and the Negro minister to see the cause of this new excitement. For different reasons, laughter rippled through both mobs. A Negro youth sat down on the other side of Boggs, and soon others had joined him. Their voices took on a new, exultant note.

Gann felt sick. If it had been Pete's intention to set the crowd rioting once again, he could not have acted with more cunning. At this point, clearly, there was no remedy but the State Police. He looked about for the patrolman he had glimpsed when he'd entered the station. Now he was beyond the ticket windows, standing by a bank of phone booths at the very rear of the building. He ran over to him, self-conscious in his swirling silks.

'Have you called in more police?' he asked hopefully.

'Can't,' the policeman said smugly. 'Those niggers have cut the lines.'

'There's another booth outside, on the corner.'

'My job is to prevent nigger violence right here in this building. I can't go traipsing off *now*. That's just common sense.'

Owen blushed with anger, though he'd expected no other

answer than this.

'Besides,' the policeman went on confidentially, 'Farron Stroud told me to let him handle this, him and that big-wheel friend of his. So what can I do? Farron stands a good chance of being our next sheriff, of being my boss.'

Owen left the bus station by Gate 4, the rearmost exit, then circled it on the boarding platform, passing the two parked buses. He did not run for fear of attracting attention to himself —though he could hardly hope, wearing Klan regalia, to melt into the crowd.

Here outside the station, however, there were no crowds at all. Up and down the empty street flags and bunting flapped desultorily in the salt breeze—and that was all the activity there was.

'Where you going, Gann?' said the Knight-Hawk, Jenks, stepping out from behind a parked car. Caught downwind of him, Gann's impulse was to choke.

'I've gone ... I'm going to call the State Police. There's getting to be too many niggers around here. We're outnumbered. It isn't safe.' It was not, he had to admit to himself, very convincing.

'Is that so?' said Jenks, exhaling powerfully. 'Is that so? I think I'll come down to the corner with you, if you don't mind. With that robe on, you stand a good chance of getting in trouble yourself. But with me along ...' Jenks raised the barrel of the shotgun concealed beneath his robe '... you won't have anything to worry about.'

Owen felt uneasy about the Knight-Hawk's easy acquiescence. Outside the phone booth he lifted his robe and found a dime in his trousers pocket. Jenks took a position several feet from the glass door. He was peering up and down the empty street as though looking for someone ... or as though making sure no one was there.

Owen understood, too late, what Pete had been trying to tell him: *they know.* The Klan had found out that he had been spying on them. In fact, it had probably been Boggs who'd figured it out. And when the Klan found itself betrayed there was little question how they would deal with the traitor.

At the double tinkle of the dime entering the coin-box, Jenks stiffened like a Pavlovian log. He lowered the shotgun barrel till it pointed at the sidewalk rather than at Gann, who quickly dialled O for Operator. Jenks seemed to regard the telephone as a potential witness to the murder he was about to commit.

'Operator,' said the operator.

'Operator, I want to be connected with the State Police,' he said. 'This is an emergency—please connect me directly.'

After a very short pause a male voice drawled, 'State Police, Norfolk. Sergeant Bradford here.'

'Hello, this is Owen Gann. I am an agent for the Federal Bureau of Investigation.' Gann and Jenks exchanged wintry smiles. 'And I want to report a race riot at the Green Line bus station in Norfolk.'

'Fine. We'll check into that.'

'*Check* into it!' he echoed indignantly.

He was about to read the riot act to Sergeant Bradford when he saw his chance for escaping from Jenks. A Buick turned the corner sharply and stopped only a few yards away, double-parking. Owen hung up the phone, and Jenks took a step forward but without raising the shotgun. The driver got out of the car and walked towards the bus station. He glanced over his shoulder at the two Klansmen curiously, an ironic smile playing on his lips. At first, because he was not wearing his toupee, Gann did not recognise him. When he did he swore.

'You can say that again,' said Jenks.

Gann set off after Roderick Raleigh, intending to question him. Perhaps the man was still trying to get his daughter back from the kidnappers. Or perhaps (as his disappearance and the double murder in Bittle's cabin made it seem more and more probable), he *was* one of the kidnappers. In either case . . .

'Where do you think you're going?' Jenks asked.

'I've got to follow that man,' Owen replied, not without a sense of how ridiculous he sounded.

Jenks laughed odorously. 'You ain't going to do *nuthin*', Owen Gann, except get killed.'

Another car rounded the corner and Jenks lowered the shot-gun, commanding Gann to stay just where he was. This car double-parked behind the Buick, and four uniformed men got out, State Police. Gann, it seemed, had not been the only one to phone for them.

One trooper, in Air Force sunglasses, approached Gann and Jenks. 'All right, all right, all right, what's going on here?'

'This man...' Gann explained, over-riding Jenks' growl. 'This man has just threatened to kill me. He's concealing an illegal weapon beneath that robe.'

'That's no surprise. Okay, Goblin, hand it over.' Swearing restrainedly, Jenks surrendered the sawn-off shotgun to the state trooper. 'That's what you call yourselves, isn't it?' he jeered, once the gun was safely in his possession. 'Goblins and dragons and wizards? Chrahst, if you want to know the truth, you Klansmen are a bigger pain than all the niggers in this state put together. Come on, come on, let's look for the little black wagon. I'll tell you something, Goblin: I don't exactly love niggers—come on!—but I sure as *hell* don't love you bastards. Shooting people. Inciting to riots. Running around dressed up like a bunch of goddam fairies. Chrahst!'

Once again Owen set off after Roderick, who had entered the station.

'And where do you think *you're* going, little friend?' the trooper asked.

'Excuse me, Officer. I took it for granted that you under-stood I'm not a Klansman. As this man can assure you, I'm an agent for the Federal Bureau of Investigation.'

'And he is too, I suppose? Or did he come from the Attor-ney-General's office?'

'C.I.A.,' said Jenks.

'Officer, this man was on the point of killing me the moment you arrived. He had found out, you see, about my...'

'I believe it, I believe it,' the trooper said, snapping open a pair of handcuffs.

'It's *true*. There's a man in that bus station I must find now. He may be dangerous. That's his car, that Buick. He's wanted by the police for questioning.'

'Come along now, the both of you.'

'Officer, here—these are my credentials. Look.'

'Chrahst, what we have to put up with from you bastards!'

'This is my *badge*.'

'And this is *mine*, wise guy. If you want to be booked for resisting arrest on top of everything else . . .'

'On top of *what* else? Name one reason for arresting me.'

The trooper took off his sunglasses and stared at Gann. 'Well, Jee-sus Chrahst Almighty! Nobody's ever going to believe this.'

Owen could see it was useless. He let himself be led off to the wagon, handcuffed to Jenks, who was enjoying himself immensely.


In the commotion that the mad Klansman had caused by sitting down beside the coloured minister, Bessy had been able to get Clara out of the bus station, but Clara was not in any condition, with her head bashed and bloody, to be carried farther, nor was Bessy, wheezing and dizzy, in any condition to carry her. She and Fay laid Clara down on the concrete of the boarding platform.

'Oh Lord!' said Bessy, glancing in through the glass door of the station. 'It's him, it's that F.B.I. man—and he's talking to a cop.' For a moment she considered sending Alice to him, but she feared that the girl, despite the promise she had made, would betray her for she knew, from long experience with Fay, how easily a child can turn traitor, or simply forget. 'Come along, Fay, Dinah—we got to get moving again.'

'Moving *where*?' Fay asked petulantly. 'I think you've forgotten all about the circus.'

'On to that bus.' She reached up and pulled at the chromed bump protruding from the side of the bus, and the door opened. Alice scampered in; then, all three of them groaning—Clara in pain, Bessy from the exertion, and Fay imitatively—she and Fay hoisted Clara to the long seat at the back of the bus. It was a touring bus, the back seats being raised a few steps above those in front, and they could not be seen by anybody on the platform.

'Are we going on a trip now?' Fay asked.

Bessy nodded.

'But you forgot our suitcases.'

Bessy reached into her bosom to touch the money Roderick had given her, wedged securely into her bra. She smiled. 'We don't have to worry about those suitcases, honey. We got enough other things to worry us.'

Clara groaned. Kneeling beside her with difficulty (why did they made the aisles of a bus so narrow?) Bessy felt her pulse. It seemed faint and rapid. Was that a good sign? She could not remember what *Feminine Hygiene* had said to do in cases like this.

'I want a drink of water,' said Fay loudly. 'I want a . . .'

Bessy clamped a hand over her mouth. 'Hush, child! We got to stay here sitting on the floor and be quiet as mice until them men that hurt Clara go away. Dinah, that goes for you too.'

'But I want a drink,' Fay whispered.

'We'll just have to wait,' Alice counselled, whispering too. 'But *now*, here's your baby. She's thirsty, too, you know.' Alice handed Fay the plastic doll. Fay began to nurse it, cooing.

The bus grew hot. It smelled of sweat and dust and cigarette butts, but Bessy feared to open a window. More to calm herself than to ease Clara, she began wiping the blood from her face with a handkerchief. There were several deep cuts. Alice, watching this, started to cry. *Lord*, Bessy thought, *in another minute I'm going to be crying myself.*

Outside there was a shriek of sirens. A new hubbub broke out in the station. The sun, approaching noonday, beat down through the tinted rear window of the bus. It got hot as hell.

*I'm going straight down to hell when I die*, she thought, *and I'll deserve it. And what was the price of my soul? The vanity of a bronze casket and a marble stone. A lot of consolation they'll be when I'm burning in hellfire. Vanity of vanities!*

She pushed herself up to her knees and started praying for all she was worth. There really wasn't anything else she could do.

Alice, embarrassed, turned to look out of the window. There were people swarming all about the bus. In the midst of them was her father. He was searching through the crowd—for her, certainly.

She knew she should hide herself down on the floor of the bus but she stayed at the window, fascinated with horror. At last, he noticed her there.

Smiling, he beckoned for her to come out of the bus.

The demonstrators were herded, against their protests, back into the bus. Those who refused to leave the station of their own volition were carried on. A state policeman rode in front beside the driver. He was to stay on the bus with them till they reached the Virginia–Maryland line. At the last possible moment, as the bus was pulling out, the police stopped it and helped Peter Boggs, still in his Klan robe, to board it.

'But this man has been injured,' the minister protested.

'If he stays in this station he'll probably be injured a lot worse,' the policeman explained. 'For his own sake, you'd better take him with you. Besides, he's the one that insists on going with you. You can leave him—and anyone else who's been badly hurt—at the state patrol emergency aid station, just the other side of the tunnel. But the rest of you people are going back to Washington, and it won't do you any good hollering about it.'

'We'll take you to court on this, I promise you.'

'Right. And you'll owe it to us, mister, that you'll be alive to go to court. Good-bye, Reverend.'

Leaving the city, the bus stopped and started with unwonted abruptness. No doubt the driver was expressing thereby his own protest at being pressed into service. At the fifth wrenching halt, Clara's eyes opened. 'What the hell?' she said.

'It's okay, Clara,' Bessy said, touching her hand. 'We're taking you to a first-aid station. You rest now. You're going to be all right.'

'Shit,' said Clara, her voice almost girlishly weak. She closed her eyes.

The young white couple in the seat ahead of them turned round to peer over their headrests. 'How is she, do you think?' the girl asked.

Bessy shook her head. She didn't want to talk to the demonstrators, fearful lest they discover that she was not one of them.

'They *could* have got her a doctor right at the bus station,' the girl said indignantly. 'She might *die* before we're able to get her to the emergency aid station.'

'Like Bessie Smith,' the boy added.

'It's shocking,' said the girl.

'But even so, you have to admit that the cops treat you better here than they do in Georgia, for instance. Americus was bad news.'

'What about *Selma*?' the girl asked.

'Man,' said the boy. 'Yeah, Selma.'

Though both were clearly Northerners, their accent was strangely hard to place. As they went on comparing notes on the jails they'd visited, Bessy began to get the paranoid suspicion that they were making fun of her own thicker speech.

'How come,' she asked, when she could no more contain her curiosity, 'you two come down here and let folks kick you around and get put in these jails? How come you don't stay at home?'

The boy's smile included Fay, who was sitting across the aisle from him. 'I don't know myself sometimes. Sometimes I think I'm just being dumb. Other times I know that I do it because I have to.' He seemed quite sad.

'I'm dumb too,' Fay said, smiling back. 'And *I* do it because I have to.'

'Hush,' said Bessy.

'This your first demonstration?' he asked Fay, who knitted her brows with earnest incomprehension. 'Is this your first sit-in?'

'You'll have to ask Bessy,' Fay said cautiously. 'And I can't do anything unless you pay first. Hey!'

'What?' said the boy, rather startled.

'You've got *chin*-whiskers!'

With an embarrassed laugh the boy turned away to gaze out of the tinted window as the neon-lighted walls of the tunnel flickered past.

At the first-aid station everyone was allowed off the bus to have coffee and sandwiches inside a wire enclosure. Fay, Bessy, and Alice were allowed into the little brick building to see Clara, who was lying on the cot next to the renegade Klansman. He had stiff, spiky hair, white with streaks of yellow, like a nicotine-stained moustache. Like many of the demonstrators he had been wearing only overalls and a denim shirt beneath his white robe.

A doctor came and examined Clara and the Klansman. He said that they were neither in any danger, but that they would have to go to the hospital for X-rays and a short rest. He touched the bumps swelling on Clara's face, and you could see how much his touch hurt her, but she didn't say a thing. Alice started to cry again, sympathetically.

'Clara,' she said, reaching over hesitantly to put a hand on hers, 'I'm sorry. I really am.'

'So am I, kid,' said Clara, with something of her old manner, and winked.

Alice realised that Clara was smiling. Actually smiling. Not in any sarcastic way nor out of that unspoken inner pain that customarily gnawed at her but a friendly, cheerful, well-intentioned *smile*. It was queer, she reflected, that the very first time she'd seen Clara spontaneously nice to other people was now, with her head all bloody, after people had been so very bad to her.

'Time to go,' said the state policeman coming into the little brick building.

'Oh, but I can't go,' Fay protested. 'Not unless Clara can come with me. I have to look after her. She's hurt. And this poor old man here too. I'm the nurse, you see.'

The poor old man rolled over in his cot to stare raptly at Fay. 'The name is Boggs,' he said in a shaky voice. 'Peter Boggs.'

'I'm very glad to meet you, Mr. Boggs. My name is Fay.'

'Time to *go*,' the policeman repeated.

'*Are* you a nurse?' the doctor asked of Fay, with considerable scepticism.

'Of course I'm a nurse!' Fay said, offended. 'And Clara *needs* me.'

'I need her too,' said Peter Boggs, and with such earnestness that the policeman could be seen to relent. The doctor, however, remained unpersuaded. Fay began to run a comb through Pete's spiky hair, being temporarily unable to think of any more nurse-like task.

Bessy went to the doctor and whispered in his ear. 'All right,' he agreed at last. 'We'll let that nurse stay with them.' Fay clapped her hands delightedly.

'The nurse stays,' the policeman said. 'But you and you'—indicating Bessy and Alice—'have got to come along. Everyone else is in the bus, waiting.' Bessy obeyed him unthinkingly. After a squeeze of Clara's hand and a whispered word of advice to Fay (who was obviously tormenting the poor old Klansman by running her comb across his bruised head) she led Alice out to the bus.

At the very last moment Alice ran back into the first-aid station. Bending down over her cot Alice planted a light kiss on Clara's chin. 'Good-bye, Clara.'

The Negress looked surprised. Then, grinning, she made a thumbs-up sign just like a wounded pilot on the Late Late Show assuring his buddies in the Flying Tigers that he'd be back up in the air in no time. 'So long, kid. Keep fighting.'

Shortly after the bus pulled away, Clara was unconscious

again. Fay turned her attention from her to her new-found friend, Peter.

'May I ask,' he asked shyly, 'what your ... uh ... last name is?'

'MacKay,' Fay replied, with some uncertainty. She seldom had occasion to use her *last* name.

'Miss MacKay, I don't think what you may think of an old man like myself, and I know I have no right to ... uh ... to ask ...'

'Oh, I think you're *nice*,' Fay protested earnestly. And truly, she always had liked men better who were shy.

'You'll probably think I'm off my rocker, coming out with a question like this when I hardly know you. But you see, it's as though you'd stepped down from heaven. Yes sir, you're just like an angel from heaven. And I'm afraid you're going to disappear just as sudden as you came.'

Fay squealed at the unaccustomed compliment.

'I can hardly believe you're real. An Angel. Miss MacKay, do you think you might ever consider marrying ... an old man like me?'

'Why, Mr. Boggs, I'd *love* to! And can we have lots of babies?'

'I sure hope so.'

She clapped her hands with anticipation. 'Can we get married *today*?'

'The courthouse is closed for the Fourth, but I reckon we can find a minister somewheres.'

Fay embraced the old man and devoured him with kisses. In an ecstasy of mingled pain and happiness, he swooned.


Some were singing folksongs, some were sleeping, Bessy among them. It was beastly hot. Alice stared out of the window at the unending dullness of the highway. Occasionally she would be overcome with a strange sense of *déjà vu*, since the bus was taking the same route her father had driven last night. A sign announced that the toll bridge across the Potomac was only a mile ahead. It would be such a *relief* to leave Virginia! Once in Washington Bessy had agreed that Alice might turn herself in to the F.B.I. headquarters. Why, with luck she might even be able to meet J. Edgar Hoover and get his autograph!

Within sight of the bridge the bus hissed to a stop. There were three police cars parked on the shoulder of the road ahead of the bus—and soldiers everywhere, with bayonets on their rifles. Was it possible that these were the soldiers of Maryland trying to keep the demonstrators out of their state? Civil rights could become very confusing. While the driver, the policeman, and the leading minister left the bus, everyone woke up and the close, hot air buzzed with conflicting theories.

The minister and a white man in a grey business suit came into the bus and conferred with some of the other leaders of the demonstration. Someone made a joke, and for the first time since they'd left Norfolk there was a sound of honest laughter in the bus. The minister said they could all go out and stretch their legs, but not to go very far.

'Ain't you coming out?' Bessy asked Alice.

Alice shook her head. She could remember, too clearly, her father beckoning her to come off the bus. So long as she stayed inside she felt safe.

'Well, I got to find out what's going on. If you're staying in here, you just say a prayer that this bus goes on to Washington, hear?'

The air-conditioning in the bus was off again, and it became hotter and hotter. Outside everyone was arguing. The soldiers argued with the state police, the bus driver argued with the soldiers, and *then* he argued with the police. Alice eavesdropped on some of the conversations through the bus's open windows, but she could only grasp faint threads of the controversy. The man in the grey business suit was, it seemed, from the Attorney-General's office, and he was more or less on the side of the demonstrators, who wanted to make the bus go back to Norfolk. The police (and the bus driver, at first) wanted to take the demonstrators to the other side of the toll bridge, then leave them there in Maryland, standing beside the highway. As for the soldiers, they seemed to favour both alternatives alternately, and it was their vacillations that kept the bus from going either forwards or back. Dinner time came and went, but the only food Bessy could find for herself and Alice was peanuts and soda pop from a near-by filling station. The young couple in the seat ahead offered to let Alice and Bessy share the little water melon they'd brought with them in honour of the Fourth.

At seven o'clock everyone was gathered back into the bus. The state policeman was no longer riding with them; the man from the Attorney-General's office had taken his place. They were returning to Norfolk.

'Oh *no*!' Alice said, on the verge of tears. 'Oh, *no*!'

'I'm sorry, honey. I prayed we'd go on to Washington, but I had four preachers praying the other way. There wasn't no help for it.'

'Bessy, he *knows* we're on this bus. He saw me through the window, back at the bus station.'

'I know, child. When I went out of the bus I saw him too. Wasn't more than half an hour ago. He was just driving back and forth. He's got a new car, but it was him all right. I guess the time's come for me to tell them all just who you are.'

'No!' Alice said, for she knew that this would also mean Bessy's arrest. 'If you tell that to anyone I'll say you made it up. I'll say I'm just a little black girl and that you're *crazy*. I'll say that *you're* my mother.'

Bessy chuckled and rumped Alice's wiry curls. 'You're a sweetheart,' she said.

Alice burst into tears, and at the same moment everyone on the bus started to sing *Bringing in the Sheaves* in a merry, deafening chorus. This time Bessy joined in. Drying her eyes, Alice couldn't help but wonder: what in the world *were* sheaves anyhow?

Chapter 21

*Come, thick night,* Roderick whispered, *and pall thee in the dunnest smoke of hell* ... But what came after that? For the life of him he couldn't remember. Small difference for already, quite uninvoked, the darkness was well advanced: the western horizon was tinged by only the slightest slimmer of indigo. How about: *Come, you spirits that tend on moral thoughts! unsex me here* ...? No, fine as it was, that wasn't quite what he wanted either.

Remarkable, how one always seemed to come back to William Ernest Henley's *Invictus*!

Things had not been going exactly the way he would have liked. Things seemed to be getting rather out of hand. He wasn't worried, not at all ... but did feel slightly resentful at having to make such an *effort*.

The African Church was a small, white-frame structure set back agreeably from the street and shaded by two gloomsome oaks. On each side of the church were vacant lots; the buildings formerly occupying these sites seemed rather to have collapsed than been torn down, for something vaguely architectural still lingered on at the centre of each lot. Roderick had parked his newly acquired '61 Dodge (rented from its astonished owner for a price far exceeding what he could have sold it for) on the farther side of the small park fronting the church, and he sat in it now, waiting.

The night was going to be clear, but moonless: the luck wasn't *all* against him. In fact, since his escape from the closet he'd had more than his share of good fortune: sighting Alice at the bus station; being able to find, so quickly after abandoning Bittle's cursed Buick, a replacement; and—his best piece of luck—finding out from the young highway patrolman, when he'd been stopped after his third or fourth passage before the stopped bus, that the demonstrators were to be returned to Norfolk, not the station but directly to the doors of the African Church.

That the patrolman had not recognised him meant that his description was not yet being generally circulated. Soon, inevitably, a search would begin for him, and by that time he had to be sure that Bessy and Alice were disposed of.

And then: was it better to buy a forged passport and seek

comfortable oblivion in Rio or to take the risk of returning to Delphinia? With Alice dead, her trust funds would be dispersed among the several charities specified in Morgan Duquesne's will, so there was no material advantage to be gained. There were, however, considerations of a more idealistic nature: if he returned to Baltimore and suffered the indignity of an inquiry into Alice's kidnapping and death (and nothing, surely, would be proven against him, though much might be suspected) then he need not abandon his identity and good reputation to lead a life of exile and disgraceful anonymity. Besides, what was the use of committing a perfect crime if immediately afterwards you made tacit confession of your guilt by absconding? Indeed, the whole *point* of murdering Alice was getting away with it. Nietzsche, somewhere, had said something much to the same effect, had he not?

Roderick was *very* tired. Hadn't slept for ... how long? Macbeth, as he recalled, had also complained about not getting enough sleep. Heroism took a lot out of a man.

The trampled patch of parkland between Roderick and the African Church was not entirely empty tonight. As the darkness deepened, the number of sheeted woodland figures—Klansmen certainly—increased. They flitted among the trees and teeter-tottered like so many midsummer sprites. Roderick, in his heart, welcomed them. They boded confusion, rioting, opportunities.

The bus arrived, and the busy sprites hid themselves behind trees and parked cars. The church doors opened and the demonstrators filed out of the bus and up the half-flight of steps. By some quirk of group behaviour, each person upon reaching the entrance stopped and turned halfway round to glance at the darkness of the park. At such moments, with the light behind them, they were exemplary targets. Roderick left his car and advanced through the park. He felt the same godlike calm descending upon him that he had known in Bittle's cabin, the same absolute self-possession.

Alice and Bessy were the last ones to leave the bus. There was no mistaking Bessy's gross, hobbling figure nor the slight dark child holding her hand. They stood at the top of the stairs, framed in the doorway, longer than any of the others had. Roderick used a tree trunk to steady the hand holding the little pearl-handled revolver. Silhouetted so, the target was an almost irresistible temptation.

'You don't want to do that, cousin,' said a voice in his ear, a voice that betrayed the barbarous accents of a redneck.

The two figures disappeared from the doorway, and the doors were closed. It was just as well: it had been a risky shot. With a sigh Roderick turned to confront the Klansman. 'My good man . . .' he began pacifically.

The Klansman laughed and nudged Roderick's belly rudely with the barrel of his shotgun. 'Come on. Tell that one to the Grand Dragon.'

As soon as he satisfied the Norfolk police that he was, as he had claimed, a Federal agent Owen called up Madding and told him of seeing Roderick Raleigh near the bus station, as well as of his suspicions concerning the manner of the Raleigh girl's 'disguise'. Madding thought Gann's theory wildly improbable, and in support Gann could only offer the dream that had inspired it. The state police, who were still, hours after the demonstrators had been shipped back to Washington, guarding the bus station, were given Raleigh's description but he was, expectably, no longer to be found in that area; the Buick, however, was discovered where Raleigh had left it, double-parked and tagged. The steering wheel and dashboard had been wiped clean of prints, but analysis elsewhere showed clear prints of Dorman, Bittle, and the child. This evidence alone seemed to confirm the father's complicity in the kidnapping plot, but unfortunately it did not suggest any new directions for tracking down either the child or her abductors.

Gann was ordered to return to Stroud's Bar where the Klansmen had reassembled to wait out the afternoon. Though the Klan had seen through his disguise, they were not aware (so long as Jenks was held incommunicado) that he knew this and their ignorance was, in a sense, his advantage. Madding regretted (he said) sending Gann into the midst of his would-be assassins like a lamb to the slaughter, but there was no one else who could take Gann's place while anyone could be detailed to continue the Raleigh investigation. Gann said he understood and, when Madding said good-bye, made a bleating sound in answer. Then he was off to the stockyards.

At the bar Farron welcomed the strayed lamb back to the fold with great conviviality and cold beer. Owen was introduced to the Grand Dragon, who was holding court to a chosen inner circle in the black-out room at the back of the bar. Here Gann spent the rest of the hot afternoon drinking and listening to selections from the Grand Dragon's inexhaustible store of dirty jokes.

At dusk the Klan formed a Klavalcade to drive through Norfolk's niggertown on the way to the African Church. Gann was to ride in Farron's car. He was given the front seat next to the driver—the death seat, he reflected, without humour.

Despite the Klan's repeated warnings, perhaps because of them, the streets of niggertown were swarming. The crowds jeered at the passing Klavalcade. 'We'll demolish them sons of bitches,' Farron muttered in the back seat. Murmuring agreement, the driver speeded up perceptibly, closing the interval with the next car in the procession. The jeering grew louder. It was a most unsatisfactory Klavalcade.

Further on, they came to a row of shops that seemed to have been looted, though they were deserted now—except for the policemen.

'Hey!' Owen called out, as they passed a sidestreet. 'Look down that way. Is it a fire?'

'Sure enough,' the driver agreed, slowing. 'But it wouldn't be any of our boys. Not down there. Not as early as this.'

'Hell,' said Farron, 'it's as plain as day—*they* done it. Like them niggers in Watts, they're burning down their own houses. Saves us the trouble and it'll keep the police away from the African Church besides. Them dumb niggers is doing our work for us.'

A few blocks farther on the Klavalcade passed within a hundred feet of another fire—at the back of a looted hardware and paint store. In the eerie blue and blue-green flames they could make out small knots of figures locked in struggle. A fat policeman appeared in silhouette clubbing a prone figure with metronomic regularity. Alsatians bayed at the speeding Klavalcade.

When they arrived at the African Church it was filled with worshippers though the bus from Washington was still awaited. There wasn't a policeman in sight.

'Beautiful,' said Farron, which was for him a highly uncharacteristic expression. 'Now here's what me and the Grand Dragon decided. A few of us is going over by that church later on, when everyone's inside, and we'll bring along a little something for the collection box.' Farron held up a gasoline can. 'I understand they're going to set off some fireworks in the park after the church service, and we'll just hurry things up a mite. But they'll have fireworks, won't they, boys?'

The boys cheered zestfully.

'Owen Gann! Don't you go getting lost again. You and me and the Kleron are volunteering to set that fire. If that's all right by *you*?' Farron's tone was almost openly jeering. There was less and less need, as the moment of his assassination approached, to keep up appearances.

Somewhere Gann had heard that of all deaths the most excruciating was to be burned alive. Despite that the evening was by no means cool, he shivered as he stooped to pick up the two gasoline cans.

'Here comes the bus,' announced the Kleron.

The church doors opened. The demonstrators filed in. When the door closed upon the last of them, Owen, Farron, and the Kleron moved forward through the darkness to the strains of *Hark! From the Tombs a Doleful Sound.*

After the hymn the Negro minister stood up and preached and like all the sermons Alice had ever heard it was very dull. If she'd been in her own church on Gwynn River Falls Drive or in the chapel at school, at least there would have been something pretty to look at, but the decorations in this church were simply silly. Right above the main altar, where the tabernacle should have been, there was a doll wearing a sleazy gold dress and a spiky gold-foil halo. It was meant to be Baby Jesus, she supposed.

She watched the minister, who was wearing a red robe like one of the Klansmen at the bus station. He had bushy white hair, pruned close on the sides of his head but thick on top like a lamb's fleece. He was talking about St. Paul.

*And do you suppose it was easy for him to turn the other cheek? Paul, who used to go around per-secuting Christians? It was easy for Jesus, you say, to love His enemies, because He had a loving nature. But the rest of the world isn't like that. The rest of the world is human and weak, and if you turn the other cheek, chances are you'll just get hit again. What's Jesus saying anyhow? Does He want us to sell ourselves back into slavery?*

There was a subdued murmur of pious *No*'s about the church, but somebody whispered quite clearly into Alice's ear: 'That's exactly it!'

Alice turned to confront the whisperer, a black girl somewhat older than herself, with braces on her teeth. Alice was rather shocked, since at St. Arnobia's it was thought very bad form *ever* to discuss anything that Reverend Burbury said. She held

190

up a finger to her lips. The girl with braces stuck out her tongue.

*When Jesus went into the Temple of Jerusalem and drove out the money-changers, how did He do it? With soldiers and police dogs? With tanks and tear gas? No—with a little switch. Those money-changers were afraid of Him, not because of that switch, but because in their hearts they knew their own guilt and shame.*

The girl with braces hissed at Alice: 'Aunt Jemima!'

Alice retaliated with, 'Atheist!'

'That's right,' said the girl, with a proud tilt of her head. 'I *am* an atheist.'

Alice was utterly confounded and no little bit impressed. She'd never met an atheist before. 'Are you *really*?'

The girl nodded. 'Really.' Then, topping it: 'And I'm a Communist too.'

*Now let's look at what St. Paul really had to say about this business of loving our enemies. Let's turn to Romans, chapter 12, verses 19 and 20. Dearly beloved, avenge not yourselves, but rather give place unto wrath ...*

'But you *can't* be a Communist! You're too little.'

'This is a democracy, and I can be anything I like. I don't always follow the party-line but I'm a lot less deviationist than my parents. They're Trotskyites. I'll bet you don't even know what that means.'

Alice shook her head, smitten with admiration.

'My name is Tildy,' the girl said, 'but I'm going to have it changed when I'm older. It's a finky name. I'm going to be called Ivan, and that's what you should call me if you want to be friends. What's your name?'

Alice hesitated. It was important what name you gave to a new friend. 'Would it be all right if my name was Dinah?'

'Sure. But it isn't a very revolutionary name, is it?'

*St. Paul doesn't promise some far-off, by-and-by heaven, does he? He says coals of fire are going to be heaped on our enemy's head. Coals of fiery shame and guilt, and when he's burned long enough under those coals, he'll be cleansed, the way the lips of Isaiah were cleansed. He's going to die—when he sees that other cheek turned to him, our enemy's going to die inside himself, roasted on the coals of his own guilt, but out of that fire is going to come a new friend. It will be a long time before white men and black are truly friends, but that time will come. That time must come. We will make that time come.*

There was a burst of sound, like ragged applause, and the window above the flimsy wood altar collapsed, knocking over the doll in the gold dress.

'Get down!' roared the minister.

'Get down!' Bessy yelled, yanking Alice from her seat on the pew to the floor. But most of the other people in the church ignored the minister's command and were thronging around the windows and the door, trying to see what was happening.

'Dear me,' said Alice. 'What in the world *is* going on?'

'They're shooting at us, comrade,' Tildy replied. She had crawled under the pew with Alice. 'A bunch of piggy ofay bastards are shooting at us. Coals of fire! If we heaped coals of fire on their heads, they'd just use them to set one of their crosses burning.'

'What does ofay mean?'

'Jesus, where you been all your life, Dinah? Ofay means *white*. White people are anack-narisms, that's what I say. They're throwbacks to the ape. It's a fact. They'll disappear from the face of the earth some day. The man of the future is black. I'm an African Nationalist, and when I grow up I'm going to join the Black Muslims.'

Alice, for the moment, was rather glad she was black. Then another explosion rocked the church and she wished, with much more force, that she were any other colour at all.

The fat Klansman stood in the shadow of a tree. The only light was a muted flicker from a street lamp filtered through rustling leaves; it was not possible, therefore, to see what colour his silk robe was, except that it was not white like the majority of Klansmen's.

'This is the Grand Dragon,' said Roderick's captor, pushing him forward to that august presence.

'What am I supposed to do—bow down and kiss his feet?' Roderick asked, out of humour.

'I found him in the middle of the park, Brother Dragon, aiming this little revolver at the niggers.' He handed the gun to the Grand Dragon who pocketed it indifferently.

'I wouldn't have thought the Klan would concern itself over a nigger or two being shot down,' Roderick said sarcastically.

'We do if it's us who have to take the blame,' the Grand Dragon replied. 'Sam, you can leave us alone together. He knows which side of this shotgun he's standing on—he won't

192

make any trouble.' When Sam had left, the Grand Dragon went on: 'By the sound of your voice, I'd say you were a Northerner.'

Roderick made no reply, for there was something ... something about the man's voice ...

'Sounds to me like you're a Yankee agitator. One of Martin Luther Coon's boys, I'll lay odds. And you probably got a card in your wallet says you belong to the National Association for the Advancement of Coons and Piccaninnies.'

'Probably,' Roderick said scornfully.

'Let's have a look-see. Stay standing where you are and throw it to me.'

'Rather an indirect way of picking pockets, isn't it?' Roderick said, tossing his wallet to the Grand Dragon.

The Klansman set aside the shotgun and raising his hoodwink looked through Roderick's wallet with a pen torch.

'Roderick Raleigh,' he read from a driver's licence. He took the money out and tossed the empty husk back to Roderick. Then, coming a few steps closer he aimed the beam of the torchlight at Roderick's face.

At first he was dazzled, but soon he was able to see, dim in the backwash of light, the fat weary face of the Grand Dragon, all pouches and jowls. The grape-cluster lips were puckered in a fleering smile, just as Roderick had always remembered them.

'Donald Bogan,' he whispered. 'You.'

The torchlight went out, and in the intenser darkness that followed Donald Bogan hooted like an owl. 'Well, Roderick, my brother, long time no see. Can't say I haven't been *hearing* about you though. Matter of fact, one of the reasons we're out here tonight is because that Nigger-boy Bittle made off with you and your daughter. We're revenging you, brother. That's what it said in the newspaper, anyhow. Of course, Nigger-boy Bittle will never tell anybody different. He's paid the price for his deed already. You wouldn't know how that happened, would you, Roderick my brother?'

Roderick cleared his throat, to no better purpose than to punctuate the awkward silence.

'Remember, Roderick, that night in the fraternity house? Good old Kappa Kappa Kappa—those were our golden days. Remember that night that you'd just got done reading *Crime and Punishment* for Humanities 1-2-3, and we were shooting the breeze about whether it was possible to kill a person just for the hell of it and not feel guilty afterwards? I remember that night very well, Roderick, because it was one of the few times you and I were in agreement about anything. Do you remember?'

'I remember,' said Roderick.

'Well, how about it, Hot Rod? Do you feel guilty or not?'

'Not in the least,' Roderick said aloofly. 'I don't know what you're talking about.'

'Like hell you don't! You're going to make me a rich man, you horse's ass! Where you got that million dollars hid? You got a car around here? Is it there?'

'As I've been sensible enough to hide it elsewhere, you're welcome to look in my car. Don't worry, Bogan—I'll cut you in. I always *have*, haven't I?'

'Cut me in! Why you stupid asshole, you're going to *give* it to me. All of it.'

'That will be as it will be. A strange thing, Bogan, but as it happens I was asking after you only the other day. I'd been under the impression, for some reason, that you were dead.'

'Might as well have been. Dad cut me out of his will—not on account of that fiasco at the cathouse but for something serious that happened later on, and afterwards he told people I was dead. He probably believes I am by now. It's been eight years. Eight rotten years. But you—you haven't had it so bad from what I gather. Marrying that Duquesne bitch . . .'

'And being cut out of her father's will. Oh, I've done very well!'

Bogan chuckled. 'I heard about that, too. Serves you right.' He bent down to retrieve the shotgun he propped against the tree trunk. 'But we've got the rest of our lives to reminisce in. Just now we should be shooting niggers, right? Right! You wouldn't like to join our little turkey hunt?'

Roderick realised that Bogan was holding out the shotgun to him. Was it going to be as easy as *that*? He accepted it, with sincere thanks.

'Mind you don't take a shot at *me*, now.' Then the dumb bastard deliberately turned his back. Didn't Bogan realise how many *years* he as fantasied such a scene as this? Had his position as a leader of the Klan in some way given him delusions of invulnerability? Only outright madness could explain such folly.

'First thing we do,' Bogan explained, as he moved in a crouch towards the African Church, 'is shoot in the windows.

That's just to throw a scare into them. Aim high, 'cos some of the boys are going to be gathered round the church setting up Act Two. Raleigh? You with me, Raleigh?'

'Absolutely,' Roderick said.

'Don't drag-ass, or they'll start without us.'

The first volley of shot splintered the July night and the windows of the African Church. Roderick stepped forward quickly, pressed the gun against the back of Bogan's head and pulled the trigger.

Bogan laughed. 'Oh, you dumb bastard, I knew you'd try that. You didn't think I'd hand you a *loaded* gun.'

Roderick swung at Bogan's head with the shotgun but the fat man moved faster than a fat man should. The gun barrel came down harmlessly against his shoulder. Then, quite unaccountably, Roderick's lungs collapsed and the dark Mendelssohnian scene swam before his eyes. Again Bogan's fist dug into his stomach and seemed to stop only after reaching the interior of his ribcage. Bogan was laughing. Roderick kneed him viciously—at least his intentions were vicious—but Bogan's laughter continued without a pause.

'You poor dumb bastard, Raleigh. A fellow like you is just *made* to be torn apart.' But this rhetoric made Bogan careless, and the side-hand blow that he had intended for Roderick's throat, the blow that would have driven him to his knees, ready to be kicked, glanced off the side of his head clumsily.

Considering his inexperience in these matters, Roderick acted in a manner that even Nietzsche would have been compelled to admire. Though it had been above a decade since Roderick's one and only judo lesson, his hip block worked. The heap of bones and fat that was Donald Bogan flopped, fishlike and breathless, at Roderick's feet, and Roderick's feet lashed out in alternation at that heap of bones and fat and blood. He was rewarded by the solid gnashing sound of heel against bone, Bogan's responsive cry, a prayer beseeching more pain, a prayer Roderick answered, answered with supererogation, kicking the corpse till, out of breath, he could kick no more.

He found the shells for the shotgun in Bogan's shirt pocket. He let him keep the gun and the money he had taken, for when the police found Bogan's mangled body (he would be supposed, surely, the just victim of a Negro's rage) it would be evident immediately that he, Donald Bogan, Roderick's immemorial enemy, had been the master-mind of Alice's kidnapping. There had always been superficial points of resemblance between Bogan and Roderick so that if, by some mischance, there should prove to have been witnesses to Roderick's conduct today (if, for instance, that young highway policeman who'd stopped him should remember his face), it might be plausibly argued that the witness had seen not Roderick but Bogan.

God, Roderick thought, helps those who help themselves.

Roderick helped himself to the Grand Dragon's robe and hoodwink. Wearing these, he need fear no witnesses for anything he might have to do tonight.


'Drenched, you say? The front steps too?' asked Farron Stroud.

Owen Gann replied by dropping the emptied gasoline can to the grass.

'Then it looks like we're about ready to have ourselves a little weenie roast. Got a book of matches, Kleron?'

With the over-emphatic miming of an unskilled actor, the Kleron searched his pockets. 'Damned if I do, Farron!'

'Then it seems you'll have to do us that service, Brother Gann.' All day Farron had been bearing down heavily on that 'Brother' like someone who has just discovered a new word and wants to decorate every sentence with it. 'I'll have to give the signal for the boys to shoot in the windows, 'cos it's beginning to look like something's holding up the Grand Dragon. When you hear the guns go off drop a lit match to that pile of tinder. Any questions, Brother?'

Bile, not questions, rose to Owen's mouth. Reluctantly, but with a feeling that he was performing an action for which his whole life had been a preparation, he took the matches from his shirt pocket. Strange, that he, of all these Klansmen, should be the one to light this holocaust. An irony that Farron Stroud, beneath his hoodwink, was undoubtedly enjoying as well.

Farron whistled and shotguns replied to his melody. After the echoes had died the Kleron had still not fired, though his rifle was aimed now at Gann's chest. He was not to be allowed his punishment until he had committed the crime that was demanded of him.

He struck a match against the side of the box and dropped it, flaming, into the gasoline-drenched tinder. The flames at once leaped to chest height and he stepped back.

'Just stay right *there*, Brother,' Farron called out. 'If you back away from that fire any more, the Kleron here has orders to shoot you. We'd like to see you burn though.'

There were many things he might have done but he did none of them. He realised that his bleating over the phone earlier had been more than a joke, that even then he'd been preparing himself for such a moment—or such a moment for himself.

He would have preferred, abstractedly, a martyrdom by fire —such a martyrdom as he had himself kindled for those inside the church—but his flesh, assaulted by the mounting flames, flinched, and he retreated that single step that Farron had warned against. The Kleron's aim could not fail at this range. A second fire ringed his heart and swept up the mesh of his nerves to the brain there to be extinguished in an utter and instant dark.

Against all expectation, he awoke. He was lying on his back, the whole of his field of vision occupied by the solid sheet of flame that the church had become. Through the roaring a few individual cries and screams could be heard and Owen knew a moment of relief. He was certain that no one had been killed by the fire. Had anyone died he, who would have borne the guilt, would not have been allowed to go on living, for he had faith in a Providence that governs events with strict accountancy.

Belatedly he realised that the pillar of fire on his left was no part of the general conflagration, but instead Farron Stroud in his red silk robe. Farron held up his hoodwink in order better to view the fire. The customary cruelty of his lips was slackened; the lower lip drooped in a smile of sated happiness.

No longer disposed towards a non-violent, violent death (should he dispute with Providence?), Gann reached for the automatic he kept in his shoulder holster. The Kleron's bullet had made of the gun a tangle of steel little better than shrapnel. Inside its holster, the gun had saved his life; now, in his hand, it might cost him no less; for by his gesture in drawing it from under his robe he had betrayed to Farron that he was other than a dead man.

Suddenly the air about them was filled with traceries of coloured flame. The fire had reached the store of fireworks in the basement of the church, and such of the explosives as were self-propelling had been set off, to escape through the basement windows. On green flare flew directly at Farron, tangled in the

197

folds of his silk robe and exploded into fountains of green light. Farron threw up his arms and became for a moment a flaming cross.

Roderick had hoped they would all burn up inside the church, but whoever the damn fool had been who'd spread the gasoline around it had neglected the wooden steps and the whole congregation had escaped, Bessy with the child in tow among the first. Roderick's second hope had been that the Klansmen would use their shotguns on the mob of Negroes. It was just the sort of outrageous action Klansmen seemed to be doing all the time—but not, as luck would have it, tonight.

Now Bessy and Alice were resting in the park, Bessy incongruously fitted into a swing. Alice's head was turned away from Roderick, so it was Bessy who saw him first, in the robes of the Grand Dragon, approaching.

'We ain't making no trouble, believe me!' she protested at once. 'We'se just dumb black folk minding our own business, an'...'

Roderick acted with decision. No last minute qualms could prevent his finger closing over the trigger, nor could his aim, so close as this, err. The child's corpse tumbled boodily to the ground, half her head shot away.

Bessy lurched forward to prevent what had already happened, but she took no account of how unsteadily she was perched in the swing. She found herself falling backward. Roderick repressed a snicker at the absurd spectacle of her fall. 'I'm afraid, Bessy, that I shall have to use the other cartridge on you.'

Bessy, flat on her back, her legs projecting into the air, began to pray.

'Oh, really now! *You* don't believe in that sort of nonsense, do you? Only weak people need a god to believe in. It shows a slave-mentality. Try to face death with *dignity*. You, of all people!'

'For Christ's sake, Roderick, shut your mouth and do ...' She stopped speaking abruptly as though the words had been wrested from her mouth. Her eyes widened with horror, then lowered with thankfulness as she felt the last heavy drop of pain fall from the faucet and splash into the dark pool beneath.

She'd always somewhat blamed the Lord for giving her a bad

heart. Not till this moment had she known it was meant to be a blessing, not till the moment it stopped.

Roderick pressed his hand into Bessy's immense bosom, searching for a heartbeat. 'Dead,' he announced to the night air.

Overhead, as though in honour of the deed, the fireworks began to explode, not serially as at an ordinary Fourth of July exhibition, but hordes of them in the space of one minute—red, white, blue, green, gold—cannoning, illuminating the night for that moment more brightly than even the fire.

*A pity*, he thought, *that Alice can't see this. Fireworks are meant for children.*

He regarded the child bleeding at his feet with some tenderness. She had collapsed into an awkward position, and Roderick bent down to dispose her limbs more becomingly. She seemed oddly *larger* dead than she had been alive. Ordinarily Roderick would have expected the reverse to be true: that a dead person would seem smaller.

He crossed the two hands upon the never-to-ripen breasts, realising with some solemnity the *enormity* of the thing he had done. He had gone beyond—oh, well beyond!—mere good and evil, transcended the human, all-too-human limitations, of other men. Human? It was a word that scarcely could be said to apply to Roderick Raleigh. To him humanity was no more than an object that he could use as he saw fit—an object no more innately significant than the bauble he toyed with in his fingers, the identification bracelet on the girl's wrist.

Alice had never had an identity bracelet.

He read the name engraved on it by the light of the blazing church: *Matilda James.* As the suspicion of his error grew, Roderick became distinctly upset. Then, persuading himself that this had been part of Alice's 'disguise', he relaxed. A clever idea—cleverer than Roderick would have given Bessy credit for. It showed a sort of Germanic perfectionism not at all like the old woman.

Now he seemed to see everything about the child askew: her clothes, her face, even the size of her body seemed *wrong*. He pulled her into a sitting position by the braid across the top of her head. The dead girl's mouth gaped open and Roderick saw the braces on her teeth. With a cry almost of horror Roderick stood up. The hand that had held the braid came away sticky with blood, which he wiped on the silk of the robe.

Had Bessy *deliberately* tricked him? Had she, during the panic in the church, caught up the wrong child by accident or on purpose? Had she meant this child to be a scapegoat for Alice? Had she been ready, in her anxiety to save Alice, to sacrifice one of her own people? Roderick cursed the dead woman for having once again made a fool of him—and for having fled so far beyond retort.

An alternative explanation occurred: Roderick saw, coming around from the side of the church, a Klansman in a white robe that was ripped down the back. The Klansman ran to the top of the steps and stared down the fiery aisle. Through the tear in his robe were visible most of the letters composing the trademark of Spengler's Beer. Madness? Hallucination? Certainly it was too much to suppose that the F.B.I. man pursuing Roderick was a member of the Ku Klux Klan?

But when this utterly improbable phantasm came bounding across the street into the park Roderick ignored the improbability, ignored the demands of an heroic morality, ignored everything but the adrenal fear that overwhelmed him, and, stumbling over Matilda James, he turned on his heel and ran towards his car.

It was the most terrible thing, terrible beyond belief. Burning down a church and killing people. Because they were black. For no other reason than that. They had done no one harm. They had all been in church. To set a *church* on fire! And killing people, children, me.

She tried to think, to make sense of the madness going on about her, but the madness was too extreme. It scattered distinct thought like a hammer shattering a looking-glass: afterwards nothing could be made out in it but the pattern of the fractures.

The old man who had taken her by the hand when the panic started in the church had paused beside the car to catch his breath. He had been hurt where the Klansman had clubbed him, and though he told her to be brave there were tears in *his* eyes. Despite his blackness, he reminded Alice of her uncle. He was even older and more wrinkled than Jason, even more infirm, but beneath the weakness that came of age there was a strength that was also the product of age, though not so invariably.

Another Klansman came out of the park. Alice wanted to run from him, but she did not wish to leave the old man who had been so good to her all by himself. This Klansman's robe was darker than the others', though in the murky glow from the fire, it was hard to see what colour exactly ...

Green! Then was this the terrible man who had tried to hit Fay at the bus station? He seemed to have become smaller, to have shrivelled like a green grape that has been put in the oven.

Silently (and it did not seem quite right, somehow, for a Klansman to be so long silent) the green Klansman wrested Alice away from the old Negro, who had very little strength left for any sort of battle. The Klansman's hand circled Alice's upper arm, and he dragged her away from the car and out of the park. She screamed, but among so many other screams hers was inaudible.

She knew him now, this green Klansman. She knew the soft-skinned hand with its onyx ring; she knew the pointy-toed shoes with perforated patterns that tripped on the hem of the over-size robe; she knew the hasty stride that forced her to run along at his side, taking three steps for every two of his. They had been through this same scene already, in another place and context: he had dragged her home once in just this way from a birthday party at her dearest friend's house. She remembered how, on the former occasion, he kept muttering, 'You just wait. Just wait till we get home!' She remembered the incredible injustice of it.

They stopped. They were on a street of ramshackle houses. The windows were dark and the Klan had shot out the street-light at the corner. Alice tried to squirm free but her father kept a firm grip on her arm. It was quieter here so she began screaming again. He slapped her across the face.

Then he let go of her. It happened so suddenly that she was mistrustful. Why would he let her go so easily unless, for some reason, it suited him? She did not notice the ring of men who'd gathered around them until she bumped into one of them and even then she continued to scream, unable to grasp the fact that she was no more in danger.

'Raping little girls now, Mister Dragon?' one of the men said. He took away Roderick's shotgun. He ripped off the hoodwink from his head, and the toupee came with it. Roderick tried to retrieve the hairpiece, but when he bent over one of the Negroes hit him in the face and another kicked him from behind. 'So that's what a dragon looks like, is it?' the first man went on. 'I hope I got your title right—you're the Grand

Dragon, aren't you? Of the Invisible Empire?'

'No, I . . .'

'*He* calls himself a Grand Dragon, but *I* call him a child-rapist, a gangster, a goddam mother . . .'

'I'm *not* a Klansman. For heaven's sake, I wish you'd give a person a chance to explain. Don't judge by appearances.'

'Sure enough, and *we're* not niggers. It's just appearances that are against us. Oh, I'd like to kick in your clean white face. Instead, I'm just going to blow if off your neck with this shotgun, the way you blew out the brains of that little girl in the park.'

'No. Listen to me . . .'

'I'll bet you didn't think anyone was watching you there? Well, that's one advantage of being a nigger, Mister Dragon. Niggers are hard to see in the dark.'

'Oh, pow'ful haahd tuh see,' mocked another of the men.

'Stop making jokes,' a third said gruffly. 'Shoot the bastard, Tommy, and let's get out of here.'

'I'm *not* the Grand Dragon. Really, you boys are making a tragic mistake. And as for your notion that I'm a child-rapist, well, I must say! That girl there—she's my *daughter*.'

Silence could be the only response to so stupendous a lie.

'Ask her! Alice, tell them you're my daughter.'

The Negroes looked at Alice. 'Yeah, tell us that!' one said mockingly.

She lowered her eyes. 'My name ain't Alice,' she said. 'It's Dinah.'

'Alice!'

'And my father's back there by the car. The old man that he pushed down. My father's a *black* man.'

'Got anything else you'd like to say, Grand Dragon?' the man called Tommy asked, raising the shotgun he'd taken from Roderick.

'Alice! Alice, have pity on me! I'm your *father*!'

She looked up, smiling at Roderick's mistake.


'Hold it!' A white man in overalls that advertised Spengler's Beer stepped into the circle of men gathered around Roderick. National Guardsmen followed at a distance. 'Congratulations, men, on capturing this man. He's a killer wanted by the F.B.I., and as I *am* the F.B.I. that winds things up for tonight. If you'll disperse at once, we'll forget that you were threatening this man when I arrived. As a matter of fact, I don't much blame you. He's a son of a bitch.'

Alice waved good-bye to the black men. The soldiers put handcuffs on Roderick. The Spengler's Beer man was talking to her about something, but since she knew she was safe at last she didn't really have to listen.

'Miss Raleigh, try to understand. You're going *home* now—to Baltimore.'

'Oh no, *you* don't understand. The very first thing I must do is to find Bessy. To thank her for saving my life.'

'Bessy's dead,' Roderick said. 'I killed her.'

'No! That isn't true. She was in church with me, just minutes ago. Please, *you'll* say it isn't true?'

But the man in the Spengler's Beer overalls would only say, to her father: 'Raleigh, you are a slimy monster.'

The soldiers began to lead Roderick away. He said, 'I'm glad of one thing at least.'

'What?' Gann asked.

'That the kid I killed was only a nigger, after all. I won't be convicted by any jury in this state on a charge of killing a nigger.'

Gann's fist came down solidly at the base of Roderick's skull. Roderick collapsed in a swirl of green silk. 'I'm sorry, Miss Raleigh. Please forgive me—you've been witness to too much violence already this evening.'

Alice shook her head. She took his hand and smoothed out the clenched fist, then put her small hand into his confidingly. 'It's quite all right,' she assured him. 'He *was* a slimy monster.'

Alice was sitting just as Miss Godwin had left her, leaning her head on her hand, watching the setting sun through the branches of the little willow.

'It's really time for us to be getting back, mademoiselle. It's a long drive, and we've stayed later than we intended.'

Alice stood up, with a queer little toss of her head to keep back the wandering golden hair that *would* always get into her eyes. 'Oh, not yet! Just five more minutes? Because this *is* the very nicest time to be here.'

'Five minutes, then. But you know how your mother worries.'

'Oh, Mother!' Alice replied loftily. (She had been reading Oscar Wilde today.) 'Mother wouldn't be *happy* unless she could worry.'

'Five minutes,' Miss Godwin repeated, ignoring the epigram with iron sternness. She walked up the gravel path, punctuating her steps with little jabs of her parasol. Lately she had had to trade upon her delegated authority more and more often; Alice was coming to look upon her almost in the light of a parent, which was from Alice's point of view not the best of lights. Mrs. Raleigh, on the other hand, seemed quite pleased with this development, finding an ally rather than a rival now in Miss Godwin. There was a deeper motive behind this *entente*, of course: since Roderick's confinement to the asylum, she had had to find, as she put it, 'Someone to lean on.' Miss Godwin's shoulder had been conveniently at hand, and it had proved in the long run to support Delphinia's weight more firmly than any other.

At the crest of the hill she turned round to look at Alice. She was shocked anew at how tall the child had grown. She was within four inches of being as tall as herself, and already at twelve and a half her breasts were beginning to form—not, to Alice's immense distress, quite simultaneously. She stood at just that stage of life represented by the young willow at the foot of the hill, uncertain whether it was a true or a shrub.

To think that it had been only a year ago . . .

*To think*, Alice thought, *that it was only a year!*
A year exactly—since this was July the 8th. Already a few

of the details of that day a year ago were beginning to fade from memory. What song, for instance, had the organist played at the end? Ah yes—*Bringing in the Sheaves*. Alice knew what sheaves were by now, of course (How naïve one would have to be *not* to know a simple thing like that!), but why harvesting should be considered a suitable subject for a hymn was something she could not understand. It was a symbol perhaps. She had to find out what Symbolism was all about. She made a mental note to ask Miss Godwin to recommend a book on the subject.

Though it was quite possible that Miss Godwin wouldn't know of any. Alice had discovered only this summer that there were some things of which Miss Godwin knew nothing at all. Dutch painting, for instance. Alice knew far more about Dutch painting (after having read a book about it) than Miss Godwin.

'Come *along*,' Miss Godwin called out. 'They'll lock us up inside if we don't get back to the gate.'

'Just one last visit,' Alice promised. She broke into a graceless, tomboy spring along the path back to the stone. It was just round the bend of the little stream. The stone cross, which had been so bright and pink and Italian all that afternoon, had fallen into the lengthened shadow of a poplar and looked rather gloomy now.

A year! She remembered, with a smile, how at the ceremony Fay had broken out suddenly into such a cataclysm of tears that her husband, the old man with the spiky white hair, had had to take her outside. The idea of Bessy's death had not reached Fay until just that moment.

*It hasn't reached me yet*, Alice thought. Death was such an impossible thing to understand at her age. She looked forward impatiently to being eighteen and understanding death. Even at sixteen one would undoubtedly possess much deeper insights into things.

'Come along! This is the last time I'll ask you.' And Alice could tell by her tone that she meant it.

She returned to look at the stone. 'It *was* a nice funeral, wasn't it?' she whispered. 'It was *very* expensive, and everything was the way you said you'd want it. I had to go into hysterics with my uncle and again with my mother before they agreed to pay for it. So I *hope* it's what you wanted.

But the stone cross had nothing to say in reply, unless the inscription on its base were to be construed as in some way an answer: *O Lord, I am not worthy!*

'Then I don't know who is!' Alice remarked.

She kissed the cross, which was still warm from standing all day in the sun, and climbed up the hill towards her impatient governess. They left the cemetery holding hands.

# FINE MYSTERY AND SUSPENSE
# TITLES FROM CARROLL & GRAF

| | |
|---|---|
| ☐ Bentley, E.C./TRENT'S OWN CASE | $3.95 |
| ☐ Blake, Nicholas/A TANGLED WEB | $3.50 |
| ☐ Boucher, Anthony/THE CASE OF THE BAKER STREET IRREGULARS | $3.95 |
| ☐ BOUCHER, ANTHONY (ed.)/FOUR AND TWENTY BLOODHOUNDS | $3.95 |
| ☐ Brand, Christianna/FOG OF DOUBT | $3.50 |
| ☐ Brand, Christianna/TOUR DE FORCE | $3.95 |
| ☐ Brown, Fredric/THE LENIENT BEAST | $3.50 |
| ☐ Brown, Fredric/THE SCREAMING MIMI | $3.50 |
| ☐ Burnett, W.R./LITTLE CAESAR | $3.50 |
| ☐ Butler, Gerald/KISS THE BLOOD OFF MY HANDS | $3.95 |
| ☐ Carr, John Dickson/THE BRIDE OF NEWGATE | $3.95 |
| ☐ Carr, John Dickson/CAPTAIN CUT-THROAT | $3.95 |
| ☐ Carr, John Dickson/DARK OF THE MOON | $3.50 |
| ☐ Carr, John Dickson/THE DEVIL IN VELVET | $3.95 |
| ☐ Carr, John Dickson/THE EMPEROR'S SNUFF-BOX | $3.50 |
| ☐ Carr, John Dickson/IN SPITE OF THUNDER | $3.50 |
| ☐ Carr, John Dickson/LOST GALLOWS | $3.50 |
| ☐ Carr, John Dickson/NINE WRONG ANSWERS | $3.50 |
| ☐ Chesterton, G. K./THE MAN WHO KNEW TOO MUCH | $3.95 |
| ☐ Chesterton, G. K./THE MAN WHO WAS THURSDAY | $3.50 |
| ☐ Crofts, Freeman Wills/THE CASK | $3.95 |
| ☐ Coles, Manning/NIGHT TRAIN TO PARIS | $3.50 |
| ☐ Coles, Manning/NO ENTRY | $3.50 |
| ☐ Dickson, Carter/THE CURSE OF THE BRONZE LAMP | $3.50 |
| ☐ Du Maurier, Daphne/THE SCAPEGOAT | $4.50 |

| | | |
|---|---|---|
| ☐ Fennelly, Tony/THE CLOSET HANGING | | $3.50 |
| ☐ Fennelly, Tony/THE GLORY HOLE MURDERS | | $2.95 |
| ☐ Gilbert, Michael/GAME WITHOUT RULES | | $3.95 |
| ☐ Gilbert, Michael/OVERDRIVE | | $3.95 |
| ☐ Graham, Winston/MARNIE | | $3.95 |
| ☐ Greeley, Andrew/DEATH IN APRIL | | $3.95 |
| ☐ Hughes, Dorothy B./THE FALLEN SPARROW | | $3.50 |
| ☐ Hughes, Dorothy/IN A LONELY PLACE | | $3.50 |
| ☐ Hughes, Dorothy B./RIDE THE PINK HORSE | | $3.95 |
| ☐ Hornung, E. W./THE AMATEUR CRACKSMAN | | $3.95 |
| ☐ Leroux, Gaston/THE PHANTOM OF THE OPERA | | $3.95 |
| ☐ MacDonald, John D./TWO | | $2.50 |
| ☐ Mason, A.E.W./AT THE VILLA ROSE | | $3.50 |
| ☐ Mason, A.E.W./THE HOUSE OF THE ARROW | | $3.50 |
| ☐ Priestley, J.B./SALT IS LEAVING | | $3.50 |
| ☐ Queen, Ellery/THE FINISHING STROKE | | $3.95 |
| ☐ Rogers, Joel T./THE RED RIGHT HAND | | $3.50 |
| ☐ 'Sapper'/BULLDOG DRUMMOND | | $3.50 |
| ☐ Symons, Julian/THE 31st OF FEBRUARY | | $3.50 |
| ☐ Symons, Julian/BOGUE'S FORTUNE | | $3.95 |
| ☐ Symons, Julian/THE BROKEN PENNY | | $3.95 |
| ☐ Wainwright, John/ALL ON A SUMMER'S DAY | | $3.50 |
| ☐ Wallace, Edgar/THE FOUR JUST MEN | | $2.95 |

Available from fine bookstores everywhere or use this coupon for ordering:

Caroll & Graf Publishers, Inc., 260 Fifth Avenue, N.Y., N.Y. 10001

Please send me the books I have checked above. I am enclosing $_____ (please add $1.75 per title to cover postage and handling.) Send check or money order—no cash or C.O.D.'s please. N.Y. residents please add 8¼% sales tax.

Mr/Mrs/Miss _____

Address _____

City _____ State/Zip _____

Please allow four to six weeks for delivery.